wandering back to you

BOOK THREE OF THE WANDERLAND SERIES

ETTA LANE

dear reader

While there are no events in here that I would consider triggering, there is role play in the bedroom and pegging.

It should be mentioned that there is illness of a parent, toxic parenting, and wildfires in this book.

Along with that, this is a reminder that this is a work of fiction. Some events and scenarios (while possible) have been embellished for the story.

I respect all wildland firefighters and their families and the work that they do, and I have tried to handle their careers and hardships with care.

As someone who has seen a number of wildfire disasters in her home state, I appreciate and value the work that they do and the risks they take.

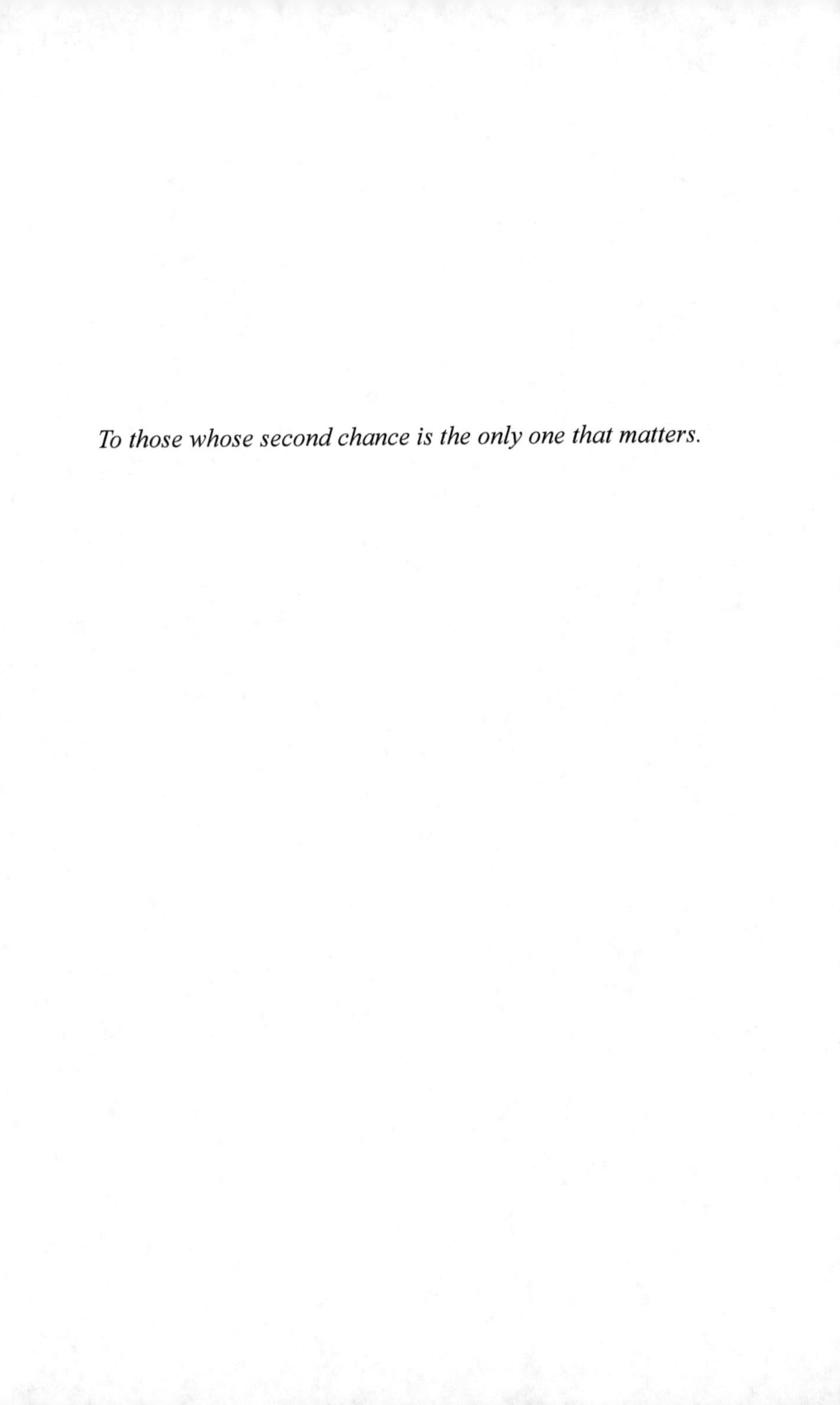

To those whose second chance is the only one that matters.

playlist

With You - Dean Lewis
Still into You - Paramore
Take on the World - You Me at Six
The Night We Met - Lord Huron
Lost Without You - Freya Ridings
Beginning Middle End - Leah Nobel
Are You With Me - nilu
Trouble - Camyilo
Block out the Noise - Johnny Craig
The Fire - Vincent Lima
Hangfire - Wind Walkers
Back to Friends - Lauren Spencer Smith
I wish u knew - vaultboy

prologue

ETHAN AGE 17

Michele is always beautiful, but tonight, she's radiant. Her honey-brown hair curls down her back, hazel eyes rimmed in black, and a pretty pink lipstick that matches her nails and dress. The dress might be my favorite part; made of simple silk with thin straps, it molds to her and ends at mid-thigh. My dad laughed when I asked if I could buy a suit jacket for this dinner, but thankfully, my mom took pity on me. I've paired it with jeans, a collared shirt, and my cleanest sneakers. I want to look good for my girl on her birthday.

"Happy birthday, Chele," I nervously croak, handing her the red roses I picked up on the way here. With a delicate grip, she takes them from me, and I wonder if I should have made the time to pick her some of the wildflowers she loves instead. "Ready to go?"

"Have her home by nine, Ethan," her dad calls from inside the house, and I nod. When Michele asks to take a photo of us first, LeeAnn, her mom, happily obliges. Michele's beauty deserves to be documented, as does her birthday dress. I never want to forget a single moment with her. Her mom waves as we head down the steps. They're good people who love their daughter, but I think they'd had enough of parenting after her brother graduated and moved out.

I rush ahead to the beat-up truck my parents bought me when I turned sixteen and open the passenger door, offering my hand to help her up. She blushes every time I do this, something I hope never changes.

There are only a few nice restaurants in town, so my options tonight were limited. Luckily, I know my girl, and I knew the little Italian place would be her favorite. They don't normally take reservations, but that didn't stop me from going in last week to beg them to save the corner booth for us. It's the most romantic and gives us more privacy.

"Did you have a good rest of your day?" I ask, navigating through town. Even though we texted all day, I haven't heard enough from her.

"Yeah, my parents made breakfast this morning. We did presents, and I got some new makeup and stuff. Evelyn took me out to lunch, which was sweet. My brother even called, which was special." Her brother, Austin, is in the Marines and doesn't make it home all that often anymore. She fidgets with the hem of her dress, and I realize I haven't even told her how pretty she looks tonight.

After pulling into a spot on Main Street in front of the restaurant, I get out and rush around to open her door again. When she steps out, I wrap her in a hug and plant a soft kiss on her pink lips, not caring about smudging her lipstick. "You look beautiful, baby. Thank you for choosing to spend this special day with me."

Michele slaps my chest playfully, but her cheeks heat again when I take her hand and lead her into the restaurant. There's a rush of cool air when we step in, the scent of fresh-baked bread and herbs permeating the space. They seat us in the booth I requested, the dim candlelight flickering in the green flecks of her eyes. She's so pretty that sometimes it physically hurts to look at her. I want to make this the best birthday ever for her. It's not every day you turn sixteen.

We peruse our menus and decide on a shared appetizer and a pesto pasta for our main. Michele's favorite color is green, which, in turn, apparently means green foods will always be her favorite. It's actually how we became friends.

This is the third place that I've lived, and the one we've stayed the longest. We've always followed my dad's career. When I was ten, we moved here, and on the first day of school, I was eating alone in the cafeteria when the prettiest girl sat across from me. She held her hand out to shake and said, "Hi, I'm Michele, and I'm your new best friend. As your new best friend, you have to let me have all the green Skittles out of that bag."

Just like that, I wasn't the awkward new kid. She really did become my best friend, even though she was a grade below me. She introduced me to River, who convinced me to join the baseball team with him, and between those two, I was hardly ever alone again.

"Do we have plans after this?" She twirls a piece of the pasta around her fork before sliding it into her mouth.

"I might have something in mind." I smile at her. I have more than something in mind. I came fully prepared to make this a memorable night. Not only do I have a present that I spent three months' allowance on, but I also plan to tell her what I've been feeling for a long time. I think I was feeling it before we started dating over a year ago.

Throughout dinner, we talk about classes and school, sports and friends. We're getting close to the end of the school year. She'll be a junior next year, but I'll be going into my senior year. It's a scary thought, trying to figure out where my life will go from here. I want to be a firefighter like my dad, and I'll likely pursue a fire science degree and endless hours of training and certifications. I've been going on ride-alongs forever, and the day I turn eighteen, I'll be able to start volunteering officially.

When dinner is done, we skip dessert, and I pay for our meal. Holding Michele's hand, I lead her out to my truck, helping her climb inside. She's quiet as we head out of town, following the overhang of trees down the backroads. Her eyes light up with recognition, and a wide smile splits her face when I turn left toward our secret spot.

"Are you doing something romantic?" she asks sweetly.

"For you, always." I pull the truck onto the dirt path and keep driving until we're in the middle of the small clearing. It's a pretty meadow surrounded by the forest. We found it by fluke last summer when I first got my license and we drove everywhere just to be together. I asked her to be my girlfriend on that very last day of summer right here in this spot. We've been coming here frequently since.

The clearing is filled with wildflowers, and overgrown grass litters the ground. As much as I hate driving over them, the center is the perfect spot. After telling Michele to stay in her seat, I run to the back of the truck and set up the blankets and pillows I have hidden there. I've even blown up an air mattress to put under it all. Nothing but the best for my girl. Last, I jog to a corner of the clearing where I know the little blue flowers are and grab a small bunch.

We've spent hours out here discovering the different flowers, but these are our favorite. Michele can turn them into a bracelet in a matter of minutes. I've tried repeatedly, but they always fall apart. She's always so patient with me, attempting to teach me and encouraging me when they're terrible and I get frustrated.

I rush back to the truck and open her door to help her out. She walks to the back of the truck, her eyes shining with unshed tears when she sees the setup. I slip off my jacket and throw it over the edge, then lean down to remove the sandals she's paired with her dress. I pull off my sneakers and lift her onto the tailgate. Before laying down, I tuck the forget-me-nots behind her ear like I always do.

She settles into my side, her five-five frame fitting perfectly against my six feet. We lie in the back watching the sun sink below the evergreens and paint the sky with an array of orange hues. The color reflects off her silky dress, making it shimmer in the evening light. Subtly, I slide the small box from my back pocket and place it on her stomach.

"What's this?"

"Open it," I whisper.

Lucky for her, May's birthstone just happens to be emerald. When she opens the lid, she gasps at the emerald-green earrings inside. "Happy birthday, baby."

She throws herself on top of me, peppering kisses over my face that turn to a slow, passionate kiss. I hold the back of her head, angling to deepen it. We've messed around, but we're both still virgins. It means we've gotten good at kissing. Like, *really good*. We make out until she's straddling my lap, rubbing herself over my very hard dick.

"You have to stop," I mutter between kisses. "That feels too good, and I have something I want to tell you."

She whimpers at the loss of my mouth, huffing a cute sigh when she sees the determination on my face. I slide her body next to me, cupping her soft cheeks in my clammy hands. I'm beyond nervous, but I can't wait a moment longer to tell her how I really feel.

"I love you," I blurt out. She stares at me in shock as I continue, "I have loved you since you claimed me on the first day of school seven years ago, and I will love you until I take my last dying breath. You're my best friend, the person who knows me best, and the keeper of my secrets. I feel you in every breath I take, and I see you in every wildflower I find. I love you, Michele Joyce VonMiller."

My hands are shaking as I wait for her to respond. She stares at me so long I worry I've broken her. Then she leans up and places the gentlest kiss on my lips. "I love you, Ethan Landon Hill." Her soft lips coast over mine again, and I feel her smile as it spreads on her pretty face. "I love you too."

When she kisses me again, I don't stop her when she climbs on top of me, nor when she pulls her dress over her head. I take in every inch of her beauty as we lose ourselves to each other for the first time, all while thinking that this is the beginning of a lifetime.

ethan

"Are you sure you can spare a few hours for me?"

I can feel River's eyes roll from thousands of miles away through the phone. "Of course I can. We fly in on Wednesday, let's do dinner in the city. You're off, right?"

"Yeah, my shift ends that morning. Anyone from your team or your girl coming?"

"Nah, Vanessa doesn't do away games anymore. Just us. It's been too damn long. We need to catch up. I'll send you the time and place when I've decided. Talk soon." He hangs up. Not fifteen minutes later, he sends me the reservation to a nice restaurant in downtown Oakland and four tickets to his game on Thursday—if I "want to bring any friends."

We may only talk a few times a year, but River remains one of the most genuine guys I have ever met. He doesn't care that we can go months without talking, and he is always the first to reach out when he hears of a wildfire near me. Out of all my friends from Cedar Ridge, he's the only one who has kept up on each of my moves and makes sure I'm safe after every large fire.

I've been living outside of Oakland, California, for the last two years—I don't love it. There's no shortage of calls, and it was necessary to gain valuable leadership skills, but I miss working with the wooded wildfires in Colorado. They're a whole different beast than structure fires and wildfires around here, which is what I truly love working with.

I've never been a city guy. I miss being surrounded by the woods. I long to walk out of my apartment and see the mountains, and smell the earth and pine, instead of the smog and sirens that greet me here. Oakland's not all bad; it's just not home. Colorado never felt like it either, but it was certainly a close second. I could close my eyes, feel the crisp breeze, and picture myself in the meadow. For that moment of memory, everything would feel okay again. It's something I haven't been able to experience since moving to California.

Ideally, I want a position with more leadership and stability. I've been looking for a way to get back to Washington. The thrill that shot through me when the spot in Cedar Ridge opened again, offering exactly what I was looking for, was immediate. All my hard work—moving and training—was going to pay off. |Two years ago, they passed me up for someone with more leadership experience, so I've been focusing on getting those skills ever since. Apparently, the new guy wants to get out of wildland fire-fighting, so the position has opened up again. When I heard about it, I jumped at the chance. I was told a decision would be made by next week, and I've been anxiously awaiting. The prospect of moving back is terrifying, yet nothing has ever felt so right. *Except her.*

It's been over nine years since I last saw Michele. I could lie and say I haven't looked her up in that time, but I definitely have. I limit myself to once every six months, just to see if she's married. Last I checked, she still looked single and as beautiful as ever. That thought equally hurts and heals. I've been away from her for so long, and no part of me wants to do it any longer. If I land this job, the promise I made to Jake will be one I'm thrilled to fulfill.

The weekend flies by, and in no time, it's Wednesday night. River and I haven't been able to get together since early last year, and that's too long. I have friends; you don't work in a dangerous job where any call could be your last without getting close to your coworkers. When it comes to wildfires, your team is essential to your survival. None of them ever sticks, though. When our shift changes or someone leaves the crew, any friendship dies. River has been my one true friend through it all.

I beat him to the restaurant, but that's not surprising. As one of the Rainier's team captains, he's always in high demand. Once seated at our table, I order a beer and glance around at the unnecessarily fancy-as-fuck decor. I feel like he's trying to wine and dine me, even though I know he simply wants to give the best to those he loves.

"ETHAN!" River yells when he sees me, not a care in the world for the other diners. He all but tackles me, his hulking frame wrapping me in a hug. I'm not small, but at six three, River is built like a tank. "God, it's good to see you." He slaps me on the back before taking a seat across from me.

"You too, man. Seeing your ugly mug makes me even more hopeful I'll get the job this time." River plays in Seattle, but that's only three hours from Cedar Ridge. Plus, his parents, brother, and nephew all live there still, so he visits as often as he can. "How's Griffin?"

"The cutest little man on the planet. Thoren said he wants to play Little League like me. Kind of thought I would be the one with a wife and kids by this point, ya know? Be the one to coach t-ball."

"Yeah, look at us, pathetic bachelors." I huff a sad laugh and finish my beer. My life truly is sad when you look at it from a relationship standpoint. As in, I haven't had one since Michele. Just like my dad, my career has been my focus. I've excelled at it; it's half the reason I don't stay in one place for more than a few years. There's always a better offer waiting for me because I love to learn. It was ingrained in me to be the best. Every new safety course that becomes available, I take. Every new certification or training course that's out there, I make it my mission to ace. My physical fitness is at the top of my priority list, so I can keep doing this job better than the best for as long as I can. But that doesn't mean it isn't lonely as hell.

"How are things with Vanessa? You've been together a long time now."

"We have," he says simply. "There's just something… missing. I know she has her flaws, but I've chosen to see the positives for so long. And she's with me for me, ya know. She comes from money, so she isn't after mine. She's never wanted the spotlight. Do you know how hard that is to find? I think I've stayed with her for so long because I'm afraid this is the best there is for me. She may be a little controlling and self-centered, but at least she's not using me." He scrapes a hand over his face. "Fuck, that's depressing to say out loud."

I hate that for him; I don't think he should settle, but it's not really my place to say. We eat in silence for a bit, unsure of what to say. Who am I to be giving out dating advice anyway?

Except, I've never settled. I simply dated the best first, and no one has ever measured up. You can't find your dream home? You settle on something close and make renovations. You can't have your dream career? You work harder and find a way to get there one day.

But your life partner? The person you're supposed to love, cherish, and wake up every day, choosing them over and over.

You should never settle for less with your partner. The person who sees your flaws and meets them with kindness and understanding. The one who sees you, the match to your soul. Find the one who brings out your inner peace, while fueling your passion. Find the one who looks into your eyes, and you know that you're home. You should never settle for someone who simply fills your space; you should find the person who *expands* it.

I can't stay silent about that, because it turns out I might be the best one to give this advice. I found that, and once he does, he'll realize settling isn't an option. "When your kids ask you one day what you love most about their mom, will it be hard to answer because there are too many things? Or will it be hard to answer because there are too few?"

"Fuck off with that," he grumbles, chasing his words with a sip of his beer.

"I understand the pain of starting over. The loneliness. The heartache. I walked away from the best thing I'll ever have. Maybe it's okay to walk away to find what yours is."

He spins the glass on the table, looking anywhere but at me. "I think I'm ready to retire."

I choke on my bite, trying not to spit it across the table. With some sips of water, I get my breathing back under control and shoot him a glare. "You can't go blurting out things like that."

"Come on. We're thirty-four, Ethan. I'm well into retirement age for baseball players. I love the game and the team, but I'm tired. My parents are getting up there in age, my mom's health is declining, and I'm missing so much of my nephew's life. Did you know Lily's pregnant again? A little girl this time. I want to be there for all that. I don't think moving to a small town and living a quiet life is for Vanessa, though. She's not even sure she wants to be a mom anymore. So I have a choice to make."

I feel for his predicament. He's been with Vanessa for over four years. At our age, it's surprising they aren't engaged. But

Riv's a family guy; he always has been. His parents are some of the nicest people I know. When we were growing up, they always seemed to have a house full of kids, but they never minded. In fact, I swear the more mouths his mom had to feed, the happier she was. I know River wants that, the wife and kids, the loud, messy house, and kids running to and from activities. He told me that if his kids didn't like sports, he would dive headfirst into whatever they did love.

Jake and Thoren always joked that Riv would end up with a house full of girls who loved ballet and art. He would get the biggest smile on his face and brag that he could be light on his feet. I mean, he isn't, but the sentiment's there. Starting over with someone new and having to wait even longer to start a family is probably half the reason he's so hesitant to leave Vanessa.

"All right, here's how it's going to go. I'm going to get the job this time around, then you'll announce that this will be your last season and that you're retiring, and you move back, too. That gives Vanessa plenty of time to decide. If she doesn't choose to move with you, then it wasn't right. It's her loss. Then we become neighbors and live happily ever after or some shit."

He barks out a laugh and throws his napkin at me. "Yeah, okay. You're getting that job. The minute Thoren told me it was posted again, I knew it was kismet. That position is made for you. It's time to stop running and face the past."

It's facing the past that both excites and terrifies me. How would I handle being around Michele again? I know she still hates me, and I have to fix that. She's one of the most stubborn and strong-willed people I've ever met, and it's equally thrilling and exasperating. If there were a way to will things into existence, she would've discovered it. Instead, she works her ass off to get what she wants and it's one of the qualities I love most about her. It won't be easy, but it will be worth it. I've been waiting years for my career to be in a place to be worthy of her. Now all I need is the job so I can fight for my girl.

River and I stay for another hour, catching up on all the new things in our lives, and he shows me his latest photos of Griffin. It hits me just how desperately I want to move back to Cedar Ridge. Of all the places I've lived, it has been the only one that felt like home. Oakland is the first place I've lived that isn't near the mountains, and I hate it. I miss the fresh air, the hiking, and the beauty in the simplicity around me.

Before heading home, Riv promises to make one of his rookies hit a home run for me. I'm looking forward to seeing the old man in action again. I tell him to break a leg, and that I'll be there to cheer him on. The whole drive home, my head is filled with thoughts of hazel eyes, pretty pink lipstick, and little blue wildflowers.

On Thursday morning, the buzz of my phone on the nightstand wakes me, and my heart rate picks up when I see the 425 area code. This could be it. This could be the call that changes my life. With a deep breath, I answer.

CHAPTER TWO

michele

Besties and the Boys Group Chat

LILY:

Just got off the phone with Riv. He got the job.

THOREN:

How does he know before me? Why do you
know before me?

JAKE:

Not the point. Don't love the group chat name,
but also not the point. What do you need
Michele?

AMBER:

I personally think it's perfect.

LILY:

Answer us Michele or we're showing up. Don't
make me pack up Griffin.

MICHELE:

I'm not helping him find a house.

THOREN:

Come on, Chele, you're better than that and
you're the best option.

AMBER:

Fuck that. If he wants to talk to her, he can do it
on his knees.

JAKE:

I… I'll be home in 10 Whiskey.

LILY:

I don't know if I should gag or applaud.
Thor….?

THOREN:

Yeah baby, I'll get on my knees for you.

MICHELE HAS LEFT THE CHAT

Cleaning has never been my happy place, but it's great for working out my frustrations. A week has passed since I found out Ethan got the job. I still don't know how to feel about it. It's been years since we broke up, and I should be over him, but I'm not. When he chose to move with his family after graduating, it broke my heart. It tore apart everything I thought I knew. Once again, I felt like I was too much and not enough in equal measures. We had a future planned; one where he promised me forever, only to rip it away.

When I flew to Colorado to visit him nine years ago, he dangled that future again, just to turn around and say nothing as I walked away. I'm furious, which I have every right to be. How dare he move back to *my* town after all these years? I haven't mustered up the strength to ask whether he's moving alone or with someone. He posts about once a year on social media, and it's usually something related to firefighting, so I have no idea if he's involved with anyone. Not that I stalk his profiles. It's simply due diligence to check, and every time, it brings an ache to my chest and a day of mental recovery.

River called last night, letting me know Ethan would be reaching out today to discuss available homes in the area, which is what has me on my hands and knees, scrubbing my baseboards. I know I'm stronger than this. But if there's anyone who can break down my defenses, it's Ethan. After wiping the sweat from my forehead with the back of my hand, I wring out the dirty cloth and get back to the task at hand. The damn things aren't even dirty. I did my monthly deep clean last week.

My phone chimes from the kitchen counter, and I freeze. I can do this. I can tell him no.

With my rag and bucket abandoned, I wash my hands in the kitchen sink before picking up my phone. My pulse is pounding in my ears, and my vision tunnels from seeing his name on my screen.

ETHAN:

Hey, Michele, I'm sure you heard I'm moving back. I was hoping we could work together to find me a place to live?

My blood heats at his casual request. As if it's no skin off his back to see me again. As if he didn't shatter me, with a straight face, even though I saw the pain in his eyes. Is the pain still there? Does his chest ache and his hands shake, knowing we'll be orbiting each other's lives again?

MICHELE:

No.

ETHAN:

Come on, Chele, don't be like that.

I scoff. He has no right to tell me what to be like. To call me by a nickname like I still mean something to him. My chest burns, and I want to scream. Why does my heart feel like it still beats for him when my head wants to tell him to fuck off like he deserves?

MICHELE:

Don't call me that.

ETHAN:

Then please help me find a house.

MICHELE:

Nah.

I know I'm being petty, but out of this whole situation, this is what I can control, and I need that sense of strength right now. He could use the other realtor in town, but she's not great. She mostly works to have something to do, not because she loves what she does, like I do.

ETHAN:

Don't make me show up on your doorstep with my bags. I'll sleep there in my truck bed like old times.

Damn him! Images of the nights we spent stargazing and planning our lives in his truck bed flutter through my mind, sending warmth through my veins. I've had a wonderful and fulfilling life since then, but those are still some of my best memories.

MICHELE:

Fine. I'll call tonight and we can discuss what you're looking for.

ETHAN:

Thanks, Chele-Bell. Can't wait to hear your
voice.

I slam my phone on the counter, more upset than I was before, but now with a horrible inkling of hope mixed with the anger. Hope that I shove deep down, because no matter how much my heart still longs for a love like I had with Ethan, I won't let myself go there with him again. He had his shot. In fact, he's had *multiple* shots. And I'm worth more than that.

Twirling a pen in my free hand, the phone rings once, then twice, before the masculine voice skates through the speakers. "Michele," Ethan purrs, the same way he used to. A shiver skates down my spine, and my rigid shoulders relax. He's always had a calming effect on me in that way. His voice carries a smile, and I try to fight the one it pulls from me. "How are you?"

"I'm wonderful. I have a few questions to go over. First, what is your expected date of arrival?"

His chuckle is deep, and I sit straighter in my office chair. I took the phone call in here to keep this strictly professional. Talking to him while snuggled on my couch felt like it crossed too many lines. Talking about anything other than what is absolutely necessary seems like a dangerous game, too. "Jumping straight to it then? You always were a straight shooter. I'm planning on being there in about three weeks. Depends on how many stops I make along the drive."

I want to ask whether he's still in California and if that's where he's coming from, but I don't. "Okay, so you'll need a rental or a place to stay until you can close on a house. What are you looking for size-wise, and any desired locations?"

"I would like to avoid hotels if I can. Riv said I could camp on his land while the house is being worked on, but there's no bathrooms, and camping by a construction site sounds miserable. I don't need anything too big. Two to three bedrooms, and preferably on decent-sized land. Not opposed to renting until the right place comes along."

In my head, I flip through all the properties that are available right now, and only one stands out. I work mainly in this town, but occasionally in a few of the neighboring ones as well. The rental market is mediocre, but buying can be tricky, too. Most homes with property sell fast because it's rare they come on the market.

"I have a rental that is on the smaller side but right by the river with no neighbors in sight. I could probably get you in it right away. An older couple owns it; they moved out over a year ago to an assisted living facility. If you're looking for over half an acre, there's not much out there right now, but I'll see what I can find."

"Anything close to you?"

My sigh is heavy, "It's a small town, Ethan. Everything is close together." The property I'm thinking of is *very* close to me, unfortunately, but I don't want to tell him that. Homes available to rent on the outskirts of town are the only ones that will have the space he's looking for. And much like the sale market, they get scooped up quickly. This one has sat for a while because it's more than a little run-down. It shouldn't bring me satisfaction, thinking of him staying in that hunk of junk, but it does.

"All right, send over whatever you find. Maybe we can do some video walk-throughs this weekend? I get off my twenty-four-hour shift at seven Sunday morning and will be free the rest of the day. Can also do Saturday if I'm not out on a call."

Despite my efforts, my heart squeezes at the thought of him out on calls. What he does is incredible, but it's also terrifying.

It's what makes me even more conflicted about his move here. The position he's taking over is unique to our area. River explained it all to me, how he would be a Fire Planner for the local hotshots. I had no idea that there were crews that fell under the National Park Service with different roles, and that's what Ethan would be doing. He would still go out as Task Force Leader during calls, but the crew here is smaller than the neighboring wildfire crews. Their focus being on the safety of the locals and tourists, and preservation of the parks. It means still doing what he loves with less risk and danger, and damn if I don't want that for him.

"Sounds good, I'll get some properties sent over this week, and you can tell me which ones you want to view." The pen in my hand is still sliding through my fingers, trying to keep my focus on spinning it and not on the fact I'll see his face this weekend.

Ethan's quiet on the other end, and I can hear him shuffling before he speaks quietly. "I've missed you."

"I have to go." I hang up before he can even respond. *What the fuck!* That wasn't a friendly "I miss you." There was heat and longing in his voice, which tells me he's as single as a Pringle and I'm in big trouble.

ethan

I had a plan.

It may seem crazy since you can't count on anything in my career, but I love having a well-thought-out and prepared design. Like the road trip I was excited to take up the coast. I had so many stops mapped out.

That was before Michele's face popped up on my laptop screen as she walked me through homes last weekend. After all this time, she still takes my breath away. Now, my only plan is to get to her as quickly as possible. To finally set down roots in the town I've always wanted to make my home. There is so much time to make up for, and I want to get settled before starting my new position. The moment my two-week notice was up, I was packed and on my way.

I decided to take the small rental since I could move in immediately, and it was cheap. It's also temporary, so I will be ready when the right property comes along. Despite the fact we risk our lives on most calls, firefighters don't make much money. The pay in Colorado, fighting wildfires was significantly less than what I made at the firehouse in California. Going back to wildfires, even in a leadership position, means another pay cut. Worth it to finally achieve the future I've been fighting so hard for.

The drive through Oregon was scenic, the overabundance of greenery missing in Oakland colored the views outside my windows. Towering evergreen trees and sprawling mountain scapes filled the trip with all my favorite things. The things I fight hard to protect in my career. It didn't even touch the feelings I had when I crossed the Washington border.

This state, more than any other, feels like home. Even the traffic hell around Seattle was comforting, in a way. Heavy smog mixed with aromas of coffee, ocean breeze, and wet forest floor permeated the air when I rolled my windows down. Every mile closer to Cedar Ridge felt like I could release the breath I've been holding since the day I left. This place is *home*. Even with similar landscapes and scenery in Colorado, the area was never my comfort zone. I was an outsider, trying to make the cities and towns I worked and lived in my home, but they never were.

Beyond Washington and its breathtaking scenery, it's the people, the small-town feel, where everyone comes together, and the deep roots and pride everyone has for the unique Bavarian town. It's been so long since I've felt this light. Pressure from my parents, from my career, even pressure I put on myself doesn't feel quite so heavy out here. The world seems to slip away as the miles pass, and I can imagine the future I dreamed of as a child playing out in front of me. A future in the job I love, in a place that calls to me, with the woman who still owns my heart.

It's bittersweet, since I'm the one who ran from this all in the beginning. Not like I had much of a choice, so many factors influenced why I moved with my family and left everything and everyone behind. That decision still haunts me, because everything would look so different if I had stayed, but I'm not sure it all would have been good.

The circumstances around why I left have changed, and I need to make that clear to Michele. She needs to know why I disappeared on such short notice, and why I thought I couldn't come back for her sooner. I apologized on the day I walked away fifteen years ago, but she deserves that apology again. She deserves to see the pain and anguish in my eyes over how everything went down.

At best, Michele has kept me at arm's length, responding to my texts when necessary, and never breaking her smooth professional exterior. She told me to let her know when I would be getting into town so she could leave the keys in the mailbox, but that won't do. I need to see her. I need to see if her body still responds to me, if her eyes still hold the warmth that reminds me of the first sparks of a forest blaze. Most of all, I need to know that she's okay.

The winding road leads higher into the mountain until the rickety wooden sign finally announces my arrival to Cedar Ridge. It's a relief to see not too much has changed as I navigate my truck through town. Main Street is still pretty empty; the tourist season not yet in full swing. Some of the stores, like the iconic hat store, are still standing, while others, like the one at the end, are new. Anderson's Fine Furnishings sits proudly on the end of Main Street. The circular sign hangs over the door; it's a beacon showing life here didn't stop and wait for my return.

That thought pulls at my chest, but I continue driving slowly, taking it all in. The gazebo in the center of town looks freshly painted, and the lamp posts are all surrounded by flowerpots teeming with colored blooms. It's charming, clean, and exactly as I remember.

My parents lived right in town, but Michele's, like most locals, lived on the outskirts. Following my GPS, I see she's still further from the town center. The two-lane road has a canopy of leafy trees covering it and cracks that really should be filled. Heavy snow in the winter and deep roots of the forest have their way of breaking up the road surface. It isn't until I'm turning into her long driveway that I realize my rental is off this road as well. When I reach down to grab my phone to see how far away I am, the trees clear, and Michele's home sits before me.

The sprawling ranch-style home is pristine, and so out of place with the other homes in the area. Yet, it's exactly what she described wanting when we were growing up. The covered wraparound porch has an abundance of little pots all with blooming flowers of every color and kind. What I'm assuming used to be the detached garage is a deep forest green with two sets of glass-paned French doors, also surrounded by planters of bold-colored flowers.

Every inch of the home and property is meticulously manicured and cared for, and immediately, I know Michele does it all herself. She's stubborn in that way. I turn off my truck, then grab my hat from the dash and slip it on before making my way to the garage. River said she had a home office, but it didn't register that he meant like this. The lack of neighbors, the fact that anyone and everyone can come here and know where she lives, has me on edge. She did all this on her own, accomplished her dreams, and made this happen. I want to be worried for her out here. I am. But more than that, I'm insanely proud.

The first set of doors opens before I reach it, and there she is. Wrapped in a light green dress, hair around her shoulders, and wedged heels, Michele is a vision. From the day I met her with her little gap teeth and frizzy hair, to now with a blinding white grin and flawless skin, she's always been beautiful.

That bright smile falls quickly as recognition sets in, the pain of that simple action stabbing deep.

"Hey, Wildflower."

She bristles, recovering quickly and donning a blank expression. "Ethan. What are you doing here?"

"I came to pick up my keys. The lease is signed, and the deposit is paid, so I figured it's fine if I'm a few days early."

"I wasn't expecting you until this weekend." Her quiet voice is full of upset, but I'm not entirely sure why. "I'll get your keys."

My long strides eat up the distance between us to follow her into the office. I'm surprised by how nice it is inside, with pale pink walls, area rugs under her desk, and a set of couches and chairs off to one side. There's even a little coffee bar set with different drink options. The subtle scent of her signature vanilla lingers in the air. It's inviting, upscale, and warm. The entire space embodies Michele.

To the right, there's a set of shelves lining the corner that draws my attention away from the way Michele's hips sway when she walks. I wander closer, my gaze trailing over photos of her with different clients, some random mementos that are clearly from the area, before my eyes fix on one item. In a small shadow box, there's a bracelet made of dried wildflowers. The glass surround has hearts etched into it, adding to its beauty. I know that bracelet instantly, and my skin heats with the significance. I was never good at making those damn things, which is why I always stuck them behind her ear instead. I spent weeks practicing at home before presenting her with the one that's now displayed.

Her shoes click on the hardwood behind me, so I spin to face her. Not wanting to push, I don't mention the bracelet, instead motioning to the space around us. "You always did have a knack for making things pretty."

A light flush travels over her cheeks as she holds out a set of keys and a folder with paperwork for me. "Thanks. I wish you had told me you were coming early."

Studying her face, I detect a hint of frustration, but let it go. I knew she wouldn't be thrilled with me showing up, but my desire to see her won out over that knowledge. Her hazel eyes are filled with as much life as I remember, shining as bright as the summer sun. She was an adult when I last saw her, but barely. Standing before me now, she's all woman with mouthwatering curves I want to trace with my tongue.

"Can we sit down and catch up? Maybe grab dinner this week?"

"I don't think so."

Rocking back on my heels, I blow out a frustrated sigh. I know she wasn't happy to leave things the way they were in Colorado, but I thought she'd at least want to try to be friends again. Being shut down like this, to even just have a conversation, hurts more than I'd like to admit. I want to be equal parts proud of her for knowing she deserves better, and frustrated that she can't even try with me.

"Please, Michele. I'm back, it's a small town, and we share a friend group. We're going to see each other. Can you at least give me a chance to explain myself?" I'm not sure what I would say to her, how to justify any of it, but I have to try.

"You had a chance to explain nine years ago when I flew to Colorado to see you. Then you show back up here for what? A year or two before you want something bigger and better again? *And* you ambush me without telling me you're coming early? I'm not doing this with you, Ethan." She turns her back on me and takes several deep breaths. "Please, just go."

No part of me wants to leave. I'm dying to take her into my arms and hold her against my chest until her breathing matches my own. To see if her hair still smells like vanilla cupcakes. To tell her that no one has ever held a candle to her, and how that might be because I've never given them a chance. Most of all, though, I want to tell her that I'm here for good, and I'm going to make things right.

"Okay, but I'll be back."

CHAPTER FOUR

michele

The crunch of my gravel driveway under his boots recedes until his truck door slams and the engine turns over. With unsteady steps, I walk back into my office and slink onto the couch in the corner. One hot tear escapes, and I quickly wipe it away.

I'm mad at myself for letting him get to me so easily. I should be stronger than this. I've been mentally preparing myself for weeks. In my defense, I thought I had a few more days. He wasn't supposed to be here until this weekend. I had time to carry out the rest of my plans and get it in my head that I would see him around town.

I didn't think he'd ambush me looking the way he did. My brain short-circuited, my skin prickled with awareness, and heat flooded my veins. There was a complete loss of words—and feelings—until he asked to see me. I'm trying not to be bitter and hold on to the hurt I feel. He's a man now, not the boy who moved away or the young adult who asked me to visit him in Colorado. But those experiences, and the way he behaved, broke pieces of me no one has been able to repair.

Maybe I was broken from the start. I've always been stubborn, sure of my ways. I had to be, growing up with Austin as an older brother. He was loud and secure, a little bit of a hellion but with a good head on his shoulders. Our parents raised him well. So well that I think sometimes they forgot they had another child to raise. Austin was six when I was born, and without any intentions, they let me fall through the cracks.

I emulated everything my brother was, hoping to get the same attention, but it often fell on deaf ears. That's not to say my parents were cruel or didn't care. They loved me the best way they could. The older Austin got, the more he saw that he received the love and effort, and I was given the scraps. I tried to do everything right; have the perfect grades, take care of my belongings, and help cook and clean. Where Austin was given praise for these things, I was given a nod and a pat on the back. So I worked harder, strived for better, always working toward that praise.

My strong will, my ability to do things on my own, to persevere, all started so young. All of that changed with Ethan. He saw me, and he appreciated everything I was. There was no need to work for his love. He gave it freely, *with* intention. I was a priority to him, and I felt that in every action and word.

When he left, it shattered that sense of stability. That sense of self I had found again.

Ethan showed up on my porch three days before school started for my Senior year.

"Hey, Chele, can we go for a drive?"

"Of course. Mom," I holler into the house. "I'll be back later. Ethan and I are going to hang out." I shut the front door before she responds, knowing one isn't likely. "I didn't know you were planning on coming over today."

He opens the passenger door of his truck for me to slide in, not meeting my eyes. When he slips into the other side, white knuckling the steering wheel, he stares at my home, posture resigned, before loosening his grip and reversing out of the driveway.

I want to tell him that I picked out my outfit for the first day of school, but something feels off. Wrong. So, I wait until he finally responds, "We need to talk."

The words no girl wants to hear. Adrenaline floods my body, my heart starts racing, and my hands start to shake. My gut is screaming at me to run. To tell him to turn around, take me home, and not give him a chance to say the words I suddenly fear are coming. Maybe I'm wrong. Please God, let me be wrong.

"Okay," I draw the word out. I know he's been overwhelmed. His dad received a job offer a month ago. There's a chance his parents are moving, and he has to figure out his next steps, our next steps, sooner than we were hoping. He turns into a park down the road and pulls into a corner spot before shutting off the engine. It's secluded, and warning bells are blaring.

We've come here to toss a football or baseball around with our friends, but never just the two of us. It's weird, and kicks my heart rate up a notch, making it hard to breathe.

I don't want to hear this.

I need to hear this.

"What's going on?"

Ethan fidgets in the seat, wiping his hands on his pants, then grips the steering wheel. His eyes flit around the park, watching the families play one last time before life goes back to the school routine in the fall.

"I'm leaving."

Time halts.

The world stops spinning.

There's no air in the cab of the truck.

Despite feeling like a porcelain doll experiencing the first crack in her frame, he keeps going.

"My dad took the job. He's going to work with me on my training to get me a position. This is a chance for me to get a head start on my career. A chance to pursue my passion without struggling. If I stayed, I would have to get a full-time job elsewhere while completing my training. While attempting to get my fire science degree. This way, I start with a leg up, and I think I need to take it. I'm sorry, Michele. There are no words to describe how sorry I am, but I have to do this. You will always be the love of my life. One day, I hope you understand that I'm doing this for us."

Somehow, I hear his words past the pounding in my ears. Everything he's told me up to this point, every plan we laid, every moment shared, feels empty. What was the point of drawing the home we wanted to build? Of talking through the struggles we would face as a young couple taking on the world right out of high school.

He's stiff as a board beside me. Hands back to tightening on the steering wheel, working in time with the clench of his jaw. It's then that I feel it. He's holding back. This isn't even the worst of the heartbreak. Another crack forms along my porcelain skin.

I have so much I want to say, things I want to ask, but my mind is stuck on one. The one I think he's holding back. "When?"

Ethan must hear the devastation in my voice because he finally turns and looks me in the eyes. There's pain etched across every feature, and glassy tears swimming in his vibrant green eyes. The look he gives me is begging me not to make him say it. He takes a ragged breath, the inhale choking him.

"Tomorrow."

Nothing.

I feel nothing.

"Take me home."

"Michele," he starts.

Another crack.

"Take. Me. Home."

"I'm so sorry. Please, Wildf—"

"Take me home!" I scream into the void of the cab.

I feel it. A moment frozen in time. The porcelain doll dropped. Her frame shattered, but frozen time is keeping the pieces together.

It's tense and silent, all the blood drained from his face, and his body still, staring at me. I never yell. Then again, I've never been broken. Carelessly dropped to the floor. The keys jingle as he turns them in the ignition. The drive home carries the same air of discomfort. Heartbreak. Anger.

I have everything and nothing warring for the top spot in my head, but all I can hear is his word on repeat.

Tomorrow.

Tomorrow.

Tomorrow.

His hands tremble so violently on the wheel that he struggles to turn into my driveway. When he parks, he turns to me, but no words escape. He looks tortured, opening his mouth, only to continue letting the silence tear us apart.

With shaky hands, I unbuckle my seat belt and open the door. I pause to turn and look at him. 'Fight,' my head yells. 'Flight,' my heart responds.

"I love you," I say, and finally step out of the truck. Before I close it, I hear him whisper, 'I'll be back.'

I keep it together walking up my porch. I keep it together while climbing the stairs to my room. I keep together until I close the door and am greeted by silence once again.

Only then, as the first tear falls, do I allow myself to acknowl-

edge that time is no longer frozen, and I'm about to be broken in a way that will never be repaired.

Pulling myself from the memory, I look around my office and try to shake the feeling of the cracks showing through the thin veneer I worked on plastering over it. Needing some clarity, I text the girls.

ethan

With the keys and folder in hand, I retreat slowly, waiting for her to turn around, but she doesn't. I reset the navigation to my new place, thrilled to find it's only five minutes away. When I turn into the gravel drive that is overrun with weeds, the house sits like a taunt in front of me. It's a piece of shit. Even knowing its state going into this, seeing it in person is somehow worse.

Taking my keys, I face the nightmare before me. The small porch steps look days away from disintegrating, and when I unlock the front door, I have to use my body weight to push it open. A fresh pine scent wafts from inside when it swings open, the living room surprisingly clean. Someone has clearly wiped down the walls and floors; even the baseboards are cobweb and stain-free.

The kitchen, which sits at the back of the house, is just as tidy. While the linoleum flooring is starting to peel in some spots, I swear it's sparkling. I almost feel bad walking over it with my dirty boots. Down a narrow hall are the two bedrooms and a bathroom. These don't look like they've been touched or even cleaned since the last tenant. There are hangers and some empty boxes in one closet, and a family of spiders in a corner of the bathroom.

I don't understand why someone only cleaned half the house, but whatever. Michele warned me it wasn't great, so this is what I was expecting. After opening all the windows, I maneuver my truck so I can detach the trailer, holding all my belongings. With that out of the way, I remove cleaning supplies from my truck bed and get to work.

It isn't until I take a break and stick my head under the kitchen sink for some water that my phone vibrates on the counter.

Free Labor Group Chat

THOREN:

When do you want us?

JAKE:

I'm free all evening. And I'm slugging you for whatever you did to Michele.

THOREN:

He hasn't seen us since high school. Go easy on him.

JAKE:

Been a minute since I've hit someone. Gotta loosen up the muscles.

THOREN:

What did he do?

JAKE:

No idea, but Amber came into the shop talking about wanting to 'deck that Ethan dude' so I told her I'd do it for her.

ETHAN:

There's a chance she was crying when I left her office. But I didn't do anything!

THOREN:

I'll bring you a case of beer if you let me hit him
first.

ETHAN:

Oh fuck off, I hate myself enough. House is
almost clean, appreciate your help whenever
you can give it.

It's been almost half my lifetime since I last saw the guys, so I have no idea whether they're serious or not. I'm not entirely sure I won't be showing up to my first day on the job with two black eyes. Pushing it to the back of my mind, I finish the last bit of cleaning, which isn't nearly as good as the living room and kitchen.

The first couple of bags are unloaded when two identical trucks park behind mine. Jake and Thoren step from their vehicles, and there's no stopping my laugh, even with the scowls on their faces. They were inseparable as kids, so the matching trucks fit perfectly.

"What are you laughing at? The fact you're living in a shithole?" Jake steps over, slapping my hand away and pulling me in for a hug. "Good to see you, Ethan. It's been too long." We've barely kept in touch over the years. Random texts and the rare phone call. Nothing like River and me.

When he pulls back, he slams his fist into my side, and I double over as the breath is forced from my body. Thoren rolls his eyes and pats my back as I wheeze, trying to suck in air. "Bastard, you said I could hit him first." He looks down at me, making sure I'm okay, before pulling me into a hug. "It's good to have you back, bud."

"I hate you both," I croak through the pain. With a mock glare at Jake, I add, "Nice to see you haven't lost your touch."

The jerk just smirks at me and then moves to the back of the trailer. He grabs a box of kitchen items and heads for the house. Thoren follows suit, scowling when he picks up a stack of smaller boxes. "When does the rest of your stuff come?"

"What rest? This is it." I'm a bachelor, a workaholic, and I move often. It seemed pretty pointless to spend my money on nice furniture or fancy things. I have all the necessities and a very good-looking 401(k). That also means my belongings can fit into a small trailer, minus the sofa I donated before I left.

"Shit, you're even more pathetic than I thought. Now I feel bad that Jake punched you."

"I don't," Jake hollers over his shoulder. "I'm coming back this weekend to help you rebuild these steps." He bounces on the middle one, and I cringe as it almost buckles under him. "That shit's going to cave under your weight."

Jake's in the house before I can respond. I'm a built guy, but he has at least three inches on me and definitely more bulk.

"When's your brother moving back? He's nicer than you guys."

Thoren laughs, stepping into the house with me hot on his heels. "This is officially his last season, but he's been coming home more frequently since Griff was born. You know we're just giving you shit, right? I mean, we haven't seen you in fifteen years, but we still showed up to help you move in."

He's not wrong. River said the town would welcome me home with open arms, and that our old friend group, namely Thoren and Jake, would help make the move a smooth transition. They volunteered to help me without a second thought or complaint. I didn't even have to bribe them with pizza and beer, even though I plan on taking them out to dinner after this. I'm so grateful, even if I don't say it out loud.

There's true, genuine friendship here. Never settling down as an adult, moving around as a kid, has led me to feel hollow. There's been no depth in my life; everything has remained surface-level. I haven't even been back in Cedar Ridge for twenty-four hours and there's more meaning to my life than there has been in years. People filling the void I didn't realize was so vast.

"Don't let him off that easily." Jake is leaning against the old counter, arms crossed over his chest. "You were like a brother to us growing up, but Michele is our girl. Not only has she helped us both throughout the years, but she's also best friends with our wives. We aren't going to let you come in here and mess with her. That includes showing up unexpectedly and upsetting her."

My mind is struggling to unpack everything he just said, focusing on one thing. "You're married?"

He holds up his left ring finger, a black band tattooed on it. "We eloped last summer. Now, back to the point, what are your intentions with Michele?" It's almost scary how quickly he can go from a goofy grin, talking about his wife, to a scowl when protecting Michele.

Besides River, these guys are my only friends, even if they're a lot more intimidating than they were in high school. It can't hurt to be honest with them, because I know I'll need their help, or maybe their wives', along the way. "I need to apologize. To explain why I left, and how hard I've been fighting to come back the right way. I didn't think showing up a few days early would upset her so much."

I'm still not sure what it was about arriving early, but I feel awful about it. Every time I talk to her feels like I'm digging a deeper grave. Probably shouldn't have used her nickname to start with. We're adults now, and a lifetime has passed, but I need to make it right. She's still who I see when I picture my future. But if *I'm* not that for *her* anymore, I need to at least make things good between us if I want a fighting chance.

Thoren's been pulling open cupboards and looking around while Jake and I have our standoff. "She clean this house for you? It's immaculate."

I scratch behind my neck. "I'm not sure. These two rooms were cleaned, but the back ones weren't."

He finally finishes looking around and matches Jake's stance. "I guarantee that's part of the reason why she was upset. She always goes above and beyond for her clients. It's kind of her thing. Stocked Lily's pantry with a week's worth of food when she moved in. Bought River a custom metal sign for the fence he ordered for his property. Showed up and planted a whole flower garden off the deck of Jake and Amber's place when they moved in together. You showing up early probably meant she couldn't finish getting your place ready for you."

Damn it. I run my hands down my face, resisting the urge to scream. Why can't I get anything right with her? There's not an ounce of surprise that she would clean this place for me, even with her deep fear of spiders and clear contempt for my return. It's just who she is; who she always has been. Giving to a fault, always putting others before herself. "How do I fix it?"

"We finish unloading your four whole boxes and then you take us and our wives out to dinner and we figure it out." Jake pushes off the counter and stalks back toward the front door. He stops just before he steps outside, looking back at me. "We're really glad to have you back, Ethan."

CHAPTER SIX

michele

Triple Threat Group Chat

LILY:

Dinner at BlueRoots at 6.

AMBER:

I'll get Natasha to close and be there.

Michele:

I'm ubering there, I need a large margarita.

LILY:

…

Michele:

Lily. Spill.

LILY:

It's the whole gang. Including Ethan.

Michele:

Nope. I'm out.

AMBER:

Okay, we need all the details. Like ALL. Change it to 5 and we can be drunk by the time the boys join. Drop Griffin with the grandparents.

Michele:

You guys owe me.

There aren't many Uber drivers in Cedar Ridge, so it's unsurprising when my brother's friend Ian pulls up in front of my house. Not only did they graduate together, but they also joined the Marines at the same time. Ian was medically separated after eight years and has been doing odd jobs ever since, Uber being his most frequent. He gives me a wave as I walk down the front steps and climb into his front seat.

"You look nice." He eyes me suspiciously instead of driving. "Got a hot date?"

My cheeks heat at the insinuation. While it may not be a date, I absolutely touched up my makeup and re-curled my hair. Thankfully, I was wearing one of my favorite figure-flattering dresses when he stopped by earlier, so it stayed on.

I shouldn't care. I don't. It's just… I haven't been with someone in a few years, and seeing Ethan today affected me way more than it should have. He deserves to look at me with longing and remorse, and a little lust.

"No, just dinner with the girls. Now, hurry up. You sitting in my driveway is costing me."

He rolls his eyes, but slowly reverses and heads into town. We talk about Austin and where he's stationed now while he navigates the back roads. I make a mental note to give my brother a call this weekend. With a six-year age gap, he was already in the military by the time Ethan and I started dating, but he knows all about our past. I'm not sure how he'll feel about him moving back.

Ian pulls up to the restaurant, stopping me before I can step out. "If you need a ride back tonight, call me. I know you're an adult now, but don't be an idiot, and tell your brother I say hi."

Waving him off, I hop out and move to his open window. "I was never the idiot; that was you two boneheads. But I will because you owe me a free ride after that slow-ass driving."

By the time I'm seated at the large corner table, Lily and Amber come striding in. Lily's precious baby bump steals all the attention when her stomach growls while we hug. She shrugs and takes a seat, immediately opening the menu. "I fed the little gremlin an hour ago. She eats more than Griff, and she's still inside of me."

Amber laughs and gives me a squeeze before sitting. "You look pretty," she says with an observing glance.

"Busy day with clients." I let the small lie slip from my lips, not ready to open that can of worms yet. "Do Thoren's parents have Griffin?"

"No, Evelyn's worn out after treatment yesterday, so I left him with Ivy. Griffin squealed his head off when he realized he would get to see Vivian. They're the cutest little besties."

Griffin is two and a half, and Lily's mini-me. He's calm-natured, empathetic, and has the brightest smile. "That's really great. How is it having someone new in your little area of the woods?"

Lily and Amber live on a little dead-end street that has three cabins. Amber and Jake own one, Thoren and Lily own the other two. They had hopes of moving Thoren's parents into it, but since they've refused, they moved Evelyn's home nurse, Ivy, in there instead.

"She's always sweet to us. A little bit of a recluse. If the kids aren't playing together, you wouldn't know she's even there."

"That's good, I guess. If you ever want to invite her to a girls' day, you can."

Lily rubs her baby bump absentmindedly. "She seems pretty cautious about leaving Vivian with anyone, and there doesn't seem to be a dad in the picture, but I will extend the invite."

That hurts my heart, but I'm grateful she has Lily and Amber around for help. Knowing Lily, she probably shows up periodically, forcing play dates so Ivy isn't alone out there. Living alone is hard enough some days, and I can't imagine the stress and heartache of raising your child as a single parent. We do what we have to, but I want to see those around me flourishing.

Amber and I order margaritas, and Lily orders a tea, the silence stretching between us. Amber's gaze pins me to the spot as she takes a slow sip. "Five minutes of truths, Michele. Where's your head at?"

That's a very good question because there's a pendulum swinging in there. I want Ethan gone so I can continue living my mediocre life, where I strive to be everything for everyone so I'm not left behind again. To go back to feeling empty despite being surrounded by incredible friends and a fulfilling career. On the other hand, I want him to stay, because there's been a hole in my heart from the piece he took and never gave back. I've fully accepted he was my one true love, and I was lucky to have him, if only for a short while. I've dated since he left, and there was one I could have seen myself staying with. The thing is, I knew I could never give him my whole heart, and that wasn't fair, so I let him go.

"I don't know. I'm pissed that he's here, trying to step back into my life like he didn't walk away from me fifteen years ago. The bastard even came early without telling me, so I couldn't finish cleaning his house or get a chance to plant some flowers out front." The sip of my margarita does little to cool my heated cheeks. "He walked into my office like he didn't shatter me. Like he didn't make me question for years if love was real. How does one find the person their soul calls to, for that person to walk away? That's not love."

The conversation is getting too heavy, and my chest aches alongside the knot in my throat. I already relived the day he left; I can't do it again with them. "Then on top of that, he looks fucking amazing. He walked into my office with all his muscles on display and a backward hat like a dick. Who does that?"

Amber chuckles, shaking her head. "Yeah, fuck him for still being a sexy asshole."

My glare does nothing but make her laugh harder. "What? He's a firefighter; it's kind of his job to have big muscles. Screw him for the hat, though, that was personal."

"Right?" My arms flare out with my dramatics before I tone it down. "Anyway, the other part of me, mostly the touch-starved part that thinks with my heart and not my brain, wants to rejoice and climb the man like a tree. So that's where I'm at."

The margarita glass empties quickly, and I glare at it like the personal offense it is. Lily reaches over, placing her small hand on mine, her unique wedding ring on display. "Do you want our opinions, or do you want to move on and fill up on appetizers before the guys get here?"

"Opinions, please."

Lily nods, clearly thinking over her words. "Well, you've never disclosed the whole story, so I'm going off what I know. First, I think you guys need to sit down and have a conversation. Demand an explanation for why he left and didn't come back until now. Then, decide whether you want to be friends or not. I'm not sure how well you can avoid him, so if moving forward is what you want, figure out what you both want that to look like."

Amber scoffs, waving off Lily's opinion. "Well, I say you

jump his bones. You've already slept with him, so it's the responsible thing to recycle. If fifteen years haven't stopped you from loving him, nothing will. You owe it to yourself to see if there's still something there. You'll be miserable with the what-ifs, so might as well get yours."

Lily and I gape at her as she shrugs and sips on her drink. "You're not the same woman we first met."

Her deadpanned look is hilarious. "I'm married to Jake. What did you expect?"

"Still can't believe he's the only one you've been with," Lily mutters. We found out that little tidbit by accident one night, and I was shocked to my core. She got lucky nailing it the first time, pun intended.

I'm still not sure what I want to do with Ethan. Lily's right; I can't hide from him forever. Not only do we share the same friends in the same small town, but I know he will seek me out. Not to mention I'm about to have dinner with him, and I'm not prepared. His intentions are what I don't trust. Is he here for now, only to move when he gets a better offer somewhere else? Is he trying to find someone to warm his bed until that time, or does he still feel as deeply as I do?

He made promises and plans with me before that were all thrown to the side. The only way to know for sure is to have a conversation and go from there.

"Can we order appetizers now?"

ethan

I park my truck next to Jake's in front of BlueRoots, already regretting not swapping shirts. I refreshed my deodorant and sprayed on some cologne, but my tee is wrinkled. I didn't think about it since the boys are in T-shirts as well, but now I'm realizing it's not the best first impression for the women I'll be asking to help me win my girl back. The minute my trailer was unloaded, the guys were ready to go, eager to get to the restaurant to see their wives.

I tried not to let the bittersweet thought of that sting. They're the same great guys I grew up with, and they deserve love and happiness. Besides, do I even have the right to be jealous when I haven't given a single woman a shot since Michele?

Jake knocks on my window, pulling me from my pity party, so I step out of my truck. Clearly, I've been sitting there longer than intended because Thoren's already inside the restaurant. "Remember that talk we had almost three years ago?" he asks as we step onto the sidewalk.

I grip the back of my neck. Right after he found out I was passed over for this job the first time, Jake very bluntly told me that if I planned to come back, I needed to be sure that it was for good. "Yeah."

His eyes hold mine for an uncomfortably long time before he nods. "Just checking."

With that, he walks into BlueRoots with me on his heels. My eyes take a moment to adjust to the moody lighting, instantly stalling when they find hazel eyes across the room. Time stands still, the chatter of the restaurant gone. There's only her and me, and the erratic beating of my heart. I saw her earlier, but it wasn't enough. It will *never* be enough. I will always have this reaction upon seeing her. A quiet mind. An erratic heartbeat. And a feeling like I'm the luckiest man in the world for having known her love.

She blinks, breaking the spell, as the noise from the restaurant filters in again. Neither of the guys told me Michele would be here, and by the look Thoren gives me, this was his plan all along.

Jake wraps a pretty blonde in a hug before pointing at me. "Ethan, this is Amber, my wife. The one shoving mozzarella sticks in her mouth is Lily, Thoren's better half. Ladies, this is Ethan."

He takes a seat next to his wife, leaving the only available seat across from Michele. Her heated gaze rakes over me before she turns back to her friends. There's a flash of irritation, then resignation. I really regret not putting on something nicer. I reach across the table to shake hands with both women before sliding into the chair. "It's nice to meet you both."

Lily's smile is warm as she takes me in. "You too. Did the guys help you get settled?"

Thoren snorts as he flips through the menu. "He had less stuff than Jake. We had it unloaded and put away in under three hours. Someone took the term bachelor pad to the extreme."

"Thanks, pal."

"It's the truth," Jake adds. "He doesn't even have a couch. At least he's civilized enough to have a bed frame."

Everyone gets a good laugh at my expense, and somehow it only makes me happy. I'm the outsider here, the butt of their jokes and the one who doesn't understand all the sneaky glances passed between them. It only endears me to my old friends more. These are the types of friendships I've been missing. Lifelong friends that won't fade, no matter the time or space. Friends that are close enough to call you on your shit, and you know it's done with love. It makes the knowledge that River will be here soon for the gang to be back together even better. To have my best friend in my life for good.

These are the things that I gave up when I chose my career. My mom warned me what the consequences would be when I told her I wanted to follow in my father's footsteps.

Our food arrives as the conversation flows, my eyes constantly veering back to Michele. She's doing everything in her power not to look at me, even though I know she feels my gaze.

"Have you worked with search and rescue before, Ethan?" Lily asks, leaning back in her chair.

"I volunteered with the team in Colorado when I was able. It's been a few years, though. During the interview, they said you guys typically only have a few cases a year." It's the part of the job I'm most nervous about, since I don't have real-life experience. During the wildfire 'off' season, I trained with the local SAR team, but it was inconsistent at best.

I'm not familiar with these woods the way I used to be, and coming in to lead a team that knows more than me is a risk. The man I'm replacing has struggled to form a cohesive team, which is essential when you need to work well together to save a life. I've been a crew boss for a few years. I worked in a hybrid station in Oakland, doing both structural and wildland, leading teams there as well. It's not necessarily the leadership skills I'm worried about as much as the SAR aspect, and overseeing a team with more hands-on experience than I have. Stepping in to lead a team that has been working together for years, and changing things to hopefully be more efficient, doesn't always sit well with people right away.

This position is different from any I've worked in the past. I've always worked under the Forest Service, and while they have their own hotshot crews that can work together, they're separate entities. I've been preparing my entire career to come back to my dream location, even if the role is a little different, so there's no room for failure in leading the SAR team as well. The stress and pressure attached to that isn't something I've allowed myself to focus on, but I know it's going to come for me.

"You have a good crew," Lily adds. "They saved my life a few years back."

"I'm happy to join your first few training sessions and pass on any knowledge I can. You're not alone in this, and we have your back. If you succeed, we all succeed." Thoren places his hand tenderly over Lily's, then flicks his gaze between me and Michele, and I know he doesn't just mean in my career.

"Thanks, man, I appreciate that. I'm hoping I'll get more information about it all when I check in on Monday. It's a big change, and as much as I'm ready, it's also a little sad."

"Why is it sad?" Amber asks, leaning around Jake to look at me.

"I'm more of a coordinator and leader, which means I'm not actively fighting fires. That's my favorite part: being part of the action and putting in the physical labor to cut control lines, fell trees, and coordinate controlled burns. Now I'm in charge of the teams, making the calls from a distance."

Michele's fork pauses halfway to her mouth as her gorgeous eyes finally meet mine for the first time since walking in here. There's a flicker of relief crossing her features before she schools her face and looks back down at her plate. "You'll be great," she says, so soft I almost don't hear it.

We continue our meals, and the conversation shifts again. River has talked about this group, but meeting them and learning what they do and have accomplished is impressive. Despite having busy and demanding careers and families, they all made the time to be here tonight, last minute, for me. I'm humbled down to my very bones. This is the right time for everything to happen.

Thoren and Lily mention needing to head home to pick up Griffin, so I flag down the waiter and grab the check. As everyone thanks me for dinner and starts to gather their belongings, I notice Michele sitting still, looking at her phone. There's no way I'm leaving the table before her, so with a goodbye to the others, I plop my ass right back into my chair.

Hazel eyes meet mine when she realizes it's only us left. "Are you waiting until I leave so you don't have to say goodbye?" I ask, placing my elbows on the table.

"No, my ride is just finishing up a drive, then he will be here."

She got a ride here? Yeah, that's not happening again, especially not with a man. The green-eyed jealous monster rears its ugly head. "Come on, I'm taking you home."

"I have a ride, thank you. Ian will be here in less than twenty minutes." She mirrors my positioning, eyes hard and unyielding.

My stubborn girl, never refusing a challenge. Too bad I'm not the guy she used to know. He would have backed down in an instant, simply because it's what she wanted. That guy is still in me, but I've learned that I need to meet my girl head-on. Show her that I'm willing to put in the fight, no matter how hard or how long, because she's worth it.

"I drive past your house to get home. You can hate me from the passenger seat, but there's no need for you to waste your money when I'm right here." Standing, I hold my hand out for her. "Come on, Michele. Please?"

She slowly shakes her head, exasperated, but gets up, refusing the gesture to help her up. "Fine. Let me text Ian."

My chest squeezes when she says his name again. Even knowing I have no right to ask, I have to. "Who's Ian?"

Her gaze never leaves her phone as she answers nonchalantly, "A friend."

CHAPTER EIGHT

michele

Ethan follows me out of the restaurant, his hand hovering over the small of my back. He's careful not to touch me, but I sense him all the same. The prickle of awareness, goosebumps scattered over my skin, and the calm that washes through me, knowing he's near. I've always been able to sense his presence, his gaze, his emotions. From our first days of friendship, we've been attuned to each other. It's what made the transition into a relationship so seamless.

Like the true gentleman he always was, Ethan opens his truck door for me before offering his hand, which I once again deny. My body riots, wanting to sink into the comfort of his touch. When he shuts the door to round the truck, his smoky masculine scent envelops me, like a balm to my soul.

He hauls himself into the driver's seat, and the jealousy is pouring off him in waves. While I could have clarified exactly who Ian is, screw him. Ethan lost the right to feel jealous over me a long time ago. My three margaritas did nothing to tamp down the war of emotions still rolling through me, and my talk with the girls only left me more confused.

There's no way to avoid Ethan, and it's unhealthy to hold onto the anger and sorrow. They will only fester every time I see him until one day I explode. We need to talk, to clear the air. Only then will I have a clean slate to decide how I want things to look from here. My insecurities are fighting me, telling me that, aside from him admitting he misses me, he hasn't mentioned anything about being more than friends. What if I'm putting myself in a tailspin and he's moved on, and I'm the only one still pining for a ghost?

The steering wheel creaks when he white knuckles it, before shooting a quick glance my way. "I'm sorry."

As I cross my arms, a heavy sigh leaves my lips. "That list is long. Want to specify?"

His chuckle is quiet, and he loosens his grip, navigating the dark and windy roads with ease. "You've gotten feistier over the years." When I make no move to respond, he continues, "I'm sorry for showing up early and not letting you know. I didn't want to get my keys from a mailbox; I wanted to see you. It was selfish of me."

With the alcohol simmering in my veins, my filter seems to be out to lunch. "Everything you've ever done is selfish. Making me love you, then leaving. Staying away for another decade after I swallowed my pride and let you lead me to believe there was more for us. Coming back. Demanding that I help you. I was trying to do something nice for you by cleaning your place, but you ruined it." The road blurs before me as tears line my lower lashes. I bite my lower lip and will the tears not to fall.

"You ruined *me*," I add in a whisper when he pulls into my driveway.

He puts the truck in park and turns to me, his voice filled with heartbreak. "Michele."

It's not the same voice that haunts my dreams. It's deeper. Heavier. Like the air in the cab right now. That one word says it all. The way it's etched with sorrow and reluctance.

"Don't. I'll see you around, Ethan." I slip from his truck before he can stop me, closing the door, completely numb as I walk up the stairs and into my home. It all feels too familiar. Too painful. As soon as the door shuts, my body slumps against it, and I slink down to the floor, finally letting the tears fall.

His truck stays parked for a few minutes before the headlights splash against my walls, painting shadows when he backs up and leaves. My tears stream down my face as I slide my legs up and wrap my arms around them. Now I'm certain he didn't come back for me. He came back for the job, and I've been playing it all wrong in my head.

The tortured way he said my name had all the answers I needed. He said it like he was trying to let me down. He's moved on. Of course he has, it's been half a lifetime. It's just that my pathetic heart is stuck, beating for a man who left it behind. I knew this was a possibility, but still I clung to that small ounce of hope. I'm too old for this, and I've worked too hard to let myself fall apart like this. He's the only weakness I have left, and after tonight, I'm shutting that down.

Pulling myself together, I stand and head upstairs to my bedroom. The room is soft, feminine, and all me. Creams and pale pinks, fuzzy rugs and blankets cover the space. My boots get placed back in their rightful spot, and my clothes go into the hamper. I don my silky emerald robe and wander to the bathroom for my nightly routine.

Looking around, you might think that I'm a neat freak, but you'd be wrong. I'm broken. Broken at the hands of the man who dropped me off tonight and destroyed my soul beyond what he will ever know.

When my face is clean, my teeth are flossed and brushed, and my favorite floral pajamas are on, I turn out the bathroom light and pad on quiet feet to bed. My blankets smell like my lavender detergent and vanilla body wash, bringing a lump to my throat.

His smoky scent, vibrant green eyes, and soft brown hair are only a few minutes down the road, yet they seem further away than ever before, out of reach and unattainable.

One hot tear slips down the bridge of my nose, and I don't bother wiping it away. I need to feel this pain, embrace the heartache that burns me from within, and remind myself this is my reality. When his warm smile passes me in the street, when my heart skips a beat at his presence, I'll remind myself of this moment and these feelings and push it all away.

The sun's early orange rays splay across the room through my gauzy curtains. The thought of coffee that usually drags me from bed isn't cutting it this morning. Instead, I roll over and grab my phone. The group chat with the girls has notifications from them both, asking how I'm feeling about everything. That's a valid question, but not one I'm ready to answer out loud.

After throwing off the blankets, I slide out of bed before turning to smooth the comforter in place and fluff up the pillows. I trudge downstairs and set up my coffee machine, then go back upstairs to get dressed. By the time I make it back down, my coffee is ready, so I step outside to enjoy the morning's subtle warmth.

The wraparound porch is one of my favorite parts of this house. When I bought this property, it had a one-story home that I lived in for a few years. As soon as my career took off, I hired someone to take it down to the studs and expand it, transforming it into my dream home. It's inviting, cozy, and the porch is everything I wanted.

With my steaming cup of coffee in hand, I lean on the railing and take in the little slice of serenity I've built. A gentle breeze wafts the sweet floral scent, which mixes with the morning dew, my way. I take my time, enjoying the warmth from my coffee and the way the sunlight kisses my face before moving to the pile of pots I put together for Ethan's place. Staring at it, I realize I have a decision to make. Finish the project like I'm dying to, or deny us both and keep the supplies for someone else.

Gardening is my passion, my stress reliever, and my favorite thing to do for my clients. I don't do it for them all, but when I can, I add splashes of color to their landscapes before they move in. It's another thing I have to thank Ethan for. My love of flowers started when we were kids, picking wildflowers and trying to identify them all.

Now I plant row upon row of as many flowers as I can, hoarding seeds and bulbs in my greenhouse to share that beauty with others. Since Ethan's place may only be a temporary thing, I was going to leave some pots out front with easy-to-care-for options since he may be away for long spells of time fighting fires.

If I'm honest with myself, I'm still going to bring him these flowers and the welcome home sign. It called to me when I saw it, and I hope he feels the same, that he finally decides to make this quaint little town his home, as painful as that will be for me. With the decision made, I take a breath in and let my shoulders relax on my exhale. My coffee gets discarded on the railing when I grab the first pot and head to the greenhouse, and get to work.

ethan

Sleep evaded me last night, which wasn't a surprise. Michele eviscerated me with her words before running from my truck. A small part of me is glad that she ran because I had no idea what I was going to say. Sorry would never be enough. I've been selfish; I just didn't realize how much.

Leaving Michele the first time was the hardest thing I've ever done, and it hardened a piece of my heart. Then I selfishly flew her out to Colorado because I couldn't bear to go one more day without seeing her. I know I hurt her deeply, not pursuing her back then. She doesn't know I couldn't at that point. She also doesn't know that her visiting me for the week was the first time since the day I left Cedar Ridge that I'd truly felt complete. Like what I was fighting so hard to achieve wasn't some deluded pipe dream, and I could have it all. I could fight for the career I loved and the woman who will always own every part of my soul.

Moving constantly to chase my career felt easy. It's what I knew. I had a clear path on how I was going to put myself in a position to come back and fight for the future we once dreamed of. Being back now, seeing the pain behind Michele's eyes, feeling the ache deep in my chest, I see the depths of my self-centered behavior.

So I rise as soon as the sun does, trying to get settled. Even though this house is hopefully only a short-term rental, I want to show her that I'm not that egotistical man anymore. She needs actions to back up my words that I'm here to make things better. To make things right.

The guys helped to unpack my kitchenware yesterday, so all I had left were my bathroom supplies and clothes. All of that was easily taken care of last night when I got back. With hardly any knick-knacks or decor, the place is as complete as it can be. Minus the contents of the boxes in the corner, but I haven't hung those in any house, too heartbroken to be surrounded by such devastatingly beautiful reminders. I've lived like this for years, with only the necessities, but for the first time, it doesn't feel like enough. The emptiness of the house makes it feel temporary, like it always has, and I hate it.

Doubtful that there are any stores open at six a.m., I decide to work on the house itself, instead of the decor. The bathroom sink has a slow leak that I heard dripping through the night, which is first on my list. It's a quick fix with a wrench and five minutes, so I keep looking for projects. Jake said he would help with the stairs on the small porch, leaving the terrible front door. Tightening the hinges only works on two since the third is rusted through.

That discovery leads to a list of items needed in town: weed killer for the overgrown driveway, bug spray for around the whole house, gardening tools, and wood for the little raised garden bed in the backyard that could use a refresh. I've never gardened before, but the idea of growing some strawberries or some herbs sounds fun. Maybe even some flowers that I could show Michele.

She would always get a light blush when I brought her flowers as kids, but I learned quickly that those weren't her favorite. While she enjoyed and cherished them, she preferred a garden of flowers that never got cut. "There's a beauty in watching things grow and allowing them to know peace," she once said. With that sentiment in mind, I add flower seeds to the list, below the herbs.

By the time I've walked the property and made three decent lists: hardware store, grocery store, and furniture store, it's late enough in the morning that I can make my way into town. Even though the hardware store is locally owned, it has everything I need. The grocery store is next. I brought my cooler, knowing my food may sit in the truck for a bit. I'm not the best cook, mostly sticking to meal prepping, grilled meats, and vegetables, so it's an easy trip.

It's the last stop that's the trickiest. With a quick text to Jake, I head toward his store. Amber's head pops up from behind the counter when I step through the front door, surprising me. She's pretty with blonde hair and warm eyes, completely at odds with Jake's ink-covered body. "Hey, Amber, I didn't expect to see you here."

"I'm covering Sonja's lunch break." She gives me an inquisitive look, a question forming behind her eyes when Jake walks in from the back.

"Hey, bud. I didn't know your mom worked here."

"Yeah, two days a week when my dad's doing okay." He steps up behind Amber, cupping her neck and pulling her back to place a kiss on her lips. "You checking out my customers, Whiskey?"

I hold my hands up as she bats her lashes at him. "No. But what kind of friend would I be if I don't ensure he's up to Michele's standards?"

He growls, shaking his head in exasperation, before turning back to me. "I'm glad you stopped in. What are you looking for?"

The whole exchange happened so fast, I'm not entirely sure how to react. My side still aches from where Jake punched me yesterday, and I would not like a repeat. "Well, a couch was on the list, but I see those aren't here. There's not much room in the house, but I was thinking of turning the spare bedroom into an office. So, a desk, a coffee table, and maybe some outdoor seating?"

"No kitchen table?" he asks, walking around the counter and nodding for me to follow.

"There's only room for a small one. Since this house is temporary, I don't really want to buy one that will be too small for my forever place," I reply, letting my fingers trail over a beautifully made table we walk past. "These are incredible, Jake. You've really built something special here."

The back of his neck turns red as he clears his throat. "Thanks, man. I, uh, I have this desk over here. It's solid oak, has four drawers and one hidden," he says, pushing something under the lip of the desk, making a sleek drawer pop down. I've never been picky with furniture, but I've always bought it with the mindset that it's temporary. Seeing this stunning desk, I know it will last as long as I keep it, which I hope is forever.

"It's perfect. I'll take it. That might be the end of my shopping. I should have brought my trailer." Scratching at my stubble —I really need to shave—I look around at the rest of his furniture.

"Nah, don't worry about it. I can drop it all off when I help with your stairs." He points to a row of rocking chairs. "Michele has two of those on her porch that are her favorite... if you wanted those for outside." He crosses his arms, raising a brow as Amber laughs from behind me, causing me to flinch.

"Sorry," she says. "Wanted to put a sold sign on the desk. Sooo, do you want the chairs?"

Rocking back on my heels, I look between the two of them, eyeing me up like this is the most important decision of my life. "Yes," I say tentatively.

"Good choice." Amber pats me on the shoulder. "Now, tell me your plan to win Michele back."

"I'm not sure I have a plan," I admit. She scowls at me, and Jake looks disappointed. "I don't think step-by-step instructions are going to win her heart. I'm under no illusion that I have a lot to make up for. She was my best friend once. We saw each other for exactly who we were, and loved one another deeper because of it. I'm going to show up for her the way I used to: encourage her, support her, love her, in all the ways I know how. And then I'm going to hope that's enough."

Amber's scowl is replaced with a soft smile, but it's Jake who surprises me. He steps up to her, tugging on her hip and kissing the top of her head. It's tender, the most tender I've ever seen him be. "I think we let the man figure it out on his own," he says, looking at his wife. "Doesn't sound like he needs our help."

"Fine. But if he screws it up, I'm tagging you in for punishment."

Amber turns back to me, ignoring that they just had a conversation about me. "Come back for the coffee table once you have a couch to make sure it matches." She places a paper on my new desk and walks back to the front desk. "I'll ring you up, then you should head to Wendel's. They have a few couches ready to buy."

Jake whispers to her before clapping me on the back. "I'm swamped tomorrow, but can drop these off Saturday morning and help with the stairs. That sound okay?"

"Yeah, thanks again. Text when you're on your way." With that, he disappears somewhere in the back.

I've never had friends who volunteer to help me like it's nothing. I'll need to find a way to thank him, again. When Amber tells me the total, I know it's with a steep discount, and the guilt weighs heavily on me. I don't want to take charity from my friends.

"I see that look. He's happy to have you back, and this is his way of showing it. There is no expectation of anything in return." Something churns in my gut at her being able to read me so easily. Looking in her eyes, really looking, I can see the shadows in them, and the wisdom that comes with enduring pain. Like calls to like; it's clear this woman has known suffering and loss. "If it's something you really want to do, you can fix things with Michele. Plan or no plan. She'll need time, patience, and a lot of groveling. Please don't give up. And I suggest you start immediately."

Chuckling, I slip my wallet back into my pocket. "I'll happily get on my knees for that woman, any day of the week."

"Careful what you wish for."

CHAPTER TEN

ethan

My day of shopping was wildly successful. My new couch is getting delivered tomorrow, my groceries stayed fresh in my cooler, and I stopped at the local florist for a bouquet of flowers. While buying Michele wildflowers would be preferred, I don't have time to go hunting them down. The florist said the bouquet I bought is all locally grown, and that's a good alternative.

With everything unloaded, I am about to hop back in my truck when I remember what Michele said about me showing up unexpectedly.

Ethan:

Are you home?

MICHELE:

Nope.

Ethan:

Will you be later?

The three dots pop up then disappear again as I lean against the kitchen counter. When they don't come back, I slip my phone in my pocket and head outside to start on my projects. I've sprayed the house for bugs, and the driveway is mostly done with the weed killer, when my phone finally vibrates.

MICHELE:

After 5.

My heart skips a beat, a wide smile gracing my lips. I'm going to see my girl in an hour. Once inside, I make some grilled chicken and rice to eat on my back patio. It's not exceptionally large, maybe ten-by-ten, but the concrete is level and not cracked, so it could be worse. A rocking chair would be awfully nice, but my camping chair does the trick for now. There's a fluffy squirrel chittering at the edge of the yard to keep me company, at least.

I'll bring her dinner next time, when I've figured out just how carefully I need to tread. I can't show up to her house hungry, expecting her to feed me, and I shouldn't show up begging her to let me cook for her. I don't know how far I can push to show her she's still mine, after all this time. My shower is quick to avoid the incessant need to stroke my cock to thoughts of her. After, I throw on a T-shirt and joggers, brush my teeth, and grab the flowers on my way out the door.

Michele's SUV is parked in the driveway of her house when I pull up, bringing back the unease of the first time I came here. She has no garage, since hers is an office, and nowhere covered to park her car. Does she have anyone to dig it out of the snow in the winter, or does she do it alone? Just like how she lives alone, in this big, beautiful home, in the middle of the woods.

Knowing she would berate me for being protective and concerned *now*, I shove those thoughts aside and step out of my truck. With a quick peek into her office, I see it's dark, so I move to her front door instead. There's a pair of rocking chairs on the porch surrounded by overflowing pots of flowers, bringing a small smile to my lips. Jake and Amber didn't steer me wrong.

Her front door looms before me, and I let my fingers rub over the soft tulip petals within the mix of the closest pot. This is the fresh start I've been dreaming of, that I've been planning out for years, longer than she would ever believe. This is how I should have shown up the first day, flowers in hand, ready to let it all out so I can earn her back.

My knock sounds loud, or maybe it's the thudding heartbeat that goes along with it. I stand there, waiting, for an uncomfortably long time before her footsteps shuffle behind the door. Did she do that on purpose? Make me wait like I've been doing for half her life. I would deserve it.

When she opens the door, my mouth dries, and I have to physically fight back a groan. Michele is beautiful, always has been, but every time I've seen her since the summer I left after high school, she's been perfectly made up. In every picture on social media, her visit to Colorado, every video call looking at houses, her hair is perfectly styled, her outfit chic and pretty, her makeup done.

Don't get me wrong, she always looks incredible. But this, the woman standing in front of me right now, she is the girl I fell in love with. The one she doesn't seem to show anyone. Towel in her hair, an oversized tee hanging loosely around her thick, gorgeous thighs, not an ounce of 'put together' in sight, is when she's the most stunning to me. Perfection. Perfection, I haven't had the privilege of seeing in fifteen years.

A throat clearing drags my eyes back to hers, only to find them hard and unamused. "What are you doing here?"

Having to swallow to remind myself how to speak, I quirk my head. "You said you'd be home at five."

"Yes, and it's," she looks over her shoulder at a clock on the wall, "5:03. I just got out of the shower. You couldn't have waited a minute?"

I try to tamp down my smirk, but it pops out anyway. "I waited three."

Her lips twitch slightly before she lets out a reluctant laugh and shakes her head. "What do you want, Ethan?" She looks down at her toes and seems to register that she's in a T-shirt. Only a T-shirt. Delicate hands wrap around her middle, and she looks back up, an embarrassed grimace on her face.

I want to tell her I'm pissed she opened her door wearing that, but grateful at the same time. I want to tell her she looks even more beautiful than the last time I saw her, and the vanilla scent wafting from her is making my mouth water. I want to tell her my heart has been beating out of sync for the last fifteen years, but it is now perfectly in rhythm from being in her presence.

I haven't earned the right to say any of it yet.

"I wanted to talk," I say instead, holding out the bouquet of flowers. "Can I come in?"

A torrent of emotions flashes over her soft features before she points to the porch. "You can wait out here while I get dressed."

"You can put all the barriers up you want. I deserve them. But they won't stop me from knocking every single one down. Go do your thing, I'll put these in water then wait on your porch," I reply, nodding to the flowers. She looks at me incredulously, so I knock her lightly on her hip with my knuckle. "Go on."

My gaze follows the sway of her hips and the shirt clinging to her ass with every jiggle of her steps. Biting the inside of my cheek to hold back my groan, I finally step into her home and close the door behind me when she's disappeared upstairs.

It's exactly as I pictured, warm with soft colors, homey. Not a thing is out of place, the pillows on the couch artfully placed, and the throw blanket draped over the back. Everything is so meticulous, I almost wonder if she even lives here, or just treats it like a museum of untouched perfection. She liked order in high school, but this is an entirely different level, and it's a little alarming.

No one is *this* perfect.

In the kitchen, I search cupboards until I find a vase in a cabinet below the island. Once I fill it with water, I find the scissors and cut the stems before adding them to the vase and placing it on the counter. Even her cupboards are organized to within an inch of their lives, so when I'm done, I make sure to wipe down the countertops and ensure the centerpiece is perfectly centered.

Back on the front porch, I take a rocking chair and contemplate everything. Something changed in her life to make her this way. Is it a choice, a condition, or a desire?

Soft footfalls pad on the porch before she sits next to me. I don't have to glance over to know she's made herself what she feels is presentable. Something she never used to bother with, for me or anyone else. Michele was always comfortable in her skin, confident in who she was. She's great at putting on a mask, but I see the insecurity behind her eyes.

We sit in silence, only the gentle breeze and the creaking of the boards beneath our chairs as we rock. She's waiting for me to talk, and I will, once I decide where to start.

"It smells better at your house. Fresh, earthy, but floral. My yard just smells like dirt."

Her chuckle is light, airy, and it wraps tight around my heart. "That sounds like a you problem."

"Hmmm," I acknowledge. Leaning forward, the rocker moves with me when I rest my elbows on my knees. With clasped hands and my head settled on them, I finally turn to look at her. I was right, she's in leggings and a T-shirt, both clean, wrinkle-free, with her hair in a perfect bun on her head and light makeup on her face. Her finger and toenails are painted a pretty sky blue.

She's looking down at me, watching cautiously as I appraise her. Does she still care what I think, or is she this way with everyone? The old Michele would know, without a shadow of a doubt, that I think she's amazing. Smart, kind, funny, every ounce of her is incredible.

"I didn't come back for the job." Her eyes flare, but she remains silent, waiting for me to continue. "I came back for you, Chele. The job just allowed me to come back—the right way."

"The right way?"

A lump forms in my throat, the weight of my confession hard, because I know it will be a blow to her. She won't see it the way I do. "I couldn't come back for you with nothing to offer. I had to do it right, in the way *you* deserve. You've made this wonderful life for yourself with a thriving career, our dream home, and great friends. I couldn't come crawling back with nothing to show for all my time away, begging you to still love me."

I can't look at her, afraid of what I'll see. Instead, I focus on my old sneakers and joggers from two fire stations ago, completely at odds with the woman next to me. The one I will never measure up to, but I'll never stop trying to. "I've been trying to come back; the timing just never worked until now. This place." My hands run over my hair, pulling on the short strands. "This place is where I belong. With you."

Unable to hide any longer, I sit up and meet her gaze. She's stock still, her hazel eyes glassy and filled with emotion. "I'm not here for a while, Michele. I'm here for good. And I'm going to fight for you, because my heart… it still beats for you. It's never stopped beating for you."

CHAPTER ELEVEN

michele

The air is too thick, too full of the heavy words Ethan just put into existence. Words I can't accept, because they're simply that. Words. I've heard them before, maybe not these exact ones, but I don't trust their weight. They feel heavy now, but what about when he sees beneath the facade I've put up? When he realizes my new curves come with cellulite and stretch marks that I hide underneath pretty clothes. What about when this job loses its excitement, its shiny new offerings? Because it will. Who's to say that his words will hold their weight then?

Who is he to decide that I need something from him? That bullshit toxic masculinity that I know his dad put into his head. All I've ever wanted, all I've ever asked for, is his love and devotion. I wanted to be enough for him to stay. That's it. I wanted to know that I, Michele Joyce VonMiller, was enough for him, exactly as I was. That I was enough for him to stay. To love. To pursue.

My heart was in my throat when he admitted he came back for me. The bone-deep relief hit me like a freight train. I've waited fifteen years for him to come back for me. Fifteen years, I've longed for him to show up at my door in a grand gesture, telling me his heart was still mine. I craved that, dreamed about it, cried over it. I thought that's what he was going to ask in Colorado, only to be let down again.

Hope is a fickle thing, and the longer he waited, the less hope I had. Now, anger flows through my veins. Even though I want this, there's no apology for taking so long. No explanation why he left in the first place. He's being selfish, once again, to tell me this without asking how I feel or what I want.

"I wanted you to stay fifteen years ago. I asked you to come back for me nine years ago. Nine, Ethan. It's too little, too late. Your words hold no value for me." My voice comes out steady, if not harsh. That's good. That's better than the soul-shattering pain I'm pushing down.

His face morphs from pain to hurt to sorrow. "I know. I *know.* But I'm still going to try. I'm so sorry for how long it took, but I promise I'm going to show you." He stands slowly, his gaze raking over me one more time, eyes softening as he takes me in. "I'm not done fighting for you. I'll never be done. Once upon a time, I promised until my last dying breath, and if there is one promise I never break, it will be that."

My heart trips over itself, sucking the air from my lungs. I can't face him with that confession. He's carried my heart for fifteen years, and he's now telling me I've had his for this whole time, too? That simply can't be the truth. No one voluntarily walks around with a hole in their heart for *fifteen* years.

"I won't say the words until you're ready to hear them, but I will try to make sure you feel them every day in between."

His footsteps fade as he walks down my steps and back to his truck. I'm stuck, unable to move while he reverses out of my driveway. I'm still stuck when the sun starts sinking, and I know I should be making dinner. I'm stuck until the daylight fades into the inky dark of the night skies, the stars twinkling all around me.

That night, for the first night in over a decade, I forgo my nightly routine and climb straight into bed.

I don't plan to see Ethan again, diving into work as a distraction. The only downfall of my career is that if I have no clients or homes on the market, my workload can be light. I discovered that early on and took on a side business for those instances. My brother is the only one aware, since he gave me the idea.

He dealt with heartbreak early on in his military career, falling for a woman who couldn't be faithful while he was on deployment. Instead of dwelling on it, he found hobbies to take up his time. Gardening quickly became my hobby that he helped me turn into a business, since I wanted to do it on a grander scheme than my backyard.

That's how my property down the road came to be. It has no house on it, only a small storage facility, a shed, and a greenhouse. And row upon row of flowers. It's just over five acres, two of which are currently active flower gardens with beehives in the back. I have plans to fill it all, but for now, it's open space and some woodland. Over the years, I've expanded the gardens with a variety of flowers, but it's at a standstill until I either hire another employee or schedule more of my time spent here.

Imagine my surprise when Ethan dropped off a bouquet yesterday filled with flowers from my nursery. There was a sense of pride, seeing the medley he had chosen, but also a little heartbreak. My love of flowers started with him and our hunt to learn about every native wildflower we could find. He would love my flower farm and the mix of colors and plants I have found success with.

Except, he has no right to know about it, like he has no right to ask for another chance. No matter how badly my heart and body want to give it to him, my head won't get on board.

Anna's car is parked by the shed when I arrive, but I don't see her anywhere. My guess is she's busy with her bees. While she also helps me tend to the land and flowers, her real talent lies with the bees. She loves them and is a true apiarist, growing our hives and tending to them like they're her children. I've learned the basics, but they aren't my specialty. I help to package and sell the honey, but the rest is up to her.

In the shed, I change into my work boots and grab my shears, gloves, and a bucket before I make my way to the rows of tulips. They're in bloom, so I've been doing deliveries every three days to the local florist and grocery store. A few of the local hotels also purchase flowers from me, but they typically request flowers that stay in bloom for a week, and tulips can be tricky.

This venture may never make me wealthy, but it heals my heart in a way nothing else ever has. By the time my bucket is full, and I'm exchanging it for an empty one, Anna is hanging up her beekeeper's suit. "I hope you're ready for a long day because the honey is flowing and the roses, daffodils, and lavender all need weeding and the early blooms cut."

"Honestly, that's the best news I've heard all week. I could use a distraction."

She eyes me over the workbench, her dark eyes scrutinizing. "Everything okay?"

Anna has been with me for the eight years that I've been doing this, and while we've discussed our lives a lot, I've never told her about Ethan. She's ten years older than me, so she wasn't privy to my disastrous life before we met. "An old ex moved back to town." Grabbing leather gloves to shove in my new bucket for the rose bushes, I avoid her scrutiny.

"Hmmm, the one who got away?" My gaze shoots up, seeing a small smile on her face. "I'll tell you what I told my son last week. I have a mother's intuition, and your dating life, or lack of one, screams broken heart that was never repaired."

Heat creeps over my chest and up my neck at her insinuation. She's not wrong, but it's mortifying all the same. Being known as the one who was left behind, unable to move on, despite how hard I try to have the perfect life. "Is it that obvious?"

"No, I'm observant, and I've worked with you long enough to see. When did he move away?"

Clearing my throat, I keep fidgeting with the tools. "After his senior year."

When she's quiet for too long, I chance a look, but instead of finding pity or judgment, I see understanding. "Young love," she finally offers, quietly. "I'm sure people have lots of opinions. As someone who married her first love and is celebrating her twentieth wedding anniversary this summer, I can tell you that sometimes you get it right the first time."

Anna moves around the bench, taking my hands in hers. "It's okay to feel however you're feeling. Hurt, happy, broken, complete. Every emotion is valid. Just be kind to yourself. You're dealing with the heart of a woman and the hurt of a young girl."

My throat burns, but I refuse to cry, even in front of someone I consider a friend. I don't see tears as a weakness. In fact, I cry when I'm angry *and* when I'm hurt. But crying over a ghost, a love that still haunts me, is something I've done too often. I have certain things I'm used to keeping to myself. It wasn't intentional at first. My parents left town the minute I moved out. With my brother off serving, and Jake, Thoren, and River at college, I was on my own. I knew people in town, of course, but I had spent all my time with Ethan, so I didn't have girlfriends. I learned quickly to bottle up my heartbreak over Ethan simply because there was no one here to discuss it with. Now, it's a habit. I don't know how to explain what he meant to me, and how his leaving impacted who I am down to my very core.

It's similar to this nursery. When I opened it, I didn't bother telling my parents. My accomplishments never seemed to matter one way or another to them. Jake and Thoren had moved back, but it felt silly to announce my side hustle over one of our monthly dinners. I didn't mean to close myself off in this way, but now it's all I know.

"Thank you," I manage to croak out. "Where should we start?"

She takes the subject change for what it is, giving my bicep a light squeeze before grabbing her supplies. "Roses are furthest back. Let's start there and work our way forward. The honey can wait until this afternoon, when it's too hot to cut the flowers."

Together, we work tirelessly, breaking only shortly for lunch and drop-offs, not getting in our cars to leave until almost six. It is grueling and dirty, and the perfect distraction I needed.

CHAPTER TWELVE

michele

I pull into my driveway, turn off my car, and just… sit. I'm beyond exhausted, my body aches, and I'm covered in soil. Yet, all I feel is fulfilled. I was planning on making tikka masala tonight, but I think a bubble bath and something quick is calling my name instead. After placing my shoes into their basket by the door, I trudge to the laundry room to carefully remove my clothes.

I'm about to head upstairs to start the bath when someone knocks at my door. Trying not to panic over the fact I'm in nothing but a bra and underwear, I search the room for something to cover with. My raincoat is the only thing long enough, so I wrap it tightly around me and tiptoe to the front door. I peer through the peephole and let out an incredulous huff. If this were anyone else, I'd hightail it upstairs without a sound. I consider it with him, but my need to people-please wins, and with a false bravado, I pull open the door.

"Is this going to be the new normal? You showing up here every day?" I ask with pink cheeks.

Ethan grins at me, eyes lowering for only a moment. "Did I catch you at a bad time?"

"Actually, you did. Bye, Ethan." When I start to close the door, he stops it with his foot. After looking down at it and back up at him, I notice the bags in his hands, raising an eyebrow impatiently.

"I'm here to make you dinner. You can finish whatever it is you were doing. I'll be in your kitchen." His smile widens when I stare, deadpan. There's a decision to be made here, the smart one probably being to remove his foot and shut the door. The problem is, I'm tired, my emotions are fried, and not having to cook sounds amazing.

Reluctantly, I allow him to push the door open enough to step inside and shut it behind him. He kicks off his shoes, toeing them to the side, which I appreciate. Without acknowledging that he bombarded me in my home like he owns it, he moves into the kitchen with ease.

"Go do your thing," he says over his shoulder, his eyes lingering on my exposed thighs. "Dinner will be ready in thirty."

Okay, then. Trying not to dwell on whatever is happening here, I hug the coat around me and dash up the stairs. I close my bedroom door and let my body slump against it. What have I done? He has no right showing up like this, so why did my heart skip a beat when he smiled at me?

Bath, I remind myself. A bath will fix all my problems. While the tub fills, I add some bubbles and salts before scrubbing my face clean. After peeling off the rest of my clothes and hanging the jacket in my closet, I tiptoe back to the bathroom and slowly sink into the scalding water.

It stings and soothes all at once as my toes pop out the other end and my shoulders become engulfed in bubbles. Sitting in the tub after a long day in the flower fields is the only thing that can relax me and ease the tension in my muscles. Well, that and a quality orgasm.

There's a clank of a pan from downstairs ruining my thoughts of forgetting he's here, so I turn on a random playlist on my phone to drown him out. The first song plays, All of Me by John Legend, which only brings my focus to Ethan. He's in my kitchen, cooking our dinner after work, like it's any normal week-day. Suddenly, I can see it. The life we could have had, if he hadn't left. The life I've yearned for that he said he came back here to have with me.

Cooking together, drinking coffee on the porch in the morn-ing, and sharing a beer in the evening. Quiet nights on the couch watching River play ball, dates in town, hikes to our favorite lookouts. Growing and changing every day, and choosing to do it with Ethan by my side. Ebbing when he flows, as we navigate the waters of life. It would be so easy to fall into that routine. To demolish my walls and let myself experience care from a man who owns my heart as equally as my body.

After a full body scrub, I close my eyes and relax into the warmth. My mind tries to wander to the man downstairs, and no matter how hard I fight it, he's all I see. His alluring smile and vibrant green eyes that twinkle, as if they know all my secrets. The way his shirts cling to his broad shoulders and the raw power he exudes, in whatever clothes he wears.

My hands wander, sliding over my sensitive nipples, tugging lightly at the little bar piercings. The whimper it draws is imme-diate and unstoppable. My nipples have always been sensitive, and it only compounded when I got them pierced. Every brush against them brings them to stiff peaks. It was one of the greatest decisions I've made for myself.

One hand drifts lower, except in my mind, the hand is not my own. It's the hand of the man cooking me dinner downstairs. We were each other's firsts, and took the time to get to know each other's bodies. I can only imagine the way those rough fingers would feel pressing down on my clit now. The skills he must have picked up after all this time. Could he still make me come with one finger and his tongue?

Squeezing my eyes shut, I push two fingers in, stroking myself while still giving my nipple attention. I'm so lost to the pleasure, I don't hear the footsteps or notice the door slowly opening. The prickles of awareness get lost in the pleasure. It isn't until Ethan's muttered *fuuuck* that I'm pulled from my daydream.

"What the fuck?!" Water splashes over the edge of the tub as I rush to cover myself, which really shouldn't be hard since my hands were in the right places.

Ethan at least has the decency to look ashamed and keeps his eyes fixed on my face. "I knocked on your bedroom door and called your name. Dinner's ready."

"Thanks for the update. You can go home now."

His eyes darken, taking in every inch of my face. "Michele," he says with so much longing, the walls I've constructed shake, just a little.

Then I remember the pain, the hurt, the absolute devastation I faced when he left me not once, but twice. Not caring that I'm naked in the bath, I sit up and cross my arms, glaring at him. "Am I enough for you now? What is it I didn't have before that you must see now? Am I suddenly smart enough? Pretty enough? Put-together enough? Successful enough?"

Each question hits him like a bullet, his recoil visible. Good. "I know it's not my body, since that's the one flaw *everyone* points out."

You'd be stunning if you lost thirty pounds.

Guys like something to hold on to, but not that much.

You have everything, just maybe work on your diet.

Joke's on them, I've never dieted. I've never seen my weight as a flaw. It's a body worth celebrating. I can love it for exactly what it is while still acknowledging there are parts of it I don't like. This is the body that's carried me through thirty-three years of life. Through love and heartbreak; through joy and sorrow.

It's sorrow that I'm feeling now, biting my lower lip to keep it from trembling. I had a weight gain from high school to when I saw him in Colorado, but it was small. The typical "freshman fifteen" even though I didn't go to college. I've put on thirty pounds since then, and no matter how much I appreciate my body, it's hard to have it on display for someone new. Ethan may not be new, per se, but this is this is the first time he's seen me with added curves. I think all women feel that way though, fully exposed for the first time.

Ethan tilts his head, flexing his hands at his side. "You've always been enough Michele. It's *me* who isn't enough for *you*. Let me show you how enough you are. Let me help you finish what you started."

michele

His voice is pure gravel, deep and filled with need. Pupils blown wide with lust as he looks me over unabashedly.

"You don't deserve to touch me."

"I know, Wildflower. Let me make you feel good anyway." His gaze implores mine, begging me to let him in. To do this one thing. And for the life of me, I can't think of why this is a bad idea.

With a small dip of my chin, he visibly relaxes and grabs my towel off the counter, before walking over and holding it out for me. Water cascades down my body as I stand and step from the tub, only to be wrapped up by him. Ethan takes his time drying me off, ensuring he soaks up every last drop, before holding the towel around me again.

Taking my hand, he leads me into my bedroom, stopping in front of my large free-standing mirror in the corner. "Sit," he commands before adding, "Please."

After adjusting the towel, I lower myself to the floor in front of the mirror. In the reflection, he moves to my nightstand, opens it and searches through. My cheeks heat when I realize what he's looking for and will absolutely find. His low whistle has that warmth traveling down my limbs as he holds up a purple dildo, and my favorite pink vibrator.

Ethan sits behind me, and he sets the toys next to his leg before leaning forward to delicately unwrap my covering. "You said I don't deserve to touch you, and you're absolutely correct. I haven't earned that yet, but I can still take care of you."

He's careful not to put his hands on me as he lowers the towel around my hips. In the mirror, his eyes travels over every inch of exposed flesh. His groan rumbles through the room as his fists clench and release. "You are so fucking beautiful, Michele. I want to kill every person who ever made you feel otherwise, myself included. Do you know how hard it is to not touch you right now? To not demand to know when you got those pretty tits pierced and to run my tongue over them the way you used to love."

I *want* to know. I want to lean against him and feel how hard everything is. "Shirt off." My voice trembles, but he complies immediately. I like that, *a lot*, knowing he will do whatever I say. With his legs spread around mine, I lean into his chest, letting my knees fall open.

"Fuck, baby." His raspy tone skates over my shoulder as his gaze stalls on my exposed pussy. I'm so busy looking at his body in the reflection, broad shoulders that make me feel small, green eyes looking like the forest at sunset, that I don't see him pick up the vibrator.

A quiet buzz echoes through the room, and he brings the toy to my nipple, circling it lightly. The vibrations are accentuated by my piercings, it's unlike anything I've ever felt before. My back arches at the sensation, the waves of pleasure shooting to my core. I can't help but wiggle, chasing the feel of it. My ass scoots closer against him, nestling his hard cock against me. His shorts are loose and soft, not hiding an ounce of his desire. "Still so responsive. Does that feel good?"

"Yes," comes my breathy reply as he moves the toy to my other nipple. His chest is hot and hard against my back, heaving with labored breaths that rock me against the vibrator.

My eyes close when he presses directly on my nipple before upping the setting. "Watch," he rumbles in my ear, making my eyes fly open again. He takes my dildo and brings it to his lips, before sucking it into his mouth. When it comes out, covered in his spit, he holds it to my pussy, gently pushing the tip of it in. "If this is the closest I can get to my mouth on your pretty pussy, I'll take it."

He pushes it in deeper as I whimper at his words, spreading my legs wider. The vibrator on my nipple becomes too much, but Ethan knows. After all these years, he can still read my body, still knows what I like and when I'm overwhelmed. His strong arms flex around my sides as he fucks me with the dildo in earnest and moves the vibrator to my clit.

I cry out at the overwhelming euphoria shooting through me. I'm so wet, I'm dripping onto the towel below as Ethan's eyes struggle to focus on any one thing. "That's it, baby. Take your pleasure from me. You look so beautiful doing it."

His hips rock, and I'm not sure he's even aware he's doing it. Sinking into his chest changes the angle, making him hit the perfect spot. "Faster, Ethan. Please."

"Oh, baby, it should be me begging." He increases the pace of his thrusts as euphoria hits and my orgasm comes within reach. "Come for me, Wildflower. Let me see you come for me."

Our eyes lock in the mirror when the pleasure crests, and I cry out in ecstasy, pussy clenching around the toy. His hips rock a few more times before he shudders and stills. After clicking off the vibrator, he tosses it to the side. With eyes locked on my pussy, he slowly withdraws the dildo and holds it in front of us. "May I?" he asks low. I'm not sure what he means, but I nod anyway. He brings it to his mouth again, and slides it between his lips, sucking it clean of my release.

"You taste even better than I remember."

Aftershocks of pleasure cause shivers to run through me. He slowly sits me up and stands behind me. It's then I see the wet patch on his shorts. Instead of talking about it, he runs a hand over my cheek, achingly soft. "Ready for dinner?"

I think about it, but I'm no longer hungry, just beyond exhausted. "No, I just want to sleep," I say with a yawn. Before I can make a move, he bends down and scoops me into his arms, carrying me over to my bed with ease.

"Do you always make your bed like this?"

I glance over at it, the sheets tucked in, comforter straight, pillows even, and throw pillows set artfully on top. "Yes."

Humming in response, he sets me at the bottom to pull the blankets down before picking me back up and laying me under them. I should fight him off, tell him I can do it, and hide myself from him, but what's the point?

Ethan carefully tucks me in, brushes my hair back from my forehead, and trails his fingers down my face. Sleep is pulling me under when I hear the faucet running in my bathroom, and before I'm fully out, I swear I feel the brush of lips over mine.

CHAPTER FOURTEEN

ethan

Jake's truck and trailer are in my driveway when I arrive home. With the events of last night, I completely forgot he was coming by this morning. Wincing, I step from the truck and make my way to where he's removing the rotting porch steps.

"Nice of you to join me," he grunts, prying up another board. "At your own house."

Rocking back on my heels, I grip the back of my neck. "I'm sorry, man. I completely lost track of time. Can I brush my teeth and make coffee? I'll make you breakfast or something."

He stands to his full height, crossing his arms with an intimidating glower. "Want to tell me where you were?"

Not particularly, but it wasn't really a question. "Talk over coffee?"

"Nah, I'm not sure I'm staying for coffee after whatever your answer is."

I suppose that's reasonable. He warned me two years ago and again a few days ago exactly where his loyalties lay. Last night isn't something I want to divulge. I've never been one to kiss and tell, and I'm getting the feeling that, for how open Michele can be, she keeps a lot of things about herself private. I'll tell him the basics, though. "I was at Michele's."

He raises an eyebrow, checks his watch, then looks back at me. I'm well aware it's 7 a.m., and he doesn't believe a word coming out of my mouth. I step around him, unlocking the door and avoiding the first three steps he removed. Jake reluctantly follows me inside, leaning against the counter while I start a pot of coffee.

"I brought her dinner last night. She went to bed before I left, and I obviously couldn't lock her deadbolt and still get out, so I slept in my truck." The truth is, after putting her to bed, washing her toys, and draining her tub, I went downstairs and put dinner in the fridge for her. When I saw the flimsy lock on her door on the way out, I was petrified until I saw the deadbolt. There was absolutely no way I would be leaving her without that safety measure.

Cedar Ridge is a pretty safe town, but after living outside of Oakland the last few years, my trust in people has wavered. I hate the idea of someone getting to her while she is all alone in these woods. It was the only choice, even if my back is revolting this morning.

"She went to bed before you left?" he asks with a smirk when I hand him a cup of steaming coffee.

"Watch it."

Jake raises his free hand in defense and chuckles as he brings the mug to his mouth. "I respect you staying. I would have done the same." He scratches his beard. "Thoren and I have a great alarm system in our cabins. Never really go to Michele's place, so I didn't think to make sure she had one. I'll order one today." When I open my mouth to argue that I can, he stops me. "She'll be a lot more accepting of me doing it than you. Take the win."

Unfortunately, he's right. Doesn't mean I'm not going to be the one paying for it. We drink our coffee in silence, and I appreciate it. Jake has never been one to fill the void with small talk, and I commend that. What you see is what you get; what he says is what he means. I can't help but feel, again, that Cedar Ridge is exactly where I'm meant to be.

After a quick bathroom trip to pee and brush my teeth, I help him replace the stairs, and we carry the desk into my office and get the outdoor rocking chairs set up. Sleep was pretty abysmal last night in the truck, so after he leaves, I pass out on my new couch watching highlights of the Rainiers.

Upon waking up in the afternoon, I realize my phone is still sitting in my truck outside. No surprise to find it's dead, so I plug it in and make myself a sandwich. When I walk back to my room to check it, I see a text from Jake letting me know the security system is ordered, and one from Michele. There are only two words, but they feel like a start. A really good start.

MICHELE:

Thank you.

Sunday brought with it a day of rain, which felt fitting. My mind was a mess, trying to sort through my feelings and fighting nerves for the meeting with my Division Supervisor, Mr. Daniels. Every new position, each new area, comes with its own set of circumstances and challenges. Although I mostly grew up here, there's still so much to learn about the new position. The end of the weekend passed quickly, and Monday came all too soon, my head still cluttered.

In the front hall of the building shared between the park rangers, SAR, and wildfire teams, my knee bounces while I wait to meet with Mr. Daniels. The drab interior is outdated and worn, but that's to be expected. As I focus on the beige couch before me, images of Michele on Friday night flood my vision.

Her body is curvy and soft, and it has been haunting my memories that I didn't get to touch and lick every inch of it. Her pierced tits, grabbable hips, and juicy ass. The way her pussy cried for me and gripped the toy so tight, I had trouble pulling it out. Fuck, I'm getting hard thinking about it. I don't think it escaped her notice that I came in my pants like a chump, but how could I not?

She didn't let me touch her, but what she allowed me to do was intimate and took trust. Her consent told me there's still hope for me, for *us*. Counting on that, I stayed away yesterday to give her time to process. If I had my way, I would be at her house every day, making her meals, telling her how sweet, funny, and smart she is, and fucking her to sleep every night. In a similar way to how I had to fuck my hand twice last night just to get to sleep.

"Ethan Hill?" A voice breaks up my spiraling thoughts.

"Mr. Daniels," I stand to shake his hand. He was part of the interview panel, and we've had a few virtual meetings discussing my transition since I was offered the job. While he's only about ten years older than me, he looks weathered and tired. Firefighting will do that to you. "So nice to see your face outside of a screen."

His laugh is boisterous as he claps me on the back and leads me down a back hallway. "The feeling's not mutual. My wife buys those damn firefighters and puppies calendars every year, and you look like you could be on it."

"I'm flattered… I think? But you'll have to inform her I'm a one-woman man and that position's been claimed." More like I claimed her and not the other way around, but I'm working on it.

He steps into the conference room and takes a seat at the table, eyeing me with a look of respect. I know the stigma, the statistics, hell, I lived through it, although I didn't find out until much later.

Firefighters cheat, the divorce rates are high, the hero worship can go to their heads.

I think I have two things working for me in that regard. There's no hero worship in wildfires. In fact, I don't think many people know what we do, nor do they know how dirty and grueling the work is. And, my mom raised me better than to ever cheat on a woman.

"That's good to hear. You're in a leadership role now, son. There's no room to be anything less than on your game at all times. This is a high-pressure position. As we have discussed, you will be leading the SAR team as well as holding the fire planner position. Maintaining knowledge of weather conditions, working with the park rangers to make sure they keep fire hazards to a minimum, and working with your team on controlled burns is just the tip of the iceberg."

My hands move to my lap so they can wring together out of his sight. This is the next step in my career, the position I've been working toward for years, but it's overwhelming. "I understand, sir."

"We convinced Reynolds to stay on for two more months to make this transition as smooth and seamless as possible. He worked with the Forest Service before the Park Services and can advise on the differences you'll encounter and see. He has a wealth of knowledge and will be able to teach you the zones we're working in, the protocols and procedures you'll be in charge of, and the system we have created to make the calls on how and where fires will be handled."

His gaze is hard, but kind. "To be frank, you have the experience in fighting wildfires that we need, but making the tough calls, following the fire line, and having the crews' lives in your hands is nothing to sneeze at. We're a team, and while my position is mostly based out of Spokane, I'm only a phone call away at any time. The safety of your crew, the citizens, tourists in the area, and the park is a big responsibility, but you have a good hotshot team. You have incredible crew bosses, so rely on them and their knowledge, too. We all want you to succeed."

By the time we end our meeting, I'm a pile of nerves. The confidence I was feeling has been taken over by the pressure to not only do this job successfully, but with no injuries or casualties, while still learning the ropes. Daniels and Reynolds showed me my office and introduced me to some of the crew. I met with Thoren and some of his guys as well, and we set up a tentative training schedule for the next month.

Despite this, I'm not sure I retained any of it. I felt like a shell of myself, floating along while my body moved from place to place. Nodding when I should, laughing when others did. When I get in my truck to go home that evening, I finally expel the breath that has felt trapped all day.

michele

In between a showing and meeting with new potential buyers, I make a quick run to Ethan's place to drop off his flowers. Color me surprised when I drive up to find new porch steps, a decently manicured yard, and two Jake-made rocking chairs out back. I wasn't trying to snoop, but I may have gone overboard with the flowers and didn't want to put all six pots out front.

The two filled with forget-me-nots went on the bottom step of his porch, while the other four went to each corner of his back patio. With some time to spare, I sat and enjoyed the fruits of my labor. The pots on the patio are filled with a mix of wildflowers, colors popping in every shade. Between that, my favorite chair, and the sounds of the creek hidden from view, this isn't a bad spot if you don't turn around and notice the dilapidated and cracked siding of the small home.

On my way back to the car, I stick the small 'Welcome Home' sign in the ground next to the porch, and head back to work. I've managed to keep my focus on my tasks until my lunch break, when I heated up the leftovers from my uneaten dinner. The man made me Tuscan chicken orzo, and it was incredible. Warmth works its way up my cheeks when I think about that night. How I let him into my home and the events that transpired. He saw every inch of me, and the look in his eyes was pure desire. As confident as I try to be in my body, of course, I worried about what he would think. There was no denying that he loved what he saw. It shouldn't matter, but it did.

Finding everything clean the next morning, and the meal placed in the fridge for me, had stupid tears falling when they weren't welcome. I wanted to call the girls and ask for advice, but everything just feels so… raw. I'm not ready to bleed myself open when the emotions are still too close to the surface.

Calling it quits at four, I lock up the office and head into the house to work on my other business. Anna and I collected almost nine pounds of honey that we usually sell in a mix of half-gallon or eight-ounce jars. We had a special request from a repeat customer who wants one-ounce jars to hand out at her wedding. Lucky me, I get to pour all eighty-five of them. At least she's putting the stickers and designs on the jars, so I don't have to do that part.

A few jars in, my phone vibrates on the counter next to me, and my brother's face smiles up at me. Using my knuckle, I answer the video call and angle it so we can see each other.

"Hey, little sis." His deep voice comes through the speakers. "What are you up to?"

"Pouring honey and making a mess of my nice counters. What about you?"

He scoffs, knowing me too well. "What's covering the counters? Towels? Parchment Paper?"

"Butcher paper," I mumble, embarrassed. When I look at the little glass jars lined up, I can feel the weight of his stare.

"You don't have to be perfect all the time, you know? People are messy, Chele-Bell." His words hurt, even though they're meant to soothe. This is the way my pain bleeds out, and he knows that. I can't control who walks out of my life, but I can control the way things are around me.

"Thanks for the advice, Tin-Tin." The nickname makes us both smile. I struggled with his name as a kid, calling him aw-tin for a long time, which turned to Tin-Tin and the name stuck.

"I talked to Ian this weekend. He had some interesting things to say." I pause my pouring to stare at the screen. "Why didn't you tell me *he's* back?"

That's the question of the century. My brother knows my heartbreak better than most. Our age gap and distance should have made us absentee siblings, but it did the opposite. We love our parents, and we both keep in touch with them, but he's always taken on the protective and proud role in my life. Mom and Dad are so nonchalant with their place in our lives, that Austin and I have clung to each other. He's my confidant no matter where he moves to. The depth of my hurt and all the ways I've tried dealing with it over the years have been expressed to him and him alone.

"I wasn't ready to admit it out loud. I don't know what I'm doing, Austin. You know my love for him isn't going anywhere. This is what I've been hoping for, for years. So why does it feel so… painful?" I grip the edges of the counter, squeezing my fingers past the point of pain. "It took him fifteen years to come back. It feels too little too late. But seeing him, right here, in front of me, telling me he's here for good… Fuck, it's ruining me in the best and worst way." My voice cracks, and I clear my throat to cover it.

He's quiet as I try to keep myself together, assessing my every move. It's his specialty, hearing what I don't want to say. "Did you let him explain why it took so long? Why now?"

Letting my head hang, I shake it, admitting the agonizing truth. "Not really."

"You're never going to be able to move forward until you know that." He chuckles, but it's not kind. "You know my thoughts and opinions on his actions. Silence speaks volumes if you listen. Say the word and I'm on the next flight out, I have some leave saved up. Give him a chance to explain, and go from there. No matter your choice, I'm here for you."

"Even if I give him another shot?" I ask with a smirk, knowing he hates the pain Ethan put me through.

"Even then, little sis."

We catch up before he has to go, with a promise to check in more frequently. I shoot Ian a quick text to yell at him for snitching and ask how he even heard about Ethan. His response simply said "small town."

When all the jars are filled, closed, and the outsides are wiped clean, I pack them into boxes and clean the remaining mess. I'm about to start dinner when there's a knock on my front door. There was a time, not all that long ago, that my nights were quiet and guest-free. I liked the predictability, but there's no denying the thrill that runs through my body as I walk to answer it.

Ethan's on my porch, hands in his pockets, shoulders slumped. He stares at my bare feet before looking up, eyes heavy and face pale. He looks wrecked, and my heart squeezes. There's a battle he's fighting inside, and I've never been good at letting my friends take on their demons alone. "Want to come in?"

His nod is slow, arms dropping to his sides as he carefully moves past me and bends to untie his boots. My mouth waters as his tee pulls tight across his back, framing every muscle. He puts his boots to the side, like last time, before standing and taking me in. The emerald of his green eyes conveying so much, yet not enough.

"Come on."

He follows me to the kitchen, slumping into a seat at the island. I rummage through the fridge, grabbing a beer and set it in front of him wordlessly, before pulling out the ingredients for dinner.

With my back to him, I hear him pop the top and guzzle some down. After chopping the potatoes at the island for a moment, I glance up at him. "Want to talk about it?"

I'm hit with the pang of familiarity. The way we're comfortable with each other, how we know what the other needs without words. There's no tension, only a sense of calm, my soul at peace. Ethan visibly relaxed the moment he entered my home. After all this time, we still seek solace in each other. This is what hurts and heals. Proves to me that my teenage heart knew, even then, what real love was. That I didn't play things up in my head, the connection I haven't felt with a single soul since.

"No," he says around another sip of beer. "Yes."

Calmly, I wait for him to continue. Ethan has always been good at expressing how he's feeling and talking through things level-headed. It's one of the many things I loved about him when we were together. His eyes trail around the kitchen again before settling on me and watching me work. "Can I help?"

"You can wash the broccoli and get out a pan for the chicken."

Surprisingly, he jumps up and moves around the kitchen with ease, doing exactly as I asked. He takes a pan and the chicken out, before digging through my cabinets and taking out random spices. When he seems satisfied with what he's found, he throws the chicken strips on the heated pan and coats them in his concoction. It isn't until he's done washing the broccoli and starts cutting it up, that he breaks the silence.

"I met with Mr. Daniels today. We talked more in depth about the job, the expectations, and what things will look like for me from here on out. It was… stressful. Firefighting is a hard job, physically, mentally, all of it. Being in charge of a team, though, knowing your calls and decisions can impact lives and the progression of the fire. It's so much pressure." He pauses, putting his hands flat on the counter, and hangs his head. Turning it slightly, he looks over at me. "I was overwhelmed, questioning myself, and then I drove home and the first thing I saw was a brightly colored "Welcome Home" sign. Immediately, I knew it was from you. The flowers on my porch, the sign, it all really hit home."

I take out a baking sheet, lining it with foil for the potatoes, while he puts together his next words. "Thank you. For doing that, and for the reminder. This is my home now, and not just for the time being. This is my forever home, but I'm scared to screw it all up." His voice is sure, but his eyes are pained. Moving to the stove, he flips over the chicken strips. "I feel like I'm screwing it up with you so much already."

"Ethan," I start, but stop when I realize I don't know what to say. Everything in me wants to comfort him, but he needs to do this on his own. I need to know he's willing to fight for me. That he's willing to push through the hard things and put in the work, even when there's fear and obstacles. I can't promise him that he can fix things with me when I don't have that answer yet.

I can't even give him pretty words, convince him that everything will work out with this job, because I don't know that. Accidents happen every day, and who's to say he won't start looking for something different when the pressure becomes too much? This can't be my battle, and that hurts. My heart aches that I can't make this right. I can't tell him that I need to see him work through this and come out stronger, pursuing me, and using actions instead of words. He's the one who hurt me; only he can fix this.

It's his turn. I need him to fight for my love. To fight for me.

Sighing, I throw the food in the oven before grabbing the wine from the fridge and pouring myself a glass. "You're welcome for the flowers. I would have also cleaned your house if you had given me proper notice. I take pride in going above and beyond for my clients."

"I don't want to just be a client," he mutters.

After taking a sip, I lean against the counter as he checks the temperature of the chicken and tenderness of the broccoli. Every time he shows up, my resolve keeping him at bay crumbles more. He's here, he's trying, and he's letting me in. I see the man he's turned into. He's brave, and vulnerable. Honorable, and kind. And more than all that, he's making a real effort. He's showing me his heart, his insecurities, and he's trusting me with them the way he always used to. That means something to me. His effort and intention were two of the things I loved most about him, and they're shining through tonight.

"New careers are scary, stepping outside your comfort zone is scary, and having lives in your hands... I can't even begin to fathom the pressure that puts on a person. But if there's one thing I've always known about you, it's that you want the best for everyone. I know you won't make any decisions lightly."

He *can* do this job, I know he can. He grew up in these woods with all of us. He cares about the people, the wildlife, and the park. On top of that, his dad has been grooming him to be a fire-fighter since he was a kid. They were always talking about the jobs he had been on, and the proper procedures. Ethan was practically raised in a firehouse, going to visit his dad there often. Part of me wants to ask how his parents feel about his move back here, but this doesn't feel like the right time.

I know this job is different, but he can do it. It's his passion, his calling, and more than that, I need him to mean what he's saying. This has to be his final stop, the place he finally settles down, and gives us a real chance. Seeing him here in my kitchen, cooking with me like it's any other Monday, and after helping with an earth-shattering orgasm last week, it's clear what my heart wants.

It wants the mundane with him. The future he promised all those years ago, in whispered words and plans we made. Nights decompressing together, mornings watching the sunrise, cooking our meals in contented silence with no pressure to talk out our feelings. I still crave his touch, his gentle caresses, the dominance he exudes, and the way he softens, only for me.

The oven timer goes off, breaking the tension between us. Using the oven mitt, I pull the potatoes from the oven while he opens cupboards until he finds plates and takes two out. "Would you like to eat outside?"

CHAPTER SIXTEEN

ethan

This isn't how I saw today ending, but I wouldn't trade it for the world. Michele has always been the only one who could make me feel at ease. No one has ever seen me the way she does. Even now, she looks at me with love and adoration; like I can do anything. It's more than I deserve.

The meeting this morning was a lot. The whole day was, really. It sat heavy on my shoulders. I'm honored to have been chosen for this position. I've earned it, and I know I'm ready for it, but that doesn't mean it's not terrifying. During my car ride home, I repeatedly told myself that fear was a good thing. It reminds me I know the stakes, and I'm taking this seriously. Whether it's making sure my SAR team is well trained, or the hotshots are in the safest and most productive positions, lives are in my hands.

When I pulled up to the little ramshackle place I'm renting, I didn't want to go inside. I wanted to go for a run, or to the bar to grab a drink; anything but sit and stew with my feelings. Until I looked up and saw the flowerpots, and the small metal sign planted in the dirt next to them, I knew immediately it was Michele's doing. She's still in tune with me, and somehow, she manages to give me exactly what I need, without me having to say it.

My feet stall when we step onto her back porch. She continues to the table to one side, setting her plate down and taking a seat. Yet, I can't follow, mesmerized by the oasis she's created.

Directly down the porch steps is a gravel path veering between six garden beds filled with herbs, vegetables, and flowers. Beyond that is a fire pit surrounded by a swinging bench and chairs. The most stunning feature though, might be the large greenhouse on one side. The walls of windows show the abundance of plants she has growing in there.

"Are you going to eat?" she asks, humor lacing her tone.

Shaking off my stupor, I take the seat across from her. "It's amazing back here, Chele. Everything you touch is incredible."

"It has to be," she mutters under her breath before digging into her dinner. I want to ask what she means but get distracted by her pouty lips wrapping around the fork when she takes her first bite. Her eyes roll into her head before the lids closing. "This chicken is incredible. What did you put on it?"

Smirking, I lean back in the chair. "If you want it again, you'll have to invite me for dinner."

She has a soft smile as she lightly kicks me under the table before she keeps eating, never taking her eyes from me. Around bites, I ask about her day, and how things are going. Her eyes light up when she tells me about the newlywed couple she's helping find their first home, and the listing for a beautiful stone cabin on thirty acres from the town over. This is when she comes alive; helping people, being successful and driven, making others happy. I want to see this look on her face all the time. I want to see it there for *her* happiness, not for others.

When we finish eating, silence lingers between us. It's the comfortable silence of not needing to speak, finding peace in being near the one you love. "Can we walk through your garden? I would love to see how many flowers you can still name."

"Sure." She shrugs, so I follow her down the porch steps. "And all of them."

Stopping on the bottom step, I stare at her. "All of them, like all of them in your garden?"

"And more." Her voice is nonchalant. She's so driven, creating and upkeeping this beautiful home, and doing it all solo, but she still won't give herself credit. Even for such a small but significant thing like knowing the names of flowers. It makes me want to praise her and please her.

As we walk through the garden, she points out her favorites, or ones that are new this year. I'm enraptured by her, following like a lost puppy soaking up every bit of attention she gives me. When we have gone through them all, she takes a seat on the center of the bench swing, so I can't sit beside her. Instead, I take the chair across from her, leaning my elbows on my knees, watching as she fidgets on the seat.

The warm evening air smells fresh, like juniper, and a hint of smoke from the fire pit. It's a scent I'm comfortable with, but that's not why I feel at ease here. It's her. Her fingers squeeze together, her pretty face scrunching in discomfort. Finally, those beautiful eyes meet mine.

"What's going on in that head of yours?"

"I'm different when I'm with you."

I pause, really taking in that statement. "Different how?"

"Softer," she says quietly, looking out at the woods. "There's no edge. No desire to fill the silence." Her curls loosen when she runs her hands through them. "I had to be everything when you left. Do everything. I'm still so mad at you, but I can't deny the relief I feel from having you near. The way my body and mind know they don't have to be loud to be seen."

Her confession hits like a ton of bricks. The typically smooth timbre of her voice is shaky, ambivalent, with a mix of relief and reluctance. My chest aches under the weight of her words. I know that wasn't easy for her to admit. She's taking a step for me, opening herself to the possibility of us. I want to go to her, wrap her up, and show her she can still feel safety in my arms.

"I miss you, too," she whispers.

The delicate words float to me like the wings of a butterfly, landing gently, letting the beauty and vulnerability speak for themselves. My heart pounds against my rib cage at her admission. I can tell myself and listen to the guys say that Michele still feels something for me, but until those words left her mouth, I wasn't sure. This is exactly what I've been wanting to hear from her, but not in this way. Not when she looks pained to admit it.

I want to pick her up and swing her around, rejoicing in the fact that this isn't over. I want to kiss her pouty lips, the only ones that have ever touched mine. I want to carry her upstairs and show her how much I've missed her. I even want to roll up my sleeve and show her the tattoo she managed not to see the other night. But I can't do any of that. Not yet.

"Tell me what to do, baby. I've spent over a decade walking around with only half my heart. There's so much I need to make up for, so much I need to prove to you. Let me do that, Michele. Tell me what to do." My voice is desperate, my eyes pleading.

I see the indecision in her eyes, the war raging inside her as she tries to figure out what she truly wants. There's no world in which I don't want her to tell me she's mine, but if that's not her choice, I'll live with it. The only wrong choice here is one that doesn't make her happy. That doesn't mean I'll ever stop pursuing her. Loving her.

I see the moment she decides, her eyes lighting up, her stature growing confident. She leans back in the swing, spreading her legs slightly. "Crawl to me."

My mouth drops open at her command, but quickly snaps shut

when my cock jerks. I've never been anything but the dominant one in the bedroom, or hell, in most situations. For her, though, submitting to her whims and desires seems to be turning me on.

Without hesitating, I slide off the chair and let my knees hit the gravel first, then cautiously put my hands down. The rocks bite into my palms and my knees, even through my pants. Still, if this is what she needs, I'll happily endure. With my eyes trained on hers, I crawl. The first move stings, but the look on her face as her lids lower and she sucks her bottom lip erases the pain.

The closer I get to her, the heavier her breathing grows, the rise and fall of her chest giving away her excitement. My hands and knees are screaming by the time I'm between her feet, but my focus is locked on her. My cock is painfully hard. I sit back on my heels, kneeling at her feet, and dying in anticipation of what she'll tell me to do next. She leans forward, caressing her hands down the side of my face, letting her nails lightly scratch.

"Good boy."

My insides melt, never having been praised before. There are a lot of things I should feel right now, but all I feel is worthy. It makes me want to worship her, please her, and make her proud. "What now, Wildflower?"

She takes her time widening her legs, dragging her feet across the gravel rocks. Pretty pink fingernails tease the hem of her dress and slowly slide it up. Soft thighs that I used to know well are exposed, inch by inch, until I can see her green lace panties. Her pussy is so close, barely covered, and begging for my attention. But I wait for permission, like the good boy she wants me to be.

"Make me come."

She doesn't have to ask me twice. I run my palms down my shirt to wipe them clean before reaching out to grab her ankle. I lift it to my mouth, placing a soft kiss there, my eyes locked on hers. Slowly, I kiss my way up her calf, licking and nipping as I go. Her body trembles beneath my touch when I ghost my lips up her thigh, spreading her wide open for me.

There's a light thud when she lets her head fall back against the bench, so I stop, waiting for her eyes to come back to mine. She leans forward again, piercing me with her glare. "Did I say stop?"

Keeping the connection, I lean in and lick a strip over her panties, kissing over her clit. "I want your eyes on me, baby. I need you to know it's me making you feel this way."

Her eyes soften, and she readjusts, lifting her hips. I take her cue and slide my hands up her outer thighs, dragging her panties down and stuffing them in my pocket. After spreading her thighs again, I give up all sense of restraint. Being near her has been as healing and eye-opening as it has been soul-crushing. She's what's been missing from my life all this time. That hollow feeling that I tried to fill with work, but still felt unfulfilled. I will never feel complete without her.

I dive into her perfect core, latching onto her swollen clit. When she cries out, I smile against her flesh. No matter the time or distance, I know what Michele likes. She's the one I learned how to do this with, after all. Spending hours learning every inch of her body and how to please her.

My hands grip her thighs and spread her even further apart, and I lavish her sweet pussy with my tongue. Teasing her as I go, licking and sucking right on the edge of where she wants me. Savoring every drop of her I've been salivating for. She tastes even better than I remember.

When she can't take the teasing anymore, Michele spears her fingers through my short hair and grips it tight. Angling my head toward her, she lets me see the pleading in her eyes. "You need more? You need me to make you come?"

Instead of using words, she nods and pushes my head into her hot center. Chuckling low, I allow it, happily drowning in her arousal. My tongue spears into her pussy, licking her deep, fucking her with it. Her moans are a balm to my overheated skin, encouraging me to continue despite the fact my cock is about to explode.

When her breathing becomes fevered, I know she's getting close. Taking one hand from her thigh, I let my gaze latch onto her sparkling hazel eyes, and insert two fingers into my mouth, cleaning them further, then slide them into her dripping cunt. She opens her mouth on a silent cry, letting out a heavy breath. I can imagine this same scene, but when I get to finally sink my cock into her perfect pussy. How it will feel to be connected in that way again, filling her, feeling as one, and the satisfied look she gets when I finally slide in.

Keeping her gaze, I work her over with my fingers, fucking her at a slower pace, curling my fingers over her G-spot with every thrust. I need to take things slow with her, prove to her that I'm here for the long haul. This isn't a sprint; it's a marathon, and I need to pace myself. To demonstrate consistency, reliability, and unwavering commitment. In the small, everyday acts of kindness and attentiveness that will truly build trust.

I can't help but drop my guard and let her see everything in my eyes. It's a risk, exposing myself like this, but I can't seem to help it. Every piece of remorse for past mistakes, every shard of pain that still lingers, every flicker of longing for a future with her, and most importantly, the overwhelming, all-consuming love I feel for her, pouring out of me with every glance. I fear it's too much, too soon, but the truth is, I'm already hers.

Tears gather on her lower lashes as she holds my gaze, taking everything in. Picking up my pace, I finger fuck her faster, watching the first tear fall. She looks so beautiful when she cries, but I don't deserve it. I don't want to see another tear fall from her for the rest of her life.

"Please," she rasps out, maybe asking for release, maybe begging me to break this hold I have on us right now.

I'll always give her what she asks. Dropping my eyes, I wrap my lips around her clit, giving her the last bit of pressure she needs to come. With a torturous pace, I worship her. Michele comes on a whimpered cry, squeezing around my fingers and flooding my mouth with her release. My chest vibrates with satisfaction. I lick every drop of her while she's a shaky mess falling apart around me.

My cock is throbbing, begging to slide into her perfect cunt that's primed for me, but I will him to behave. I'll earn that right, and damn will it be a heady moment when she finally deems me worthy of her again.

Satisfied that I've licked every inch of her, I sit back on my heels and suck my fingers clean. Michele is slouched, her dress rumpled around her waist, with delicate tear tracks down her flushed cheeks. This is my favorite version of her yet. Satiated, raw, and looking like mine. After our time together tonight, it feels like I'm one step closer to making that happen.

CHAPTER SEVENTEEN

michele

My body is mush; beyond satisfied. I should be embarrassed, letting someone see me like this. Having that someone be Ethan is both a relief and it stings, since he's the reason I'm this way. It's not a compulsion to always be perfect; it's a necessity. If I'm perfect, my life, my home, and my career, then there's no reason for people to leave me. I wasn't good enough to make Ethan stay, but that's not true anymore. Every part of my life is meticulous and organized, so I will never not be enough for anyone again.

Yet here I am, splayed out with my body on display, my dress wrinkled, and what I'm sure is makeup running down my cheeks. With all that, my only thoughts are that the boy I once knew is still inside the man on his knees before me. Ethan and I always accepted each other without judgment. We told each other everything. He would do anything for me, even before we started dating. He researched for hours so he could teach me about every flower and tree we encountered. He'd skip out on plans with the boys to sit with me while I did my homework. One night, snuggling in his truck bed under the stars, he confessed that if his sole purpose in life was to make me smile, he would be satisfied.

How wrong things have turned out if this is where we are now. I pull my dress down and adjust myself as he leans back and stands, a proud smirk on his face. How do I reconcile the two from here? The boy who loved me is still in there, mixed in with the man who left me and waited fifteen years to come back for me.

He let me see him. Every wall and bit of bravado was dropped so I could witness the sorrow and pain he feels, the love he's trying to convey. It cracked my heart open, the way he worked me over while emotionally tormenting me, all without saying a word. It's a skill only he has. The ability to affect me so thoroughly.

He holds his hand out, and I reluctantly grab it, letting him help me up. Searching around, I don't see my underwear anywhere. "Where'd you put my panties?"

"In my pocket," he says smugly, leading me back to the porch. "Let me help you clean up, and then can we talk?"

There's so much hope in his voice, but I need to collect my thoughts. There are too many emotions flooding through me. I need my wits about me for the conversation I know he wants to have.

"Can we talk another time? It's been a long day for both of us."

He lets go of my hand to pick up our plates from the porch. His shoulders slump, but he nods in agreement. Back inside, we wash the dishes together and clean up the kitchen. When the last plate is in the dishwasher, he dries his hands before turning to me. "Saturday… Can I take you somewhere to talk?"

His arms are crossed over his broad chest, head hung, staring at where he's toeing a non-existent piece of dust. He doesn't want to be turned down again, and I can't help but feel for him. I know that feeling well.

"I'll look at my schedule tomorrow and shoot you a text. I'm sure I can squeeze in some time with you."

The hope in his eyes takes my breath away. A wide smile lights up his vibrant green eyes and brings out the creases around them. He only gets more handsome with age. "Okay, Wildflower. I'm holding you to that." I shake my head with a soft chuckle, unable to restrain a smile of my own. He steps closer, reaching out to rub his fingertips over the back of my hand. "Can I hug you goodbye?"

His scent surrounds me, the smoky warmth, mixed with a tinge of sex. Swallowing my nerves, I nod. Strong arms envelope me in an instant, pulling me tight against his chest. Despite my effort to keep him at bay, I melt into his embrace and wrap my arms around him. His chest is harder and broader, but it still cocoons me in comfort, just as it always did.

He keeps one arm around my middle, securing me to him, while the other tenderly rubs up my back before settling at the base of my neck. It's a claiming hold. One that causes me to bite back my whimper. Goosebumps race up my neck in the warmth of his contented sigh, the knot in my throat growing with the threatening tears. I've never felt more at home than I do in his arms. He holds me for so long, I let my eyes close and sink into his comfort, forgetting we're standing in my kitchen.

This is what was missing with every other man I've dated. One hug, and Ethan can make everything feel right in the world. Every ounce of stress melts away, every pressure on me is lifted. With his arms around me, all else fades, and I feel complete.

Eventually, he lets go, pressing a lingering kiss to my forehead. "Text me with a time, okay?"

"I promise."

He walks to the door and slips on his boots before looking back over his shoulder. "Lock this door. Oh, and I'm keeping these." Chuckling, he pats his pocket and closes the door behind him. It takes until he's pulling out of my driveway for me to realize he meant my panties.

Triple Threat Group Chat

MICHELE:

My heart is caving.

LILY:

Is that such a bad thing?

AMBER:

Are you making him grovel?

MICHELE:

He's groveling all on his own. And it is a bad thing! I don't know what his end goal is here. I can't do this again.

LILY:

Will you ever let yourself fully move on and let go if you don't give him this chance?

MICHELE:

Probably not.

AMBER:

There's your answer. Get some more groveling first. Did you make him get on his knees?

MICHELE:

I made him crawl.

AMBER:

Why is that a hot image? Was it as hot as I think it is?

MICHELE:

Hotter.

AMBER:

Thanks for the new idea. Do something wild
next to make him really prove it. Maybe stick a
finger up his butt.

LILY:

BOO, being pregnant and having a wild toddler
around makes fun things hard.

AMBER:

I'll babysit so you can get some. Chele, I'm
serious. If he bends for you sexually, he's in it
for the long haul.

MICHELE:

When did you become the wild one? Girls' night
soon?

On Tuesday morning, I woke up more refreshed than I have in a long time. Between the orgasm and the hug, I thought I would be plagued with spiraling thoughts, but I had the sweetest dreams and a full night's sleep. Enjoying the last few moments of being cozy in bed, I scroll through my phone when a message pops up at the top.

ETHAN:

Thank you for dinner last night. Check your front
porch.

I reread the message twice before it clicks, so I pull back the covers and wander downstairs. Peeking out the front window, I don't see his truck, so I unlock the door and swing it open. Sitting on my front porch mat is a to-go cup of coffee and a small brown bag.

I pick up the cup, read the label, then take a sip of the still-hot caramel latte, my favorite. Savoring the sweetness, I pick up the bag but drop it when something soft touches my fingers. The brown bag falls with a quiet thud, the side I couldn't see facing up. Taped to the outside of it is a small bunch of little blue flowers. Forget-me-nots, to be exact. The flower Ethan loved to put behind my ear.

They're clearly freshly picked, the vibrant petals blooming bright. Out of all the wildflowers I've planted or transferred into my gardens, this is the one I've avoided. Looking at them brings back too much, too many memories.

On the bag, I see the messy scrawl of his writing that says, *'thinking of you.'* The simple words almost mean more because, from the moment my eyes opened, he was on my mind as well. In less than a week, Ethan has infiltrated my life again, and I can't say I hate it. The blueberry scent wafts out when I peek in the bag to find a muffin. With a small smile on my lips, I carry it into the house, leaving the muffin on the counter and taking my coffee upstairs to get ready for the day.

CHAPTER EIGHTEEN

ethan

Change is the one constant I've had in my life. I changed schools, homes, states, and jobs like they were yesterday's dirty socks. It's what my dad taught me. Change was good. A welcome way to learn and explore, and to never grow stagnant.

For so long, I lived by that rule of thought. The eight years I spent in Cedar Ridge were the longest I ever stayed in one place. I cherished my time there and the steady way of life we had. Even with my dad constantly complaining that his life and career felt stale. My focus was on Michele and the life I could have with her. I would have given up that desire for change had things not played out the way they did.

After I moved with my parents at eighteen, the truth slowly unraveled before me. I saw the way my dad manipulated everyone around him, myself included. He no longer hid his infidelity from me because I was a man now and could handle it. My mom turned a blind eye, having known about it all along.

Cracks began to crumble in the facade they had put in place for so long. My whole life felt like a lie, and the one person I wanted to turn to was the one person I had broken and left behind.

So I dug my heels in and fought for my future. As soon as my training was done, I was hired by a fire crew seven hours from my parents.

I ran from them the way I had from Michele. It didn't matter that the circumstances were different. The pattern of running had started again, and that's what I did. I was building a firefighting career that I loved outside of my dad's name.

Wildland firefighting found me by accident, and suddenly, I had found my calling. When they asked for volunteers on a particularly bad fire, I went, and I've never looked back. While I've worked at some stations along the way, it was all with the goal of being a wildland firefighter and making my way back to Michele.

During the first few years away, I endured so much with my eyes wide open for the first time. Between the dangers and excitement of my job and the overwhelm of being on my own and losing every person I had kept close, I didn't allow myself to process the heartbreak of having to leave Michele. Until the nights came, then the world would get quiet, and my chest would hurt so much I'd struggle to breathe.

I felt betrayed by Mom and Dad. They had their secrets, these angry and bitter feelings they kept hidden until they got me where they wanted, and then let them loose. My dad still tried to puppeteer me, thinking I would follow his path. He tried to pave that path with women, higher-powered positions; anything he could think of to control me still. I convinced myself it was due to everything I learned about my parents. Except, as time went on and I let my mom explain herself, and I tried to have reasonable conversations with my dad, I realized I was indifferent about their situation. My mom stayed, and my dad kept cheating, neither of them trying or willing to fix anything. That's not the life I wanted. Not the love I knew was out there.

The pain in my chest still wouldn't go away. I convinced myself it was a longing to go back to Cedar Ridge. The one place where life felt easy, and everything made sense. Yet, every time I lay in bed alone, something still felt off.

It wasn't until I acknowledged that I missed Michele that things changed. I didn't just miss her in the quiet dark of night. I missed her in a room full of people. I missed her when I saw a beautiful sunrise. I missed her when a song I loved came on the radio and I wanted to share it with her. I missed her on such a bone-deep level that when I finally admitted everything was wrong because I didn't have her by my side, my life changed again.

That's when everything became hollow. Empty. Numb. From that day on, every move, every decision, every plan, was made with one thought in mind. I had to find a way to get back to my girl.

Now here I am, finally back in Cedar Ridge, and I want to rejoice because I fought like hell to get here. She may not see it that way, but I do. I pieced together my heart so when I finally got to her, I could hand her something whole, not something for her to fix. I'm the one who needs to repair it all. It's me who did the breaking of both her heart and mine, and it's me who needs to fix it. That's exactly what I intend to do.

Michele is letting me in, a little at a time. I'm not taking that for granted. In fact, I'm still amazed she's let me see her vulnerable twice already. My body is still humming from getting to put my mouth on her again. Seeing her fall apart for me.

The thing that always set me and Michele apart was trust. We trusted each other with our hearts, our bodies, and every inner thought too scary to admit out loud. Having her let me earn that again means more to me now. I used to have no problem giving her my words. They're jumbled now, and I can't string them together in a way that tells her how much her actions impact me. How my view on love and life was skewed after I left here and saw the reality of my parents' marriage.

I want her to know that it's her love that's given me hope. It's the way my heart only beats in a rhythm when she's near. The way my chest doesn't ache with each breath. That every dark night doesn't seem so scary, and my hope for a pure love with respect and truth is possible because of her. No words can capture that, so I've vowed to show her instead. I know my words have hurt her in the past, and I can't undo that, but I'll make sure my actions speak where my apologies fall short. That promise has to live in the little things —every day, every choice.

After dropping off her favorite coffee and muffin this morning, I sat in the truck thinking about how much I want to get this right. That's when I decided to text River for his advice. He's been calling most days anyway, checking on what he's dubbed "Operation Wildflower," so it feels right to get his opinion. This time with a little more purpose.

ETHAN:

Before you ask, I'm leaving gifts on her porch this week.

RIVER:

Is that really enough?

ETHAN:

Yes? I want her to see she's on my mind every day.

RIVER:

I feel like you need to go bigger. Sky-writer?

ETHAN:

What the fuck. I'll try it my way first.

RIVER:

Suit yourself. When it doesn't work and you need the big guns, you know who to call.

ETHAN:

I do need a favor...

RIVER:

Anything for you two.

ETHAN:

Custom jeweler?

RIVER:

My man. I have you covered. You really think she'll marry you?

ETHAN:

She's the only one I've ever wanted, and I'm working on making her see that. She told me she missed me too. Those words coming from her... I'm going to make her see.

RIVER:

Go get your girl.

michele

On Wednesday and Thursday morning, I woke to the same text, but a different surprise waiting each time. Wednesday was a notepad and pen with floral designs, the first page with a "hope you have a great day" note. Thursday was a very messily made flower bracelet like we used to create, this one with a sticky note that said "you still take my breath away."

This morning, I woke before my alarm and decided to beat him to the punch. Grabbing one of the extra jars of honey I keep on hand, I left it on the front porch with a note that simply says "you're sweet, thank you," using my new notepad. We haven't talked outside of morning texts and informing him I would be free after three on Saturday.

His little gifts have made me more anxious but equally excited. If this is his way of groveling, I'm into it. I've been torturing him sexually, but it's been hard for me, too. While I may be the only one getting off, my desire for him has only grown. He's all man now, and that man has a body built from hard work and dedication. He's muscular in a way that makes me feel small, something I haven't in years.

Sex wasn't something he and I jumped into, either when we were teenagers. We talked about it for months before it happened. Both of us felt it would mean more with someone you love. I still feel the same. I love sex, and wish I were having it every day, but I don't want it with just anyone. It's a totally different experience when feelings are involved. That's what I've been craving. The intimacy with passion, love, and trust; I know that's what I would feel with him.

I'm giddy during my morning routine, nervous and excited to see what Ethan will say about my gift, if anything. While I love the care and intention of the gifts, I'll have to talk to him about them on our date. It's not sustainable for him to continue this, even though it's appreciated.

My watch chimes, but it's my calendar alerting me that I have thirty minutes until my potential new clients will be here, not a text like I was expecting. Maybe Ethan decided not to stop by today, or maybe he couldn't make it in time before work. Trying not to feel disheartened, since I was going to put a stop to this anyway, I slip on some heels to head over to my office.

When I open the front door, the little honey jar is missing, and a small gift bag sits in its place. This is the first gift that's been wrapped, the pretty pink bag and sparkly tissue paper make my stomach flutter. I pick it up and bring it with me next door, intending to open it after I land these clients. It's heavier than I expected, but I don't peek. There's no note I can see, but it might be hidden inside. Even without his words, my mood has instantly improved. My walls are crumbling, and this is all the proof I need. He's in my head and my heart, rebuilding the little pieces he took from me all those years ago. Pieces I never thought I would get back.

Now isn't the time to worry about that. My day is too busy, and I need to prepare for the clients, so I set the gift on the shelf behind my desk and face the day ahead.

It's after four when I park in my driveway. Today was longer and harder than I ever imagined, and all I want is to change and go work in my garden. The clients from this morning wanted to view houses immediately, so I had to rush around, trying to find homes that not only fit their criteria but that we could get into with little notice. After driving around town with them, they agreed to give me a week to set up proper home showings. My time with them left only twenty minutes to grab a smoothie before my meeting with the florist I sell to. Then I was taking photos for a new listing I recently signed.

So much for my easy Friday to catch up on paperwork. The moment I'm through the front door, I slide my heels off. I pick them up and bring them upstairs to put away. Changed into some soft and stretchy gardening clothes, I rush back down the stairs to enjoy the afternoon sun and pull the weeds that have undoubtedly been popping up over the last week.

I usually try to spend two to three mornings a week doing yard work, but it hasn't happened this week with so much going on. Having my hands in the dirt centers me, refueling my soul. Since the front of the house gets the most visitors, I start with the planters and gardens out there.

An hour later, the front of my house looks perfect, and all that's left up here are the planters in front of my office space. After finishing those, I make a pit stop in the office to grab water from my mini fridge when the pink bag catches my eye. In all the rushing around today, I completely forgot about Ethan's gift.

With the bag and a bottle of water in hand, I head to the house instead of out to the back. I need to figure out dinner, and my interest in what's in the bag is too piqued to ignore. Unfortunately, I don't make it up my front steps when a truck comes down my driveway and honks.

I still can't tell Jake and Thoren's trucks apart, but when it parks and Amber pops out from the passenger seat, I have my answer.

"We brought burgers," she announces, holding up a brown bag.

"I wanted pizza," Jake grumbles, stepping out, then grabbing a box from the back.

Confused, I look between them, then down at my watch. "Am I missing something? Is it friends' dinner night? I thought you guys were next to host."

Thoren, Lily, Jake, Amber, and I try to get together for dinner once a month, switching who hosts every time. I'm certain that my house is next month, but I've been off my game since Ethan moved back, so it's possible I'm wrong.

"Just regular dinner with us." Jake sets the box on the porch. "Can we eat out back? It's so warm tonight." He wraps his arm over my shoulder and leads me around the porch like he owns the place. "Come on, Whiskey. I'm hungry."

I can feel Amber's eyes roll, and a quick glance behind me confirms it. She flips him off, sticking out her tongue, then winks at me. Without missing a beat or turning around, Jake chuckles and says, "You'll pay for that later, baby."

Shoving at his chest, I shrug off his arm. "Gross. I'm grabbing plates and drinks. What do you guys want?"

When I come out with beers and plates, I join them at my table, passing them out. "Not to sound ungrateful, but why are you guys here with dinner?"

Jake places a burger and some fries on my plate, then cracks open his beer. He takes a long sip before answering without meeting my eye. "I was upgrading the security system at the shop and realized you don't have one out here. So, I ordered a few things for your house and office. I'll install them tonight."

"I'm just here to gossip," Amber adds.

So that's what was in the box. Austin's been begging me for years to install cameras on my property. He hates that I'm out here alone, but I've never felt scared. Cedar Ridge is a safe place. No one really comes this far out unless they live here. Plus, I run a real estate business out of my old garage. It's not like I have valuables in there. Still, my brother will be thrilled to find out I finally have one. All thanks to Jake and his protective nature. Little did I know back in school that these guys would stay my closest friends.

When Thoren and Jake moved back from college, we picked up like no time had passed. They invited me everywhere, never bringing up Ethan despite the clear desire to ask. They've been looking out for me ever since, which I've loved, but having them both married to the most amazing women now is the icing on the cake.

Austin moved out when I was twelve, and my parents moved when I left home at twenty. I keep in touch with my brother as much as we can, but my parents are more of an every-other-month phone call. I've been lonely at times, especially in the romantic sense, but with friends like these, I have never really been alone. They show up for me without question. They support and encourage me. They're only ever a phone call away, Thoren even going so far as to send his mom, Evelyn, over with soup when I'm under the weather.

This gesture from Jake doesn't surprise me at all, but I can't help but give him a little shit for it. "So why did Amber get a security system when you still hated her, yet you've been my friend for over twenty years and I'm only getting one now?"

There's a quick shared look between the two before Jake responds, "You've always insisted on taking care of yourself. Maybe I dropped the ball on this."

"Maybe," Amber whispers under her breath.

"Thank you either way. I won't turn it down even if it's unnecessary."

Dinner passes with easy conversation, catching up on everyone's work. It's something the three of us share: owning and running our own small businesses. I love that we can commiserate in the struggles and celebrate the wins we all face. Even though they don't know that I run two.

Amber collects the trash and piles our plates up when we're done, taking them inside for me.

Jake stands, giving my shoulder a squeeze. "I'm going to start on your office. I'll show you how to connect it all to your phone and computer when I'm done." With that, he disappears around the side of the house as Amber steps onto the back porch. She looks at me with one eyebrow raised, the pink gift bag hanging from her fingertips. I guess now is as good a time as ever to open that.

michele

"What's this?" Amber asks, swinging the bag side to side. "It feels expensive."

I bark out a surprised laugh. "How does something feel expensive?"

"I don't know, it's heavy." She holds it out to me, only to snatch it back at the last second. "Actually, I want to sit in the garden. And I know this has to be from Ethan, so I'm watching you open it."

Begrudgingly, I follow her down the porch steps and through my garden beds to the fire pit at the back. Amber's already turned two of my chairs to face the flower bed in the back to give us something pretty to look at. She sits in one, waiting, staring at me expectantly.

When I drop into the seat next to her, I snatch the bag and focus on the peonies in front of us. "I've always loved flowers. They're nature's expression of love. If you plant them and care for them, they reward you with sights and scents that make you happy and warm inside. And if you're really lucky, nature does all the work for you, and you simply get to enjoy the reward."

The tissue paper crinkles between my fingers when I slowly

start pulling it out. I turn to Amber, whose eyes are trained on the bag, and continue, "I also think flowers are nature's way of telling us that, while putting in consistent effort to maintain that beauty is necessary, sometimes fate brings you the right set of circumstances. The perfect soil, sunlight, weather, and rain all work together to bring you a field full of wildflowers that blooms on its own every year."

I see the little white paper inside and pull that out, setting the bag next to me. "Ethan and I were fate. The perfect conditions to grow something so amazing it takes your breath away. Now I don't know if nature is creating those conditions again, or if he's ready to tend to the garden and cultivate those flowers we both desire."

Her gaze is boring into the side of my face while I read the note.

Since we played so nicely with these the other day, I thought I would get some new ones for our next play time. Can't wait to see you tomorrow. - Ethan

I can feel my face heat as I glance into the bag and see two velvet bags. *No.* He wouldn't! I wrap my fingers around the first bag, and sure enough, it's definitely a dildo.

"What the hell is in that bag to have you blushing like that, my little sex queen?" Amber squeals.

"Sex queen?" I snort, trying to distract her. "I am far from a sex queen."

"That's not answering," she sing-songs. "Plus, it's you. The one who embraces her sexuality and doesn't let anyone shame her. The frequency doesn't matter; you're an inspiration. You're half the reason I had the confidence to hop on Jake's dick."

Just when I think she's forgotten about the gift bag I'm trying to drop to the side subtly, her eyebrows rise. "Soooo, what is it?"

I'm not embarrassed to tell her about the sex toys. She and Lily know everything, but for some reason, this just feels too personal. Something I want to keep between Ethan and me. "How about this? If you don't ask what he gave me, I'll answer any other question you have, after I text him a thank you."

She considers it before giving a single nod. I slip my phone from my pocket and pull up his contact.

MICHELE:

Thank you for the toys.

The three dots pop up instantly, so I wait for his reply.

ETHAN:

How would you feel about bringing them on our date?

MICHELE:

Depends. You played last time, so does that mean it's my turn to use them?

ETHAN:

I'll happily watch.

MICHELE:

I didn't mean use them on me.

I bite the inside of my cheek, wondering whether this will be the time he tells me no. That I'm taking things too far. I know I'm pushing his boundaries. I don't think Ethan has ever been submissive until it comes to me. This is what I need from him, though, until I feel safe.

ETHAN:

I'm yours, Wildflower. In every sense of the word.

My grin has to be splitting my face because my cheeks hurt. Amber giggles beside me, kicking her feet up on the garden's edge. Remembering where I am, I slip my phone back in my pocket and apologize to her.

"I'd wait forever if it means you're smiling like that. After all this time, he really is still the one, isn't he?"

My mood sobers a little, the smile falling from my face. "After all this time."

Amber leans over to squeeze my knee. "I didn't mean it as a bad thing. It's the love story most people dream of. A love that truly stands the test of time. Your love is woven into every fiber of who you are."

The silence sits heavy between us, only broken by the chirping of birds and the fat bumble bees that coast from flower to flower. In the distance, I can hear the faint hum of Jake's drill.

"Can I play devil's advocate for a moment?" Amber continues without waiting for approval. "What will it take for you to open up to the idea of him again? Is it him showing where his heart lies? Time? Proving he still loves you, too? Because he does." She gestures toward the front of the house. "This was all his doing."

My house, my property, and my business? No, those are all me. He fucked me up and broke me. I took those broken pieces and made a life out of them. A home. It may be an empty and often lonely one, but I did it, and I did it alone.

"What do you mean?"

"The security system. He wanted you to be safe. Protected. Did you know he's been sleeping in his truck at the end of your driveway every night, waiting for Jake to come put this in? He would have done it, but Jake thought you would be more receptive coming from us."

What the fuck?

I digest everything, trying not to be upset that this was a setup by my friends and Ethan, and focus on the other aspect. He's been going to work every day, then sleeping in his truck outside of my house every night? He has to be exhausted. He's a big man, and there's no way he's comfortable or able to get a good night's sleep. I told him that actions would speak louder than words, and if this doesn't scream that he cares, I don't know what does. This is a careful choice to put *my* safety over any thought for himself. "What do you mean he's been sleeping in my driveway? Since when?"

"I'm not really sure. I think Jake knows. The point is, he cares about you. I think he's still very much in love with you. You can choose to use that information any way you want. But as someone who fought what was right in front of her for so long because of fear, I suggest you don't do the same."

"Five minutes, then we move on?" I ask, and she nods.

"Ethan gave me one day's notice when he left. A day—after ten years of friendship and two years of dating. He was my first everything, and he gave me a day. No explanation, simply told me that when his parents leave tomorrow, he would be going with them."

I can still hear his words perfectly. *I'm sorry, Michele. There are no words to describe how sorry I am, but I have to do this. You will always be the love of my life. One day, I hope you under-stand that I'm doing this for us.*

"He shattered me. I couldn't ask why, too stunned. Too hurt. I felt utterly and completely empty. The next morning, I went to his house to beg him to stay, but he was already gone." My breath hitches when I try to continue, "Just like that. My life changed that day. I saw how easy it was for him to walk away from me. How disposable I was. How can someone say they love you, and leave in the next breath?"

The tears lining my lashes refuse to fall. "My brother left at eighteen, and it's rare he comes back to visit. My parents moved when I was twenty and haven't come back once. Ethan left, and even when I caved and chased him nine years ago, he hasn't come back until now. How am I supposed to trust him? People always leave."

"Look around you, Chele. People don't always leave." Amber's hand covers mine, and she leaves it there, allowing silence to fill the space. If there's anyone who understands the pain of losing people, it's her. They may have completely different circumstances, but the pain and loneliness are the same. Except, she's right. She and Jake are still here. Thoren and Lily, and even River, are, too. People don't always leave.

We stay silent until Jake announces he's done and it's time to go. When Amber wraps me in a hug goodbye, she lingers, finally whispering in my ear, "The most beautiful flowers are the ones we allow ourselves to enjoy. Maybe nature's trying to point you to him, maybe he's tending to the garden. Either way, if you turn your head, you'll never get to see what becomes of it."

CHAPTER TWENTY-ONE

ethan

My feet land heavy on the pavement, the rhythm that I was in breaking when I see the sign I've passed on every run. The "Hidden Meadow Nursery" sign is simple, yet elegant; it doesn't fit with the dirt track road it sits on. Curiosity gets the better of me, so I alter my route down the path. There's a private property sign, but I continue on anyway.

The dirt road eventually opens up to reveal rows and rows of flowers. There are some small buildings in front of me, and one car is parked here, but I'm focused solely on the abundance of color. I should turn around, but instinct takes over. Pocketing my earbuds, I walk toward the first row of tulips, hands on my hips to slow my breathing.

A throat clears from near the shed to my side, where a woman in a white beekeeping suit is standing. "Can I help you?"

"Sorry," I stammer. "I've run past this place a few times now and wanted to check it out. Is this yours?"

She eyes me speculatively, then slowly approaches, holding out her hand, which I take. "No, I just work here. I'm Anna, nice to meet you…?"

"Ethan. Nice to meet you, too, Anna. This place is amazing. There are bees here, too?"

Her smile grows when she nods. "Yes, we have quite a few hives. They help with the pollination and supply some of the local honey. Here," she says, moving back toward the shed, so I follow. "I'll grab you a jar. Are you new to the area?"

"Kind of," I admit. "I grew up here, but I just moved back after about fifteen years away."

Anna's hands still in the box she was grabbing the honey from, and she takes me in again. A small smile plays on her lips, like she knows a secret she's not willing to share. "That's nice. What brings you back here?"

I take the honey from her before scratching at the back of my neck. "It's complicated. A job. A woman." A humorless laugh slips out. "I'm actually trying to win her back. I'm taking her on a date this evening. Have any advice?"

Her eyes light up, and she grabs a pair of pruning shears from the wall. "Flowers."

Twenty minutes later, I'm walking back to my place with a bouquet in one hand and a jar of honey in the other. Anna followed me around and cut anything I pointed out, then helped me put it all together nicely and even wrapped it in twine for me. I might have gone overboard with the selection. I wanted a flourish of color to emulate everything I love about my girl. Yellow for her bright smile, pink for her kindness, blue for her depth, and on and on until I had every color in the field.

I was surprised by the vast variety and selection of wildflowers. She told me the nursery was a passion project for the owner, and that tending to the flowers helped fill a void in her life that had been left by someone else.

Between that and the name, I can only think of Michele. With her extensive gardens at home, I doubt she would ever have use for a nursery like this, but I can't help but wonder anyway. I will have to tell her about it on our date.

After placing the flowers in water and taking a shower, I make a pile on the couch of the things I want to pack. Next are snacks, so I move to the kitchen when my phone rings.

"Hello?" I answer, putting it on speaker.

"How's Operation Wildflower going, buddy?" River's voice plays through the phone.

Rolling my eyes, I grab another pepper and keep slicing. "I told you not to call it that."

"Only you can use that nickname? I think not. If you want my help, I'll call it whatever I want. So, how's it going? Is she on to you yet?"

I shake my head, chuckling. "I've missed you, man. Next year can't come soon enough." I put the sliced peppers into the bowl of salad I'm making. "Is she on to me trying to win her back? Yeah, I think that's pretty clear. She agreed to a date today. I'm taking her to our spot."

"You better not screw this up. We're about to have the gang back together next year, and that can't happen if you aren't with Michele. You know the guys will always pick her over you."

"Thanks for the vote of confidence. I feel like I need to give you the same one for Vanessa."

The line goes quiet, and I feel like an ass. "We talked about moving when the season is over. She doesn't want to have kids out there. I guess I have some decisions to make."

I run my hands through my hair, tugging on the ends. "Fuck, man. I'm sorry. And here I am worried over a date."

His boisterous laugh startles me. "You should be worried about the date. Michele is a wild card. That woman is sweet, snarky, and bold. You need to be on your A-game at all times to keep up with her. I don't know how you managed to tie her down the first time, but trying again after blundering it? Good luck, buddy."

"You're a prick. I'm not asking for your help with anything again."

"You love me, and you know it. I'm the only one who's Team Ethan. Go figure out your shit with Michele, and I'll figure out mine with Vanessa. Reconvene next week."

I love this big idiot. He somehow manages to offer both courage and support, as well as a heavy dose of realism and attitude. "Talk soon."

After we hang up, I continue filling the cooler with food and drinks. Everything is set and ready for our date, so I put on smart jeans and a tee, then head to her house. Michele said three, and as much as I want to be early, I won't do that to her again. When I park out front, Michele steps onto her porch in a pink summer dress, and my brain short-circuits.

She looks gorgeous, the dress wrapped tight around her tits and waist, flaring slightly at the hips. Her hair is curled, sandals on her cute feet, but her makeup is barely there, and that one vulnerability makes my cock hard.

I step out of my truck to meet her at the bottom of the steps. "You look beautiful," I manage to say, before holding out the bouquet. "These reminded me of you."

Her gaze slowly drops to the flowers, widening when she takes it in. "Thank you," she draws out. "Where did you get these?"

"I found a small nursery down the road from here on my run. There was a lady there who let me pick these for you. You would love it there. The selection of flowers they have growing blew my mind. I have no idea how such a small place manages to grow so many varieties together. It's beyond impressive."

The longer I speak, the more her smile grows, and the knot in my chest loosens. "I'm going to put these in water, I'll be right back out."

I sit on the steps until she emerges again with her purse in hand, rising to follow her to my truck. This time, when I offer my hand to help her climb in, she takes it. It may be small, but it makes my heart race. After hopping in on the other side, I turn over the engine and back onto the main road.

She doesn't ask where we're going. In fact, she doesn't ask anything; she's completely at ease in my passenger seat, seemingly unaware that I'm having an internal freak out. Is her lack of nerves a good thing, because she's confident in us and comfortable with me? Or is it because she doesn't care how this date plays out?

It isn't until I turn onto the dirt path that she sits up straighter and glances my way. "This is where you want to talk?"

I grip the wheel tighter, slowly navigating down the road I stopped by last week. "It's a date, baby. I wouldn't want it anywhere else." The meadow sprawls out before us, still familiar, but not the same as we left it. It's clearly a more popular spot now, with a large section trampled by cars and feet alike.

The sprawl of wildflowers isn't as expansive, but if you look, they're still there, spread throughout the tall grass and around the edges. I park the truck on one side where we can watch the sunset from the bed. Michele is silent when I turn off the ignition. "It's not quite the same, is it?"

She's slow to take it all in. "I haven't been back here. I forgot how beautiful it is." Her hazel eyes are more golden in this light, and she holds my gaze. "Bold of you to bring me here."

My chuckle is filled with surprise and a hint of pride. My feisty girl is coming back out. After her taunting text last night, I wondered if she was going to be all talk, but I should have known that's not her style.

Heat floods my veins at the thought she might have brought

those toys like she warned. I take a calming breath and push open my door. "Well, let's be bold together." She's stepping out of the truck before I can get to her, so I embrace my statement and wrap my hand around the back of her neck. "You may have forgotten how beautiful it is here, but I've never forgotten how beautiful you are."

I let my hand drop, watching her cheeks turn a pretty shade of pink that matches her dress. When I grab the cooler from the back seat, I keep her in my focus, watching the way she walks carefully through the grass. The tall strands and brightly colored petals seem to part for her as her fingertips trail over them with care.

This is a moment that will be burned in my brain for the rest of my life. It's a gift, being here with her, and having the chance to win her heart over one final time. Because it will be final. I'm done running, I'm done hiding. This girl is mine.

While she reacquaints herself with our old spot, I climb in the truck bed and remove the blankets and pillows from the totes. It's muscle memory, rearranging everything to make a cozy spot to sit and lie down. The totes are thrown into the back seat when I finish, only the cooler is left. The edges of the truck bed are lined with small lanterns and drinks.

Michele turns around when I jump down from the tailgate, and I love that she didn't offer to help. She only did it once when we were kids, and never again. I'm a romantic at heart, and I always have been. I want to do the grand gestures, as well as the little things that equally make an impact. That's not to say Michele doesn't do the same for me; we just show our love in different ways.

Michele's love is quiet. It doesn't need grand displays. She shows it every day in the way she cares for those around her without a word. It's in the way she feeds others, offers her shoulder to cry on, and supports people to face their hardships. Her love is constant. Steady. A river you can float down, knowing she will silently navigate you through troubled waters, always there to keep you from getting dragged under.

"Your chariot awaits." I nod over my shoulder.

"I can't climb into that like I used to."

My smile is devious. "I'll help you up." I stalk toward her, my intent clear, as she slowly takes a step back. My long strides eat up the distance much faster than her calculated retreat, and I reach her in no time. I bend and wrap my arms around her thighs, picking her up. Instinctually, her legs wrap around my waist, and her arms clutch the back of my neck.

I have to bite back the groan that wants to escape. She was made to be in my arms. Her sharp fingernails dig into the back of my neck. "Put me down, Ethan," she squirms.

"Never, baby."

She kicks her heels against my butt, trying to wiggle down. "I'm too heavy, I'll get in there myself."

Again, she mentions her weight, and again, I'm mad at everyone who has commented on it. I heft her over my shoulder and smack her juicy ass, showing that I can still throw her around with ease. "Don't talk about my girl like that. She's perfection."

Her fists pound against my back, but I don't let it bother me. I simply hold her in place with one arm around her thighs and carry her to the truck, setting her ass gently on the tailgate. She whips her hair into place, running her hands through it. Her scowl is adorable when she adjusts her dress.

"It wasn't in a negative way. It's simply reality."

I watch it all with my arms crossed and a smug smile, my pretty girl trying to right herself. This messy version of her is my favorite, her confidence shining through. Finally, her hands still, and she leans forward, swinging her legs.

"So are we talking or what?"

"I thought we could talk over food." I point to the cooler at the far end of the bed. "Your turn to crawl for me, Wildflower."

CHAPTER TWENTY-TWO

michele

Ethan looks at me with a challenge in his eyes. I don't particularly want to flash my ass in this dress. However, this man crawled over gravel for me, and if I have my way tonight, he'll be doing *a lot* more than that. So, I guess I can give him this one thing.

Without sparing him a second glance, I slip off my sandals, turn, and fully climb into the truck bed. The skirt of my dress rides up, but I don't adjust it. Instead, I place one hand in front of the other and crawl over the blankets. The groan Ethan lets out brings a smile to my face.

There's a heady weight in his stare, like a caress over my thighs. My arousal is dampening my panties. Being exposed and submissive for him holds a deeper meaning now. It requires me to submit my heart, but I'm not ready to give him all of that. I need to know he's able to do the same for me.

When I reach the cooler, I grab it, stand, and walk back to him, sliding onto my butt on the tailgate again.

He stares, a little wide-eyed, then seems to shake from his stupor and takes a seat on the other side of the cooler. Ethan brings one foot up at a time, untying his shoes and slipping them and his socks off, then opens up the cooler.

"I made a smorgasbord of options. There's pesto pasta salad, regular salad, kiwis and apple slices, chips and guacamole, pistachio cake, and, of course, Skittles," he says while pulling out containers and setting them between us.

"They're all green."

He shrugs, noncommittal. "It's your favorite color."

My resolve to keep him at bay crumbles a little more. How am I expected not to fall back in his arms when these are the things he does for me? The butterflies in my stomach are as erratic as my heartbeat. With everything spread out between us, I grab the pesto pasta salad, and he hands me a fork.

"I've never made that before, and I bought the pistachio cake, so I hope they're good."

I take a bite of the salad and have to swallow down a groan. It's incredible, the perfect blend of spices and sauce to pasta ratio. He even added cherry tomatoes and mozzarella chunks, neither of which he likes, but I do. He's watching me, almost in a trance, as I finish chewing. Looking so eager and hopeful that I like it.

"It's incredible. Want to try some?" I stab another forkful, avoiding the tomatoes, and hold it out for him. Ethan leans over and eats it off the fork.

His face lights up, and he hums in satisfaction. "What should we try next?"

We dig in, sharing food and stories; the ease between us finding its way back. The quiet familiarity of him—his hand brushing mine as he passes containers, the way he listens when I speak—makes something inside me unclench. He's here, not half-distracted, not keeping score. My guard starts to slip. I still don't know if I can trust that this version of him will stay, but I want to. Maybe that's what scares me most—that I want to believe him again.

I sense the pull, the way his steadiness could wrap around me if I let it. But for me to follow, I need him to surrender first. I need to feel that he's as open, as raw, as I am. An article I read once said that some women can only truly submit when they feel emotionally safe, and I know I'm one of them. Control is my new armor; what kept me standing when everything else fell apart. To hand that over would mean giving him the last piece of my protection.

When I lead, it's different. It isn't about power; it's about safety. It lets me remain tethered to myself while we learn each other again. But even with that control, there's a part of me that aches to let go—to trust that he'll hold me steady when I do. That's the paradox of us. He makes me want to yield, but only because he's the one person I fear could break me again.

We balance on that edge—his dominance and my restraint, my strength and his patience. Both carry weight, and neither cancels the other out. I don't want to take his power, just know it won't consume mine. What I crave is the kind of equilibrium where giving and taking blur into something mutual, where surrender feels like safety instead of loss. But the thought of losing that balance, of offering everything and watching it slip away again—that's what keeps my heart braced, even as my body leans toward him.

When we're done, he packs the containers away in the cooler, then turns to me, eyes ricocheting between mine, catching the sunlight in his forest gaze. "Can we talk about us?"

"That's what you brought me here for."

He smirks, brushing a piece of hair from my face. "I've made so many mistakes in my life. I've learned so many hard lessons. I was chasing a dream, ticking off the boxes that were laid out before more, or so I thought. But I was wrong. My dream has been right here all along. Thought up seventeen years ago in this very meadow, holding the hand of a pretty girl I loved." Ethan takes my hand, interlacing our fingers, and runs his thumb over the inside of my wrist. "A beautiful woman who still holds every piece of my heart."

"Ethan, I—"

"Let me finish, baby. While I was out there, pursuing my career goals, you were here, achieving our dream. You built the home we dreamed of. You planted the flowers that we love and watched them grow. You held it all together and made that dream a reality. You did that. I should have been here. It should have been *us*. I'm so sorry I left you to do it on your own."

His hand squeezes mine as he leans forward and places an achingly soft kiss on my forehead. "I see you, Michele. I see how hard you work. How you make sure to leave everything around you better than when you found it. How you pour everything you have into being the perfect realtor, perfect friend, perfect home-owner, leaving nothing for yourself. You don't have to do that for me. Be messy, be loud, be unapologetically yourself. Take from me, let me be the one who gives all of myself to you."

My heart is beating erratically, and I know he can feel it when his thumb stops over my pulse point. These are the words I've been needing to hear from him. A knot forms in my throat when I think of what I want to say to him. This is the Ethan I knew as a boy. The one who looked deeper and saw every part of me. Before me is the man I've been waiting for all this time. The one who has held my heart, keeping me from being able to give it to anyone else.

"Tell me this is for good. That you won't leave for something new. Something better."

Ethan shakes his head with a scoff. "My Wildflower, there is nothing and no one better. I'm here for you. I want you. All of you. Forever."

I'm leaning into him and pressing my lips to his before I have time to think it through. Ethan's hand wraps around the back of my neck in a possessive hold, angling my head to kiss me harder. My lips part, and his tongue invades my mouth, stroking against mine. I melt into him. With an ease that shouldn't be there, he grabs my hips and lifts me over him until I'm straddling his lap.

My nails run through the small hairs at the nape of his neck, causing him to shudder. I smile against his lips before diving back in, deepening the kiss, and grinding against him. His hands explore my body, rubbing down my spine, squeezing my ass, and trailing up and down my thighs. It's like he can't get enough of me, groaning between our kisses, his cock getting impossibly harder with each passing minute. Ethan makes me feel beautiful, powerful, and sexy.

He finally pulls his lips from mine, leaning back to look me in the eye. "Did you bring my present?"

ethan

Michele looks at me with wide eyes and the most perfect kiss-swollen lips. Her gaze searches mine before she cautiously answers, "I did."

My hands grip her ass tighter, the smile on my face stretching so big it hurts. I pick her up and move her to sit next to me again and hop down. Her purse is still in the passenger seat, so I retrieve it eagerly. When I come back to the tailgate, I find Michele leaning all the way against the pillows along the back.

Her dress is bunched around her waist, knees bent and spread just enough to show off her little pink panties, and the wet spot in the center. The fading light of the sun is reflecting in her hazel eyes, her skin glowing, looking like the angel I know she is.

I toss the purse to the side and climb up, stalking to her. The look in her eyes grows from teasing to anticipation as I bend, pushing her legs flat. My knees drop to either side of hers, as I reverse our position from earlier, and straddle her lap.

Michele's chest is heaving with labored breaths, and it takes all my self-restraint not to grab her dress at the cleavage and rip it open. Seeing those tits with their pretty jewelry from this angle would make my cock explode, but she would kill me for ruining her dress. Instead, I wrap my hand around her throat, feeling her pulse flutter under my fingertips, and tip her head up. When those gorgeous eyes meet mine, she lets out a shaky breath.

"Do you want to play with me, Wildflower?"

Oh, so slowly, she nods as much as she can with my hand still in place. Sliding it around the back of her neck and gripping the hair there, I tug, angling her up further. I lick a trail from the base of her neck to the spot right below her ear. My lips graze over them as I whisper, "How do you want me?"

Goosebumps skitter over her skin, but the shudder rolls through me this time. Since Michele's text last night, I've been working myself up to this idea. I'm not sure how I feel about it, but I did a little searching on the internet. The general consensus was: Do it with someone you trust. There's a vulnerability in new sexual experiences, especially one that is a little taboo.

I want all my new experiences with Michele. She already owns every other first for me. First kiss, first love, we were each other's firsts for it all, and it seems only fitting to keep it for this.

With a confidence I didn't expect, Michele pushes me off her lap and tells me to lie back. When I get settled, her fingers move to my pants, unbuttoning them. I lift my hips when she starts pulling them down my legs, and she removes them completely.

Spreading my legs, she sits on her knees between them, her thick, beautiful thighs on full display. "Are you sure about this?"

"I'm yours, Michele. Tell me what you want to do."

Her gaze trails her fingers as they trace patterns from my knees to the bottom of my briefs, before she meets my stare head-on. "I want to fuck your ass."

My pulse races, and it feels like my heart might beat out of my rib cage. I know it's scary for her to believe in me. She's putting all her trust in my hands that I won't break her heart again. Too many people have left her behind in this life, me being the first of them. Her trust holds weight.

I can be vulnerable and give this to her. Who knows, maybe I'll find a new kink in the process. Not breaking our eye contact, I slide my briefs down, carefully peeling one leg out at a time so she doesn't have to move. When I toss them to the side, she bites her lip, reaching for the hem of her dress. She tugs it over her head, revealing a silk pink bra that matches her panties.

"Stunning." I thought the sunlight glinting in her eyes was breathtaking, but Michele with orange rays of the sun shining behind her, flawless skin, and delicious curves on display for me, is an otherworldly experience.

She places her hands on my knees, lightly tickling up my thighs until she grips the bottom of my shirt. I lean forward so she can tug it off and slip it over my head, dropping a swift kiss on her forehead before settling back against the pillows. Michele takes her fill of me, drinking in every dip and line on my body. My cock is rock hard and leaking from the tip, eager and begging to be touched by her.

Soft hands with pretty pink nails wrap around my dick; she's finally touching me again. It's euphoria, being back here in this meadow, with my dream girl in front of me. A wild sense of deja vu from all the nights we spent out here.

Michele grips me tighter, spreading my precum down my length. She works me over, taking her time, drawing out my pleasure with every stroke. I love the way she grips me, having her hands on me, and the way she looks at me with so much desire.

"Spread your legs wider," she commands, so I do as much as I can. With a wicked smirk and a husky voice, she adds, "Good boy. Now, lift your knees."

I'm fully exposed to her now, the pretty goddess between my legs. It's vulnerable, and frightening, and also somehow the hottest thing I've ever done. Having Michele control my pleasure is a bucket list item I didn't know I had.

I'm starting to relax when she spits directly on my ass,

making me tense again. Michele's finger rims my hole, spreading her saliva, all while her other hand is still stroking me.

"Relax, babe," she says, circling her finger over and over. "If you need me to stop or slow down, you say it. Understand?" Her hands work together, putting my head in a tailspin. Warmth floods my veins, and I close my eyes, focusing wholly on her touch. I grip the blankets below me as new sensations take over. It's when she leans over, pulling the new vibrator and a bottle of lube from her purse, that my eyes fly open. Every part of me wants this. Wants to give her everything. Every part of me is laid bare for her, so she can see that my words hold weight, too. It doesn't mean I'm not also apprehensive about this new experience. I'm glad she chose the bullet vibrator over the dildo I gifted her.

"What's the plan here, Wildflower?"

She smiles sweetly and spreads some lube on her finger. My beautiful girl then leans forward and sucks my head into her mouth, licking the precum off. At that exact moment, she inserts her finger, causing garbled noises to leave me.

"Jesus, fuck," I blurt out, trying to take in both sensations. There's a slight burn in my ass as her finger slides in and out, until she hits a spot that makes me see stars.

This is a pivotal moment for us. Whether Michele sees it or not, she has the power here. In this moment, it's not about me pursuing her and making things right. It's about her feeling comfortable enough to open her heart again. I'm freely giving her all of me, and she's showing me she'll take it with the same care and intention she always has.

The whimper that escapes me is mortifying, but Michele hums in satisfaction, licking up the mess that is now leaking in fervor. I'm so distracted by everything going on, and the fact that I might really like this, that I don't hear the click.

She lets my cock slip from her mouth, replacing it with the small purple vibrator, sliding it up and down my shaft with each thrust of her finger. I'm overwhelmed, still unsure, but doing this for my brave, sexy girl.

"Fuuuuck," I moan when she holds the vibrator under the head of my cock. Precum is dripping out in spurts, only intensified when she works a second finger into my ass. Her fingers thrust further, brushing my prostate again. It's official, I'm into this. There's no way I'm going to last if she keeps up this double assault. "Michele."

"I know," she coos. "You're doing so well. I'll take care of you. Don't come until I say."

Fuck, I am so in love with this woman. If spending an hour yesterday researching how to clean and prep myself in case she wanted to do this doesn't show it. Or the fact I opened up something I never thought I'd explore for her to feel safe and in control. Then this, right here, is proof. I'm a whimpering, pleading mess, and here she is, praising me and making me feel like a king.

"Come for me, Ethan."

The vibrator clicks again, speeding up, and her fingers press deeper into me. My eyes roll into the back of my head, I might be drooling, and blinding euphoria shoots through me. I'm not sure if I'm yelling, or crying, or making no noise at all, as the biggest orgasm of my life explodes through me. I erupt on my stomach, spurts of cum covering me, while Michele works me all the way through it.

When I finally float back into my body, I open my eyes to find Michele taking wipes out of her purse. Of course she came prepared. She smiles sweetly at me, wiping up my mess. I should be embarrassed, maybe emasculated, but all I feel is satisfied, and so damn happy. I also absolutely have a new kink, if Michele ever wants to do this again.

She tosses the wet wipe to the side, and I grab her hand, pulling her body over top of mine. I can see the protest ready to leave her and shut her up with a kiss. There's no weight on me, Michele, holding herself on her hands and knees. Spreading my thighs and gripping the back of her neck, I force her to settle her body on me. There isn't a single thing about Michele that I don't find perfect, and certainly not her damn weight.

My hands travel over every inch of her, unsnapping her bra when I get there, and sliding it off. I want her to ride my face, get absolutely smothered by her thick thighs, but she stops me from pulling her body higher.

"Take a breath. We just experienced something new. I want to see where your head's at."

"Okay, baby," I say, pulling one of the blankets on the side over us and tucking her into my side. "Let's talk."

CHAPTER TWENTY-FOUR

michele

There's a slight breeze breaking through the warm spring air. Ethan pulls me tighter against him, wrapping his leg over mine under the blanket. The sun is grazing the tops of the trees, highlighting the colorful flowers littering the forest floor around us. I've missed this spot. Even with a yard, greenhouse, and business full of wildflowers I've grown, there's something special about seeing them out in nature, untouched.

Ethan scratches up and down my back, setting off chills, when his chest rumbles with a chuckle.

"What?"

"I was just reminiscing about all the times we've done this, and how nice it is to be back here now." He laughs again, shaking his head. "Then you got chills and your nipples got hard, poking your piercings into my side. Never experienced that back then."

He rubs a thumb over the offending jewelry and groans. "You just made me come so hard I saw stars, but one thought of these pierced tits and I'm ready to go again."

I can feel him thickening against me, but I ignore it. "Did you like it?"

"Yeah, baby. I liked it a lot."

Going into tonight, I had so many thoughts. I wanted to push his boundaries, to see if he would make himself as vulnerable as I feel with him. He's been so patient with me, not overstepping the clear boundaries I'm setting. Yet somehow, he still finds ways to show his affection. I wasn't expecting to realize I'm into this. The look on his face when he came will be etched into my brain for all of eternity.

"I liked it too. Next time, I'm really fucking your ass."

He barks out another laugh, his whole body shaking with it. "So, there will be a next time?"

"Yes, I think there will." I lean back to look at him. His green eyes are radiating pure adoration, and I'm taken aback by how quickly it makes my heart race. "Thank you for putting your trust in me. I'm scared, Ethan. My heart couldn't handle it if you were to leave me again. The first two times… It took a long time for me to recover, and I'm not sure I ever fully did."

Admitting all of this to him is scary. He knows. I know that, but putting the words out in the open, letting him hear my truth, is vulnerable. After what he just let me do, though, I can do this.

"If you want to give this a real shot, I'm in. But there are rules. I want to take it slow. We're dating, not spending every waking moment together. And you need to mean this. No running, no leaving, this *has* to be your final stop. And one final thing, when you're ready, I need to know why you left."

He's quiet for a minute before he tips my chin and kisses me. It's soft and sweet, and melts me on the spot. "This is for real," he whispers against my lips, kissing me again. "We go at your pace." *Kiss.* "I can still read you like a book, baby. I'll take my cues from you." *Kiss.* "I'm not going anywhere. I'm yours, until you tell me otherwise, and even then, I'm still yours." *Kiss.*

Ethan pulls back to stroke his thumb down my cheek. "I want to have that talk. Just not here, and not now," he admits, and my heart sinks a little. I need to know what made him leave. I have to know if it was me or something I did. I need to know it's something that won't happen again. "I can give you something else. If you think I've moved on in the last fifteen years, or if any woman has held my heart the way you have, you'd be wrong. I've been on dates, you know that, but there were no feelings involved. No intimacy. You're the only woman I've kissed. The only one I'll ever kiss. It's always been you, Michele."

Tears pool along my lashes, and a ball of emotion sits heavy in my chest. I wasn't ready for that. "Ethan—" My voice cracks, and the first tear falls.

"Until my last dying breath, baby," he whispers against my cheek, kissing away the tears as they fall. "I promised you that, and I intend to keep it."

The tears cascade in earnest now, but he simply wipes them away. After rolling me onto my back, he kisses me with everything he has. He's always been an incredible kisser, having practiced with me until he could turn me on with just his mouth pressed to mine. It's heightened, knowing he's waited all these years for me. He slides his hand beneath the blanket, rubbing his thumb over my nipples, and tugs on the little bar there.

I gasp into his kiss as he trails that hand further, over my stomach, and straight into my silk panties. His middle finger rubs my clit before dipping into my wet center. He pulls it out and circles my clit again, not stopping until I'm squirming under his touch.

"I need more."

"I know, baby." He removes his finger and pulls down my panties, discarding them to the side, and rustling around, grabbing a condom from his pocket.

He smiles sheepishly when I raise an eyebrow. "I had hopes, not expectations." When he secures it, he lies the opposite way and rolls it down his length. "Ride me, Michele."

I sit up and settle myself over his lap.

"A pretty girl like you deserves to watch the pretty sunset. It's our favorite part, after all."

Goosebumps scatter over my skin from a mix of the nip of the cooling night air and his words. The sky is painted in an array of pink and orange shades, the sun almost fully obscured by the trees. Ethan lines himself up, and I sink onto him. There's a collective moan when I'm fully seated.

Neither of us moves, reveling in this union. He's the perfect stretch, filling me so completely. He grips my hips, encouraging me to move, so I do. I grind myself against him, shuddering when my clit rubs his pubic bone. Ethan watches me with reverence, pupils blown wide. His hands move from my hips, one circling my clit while the other runs over my body.

"I'm close," I cry out.

He sits taller and pulls me into his lap, his strong arms a secure cage around me, my legs instinctively wrapping around his waist, finding purchase against the hard planes of his stomach. His forehead rests against mine, the stubble of his beard a gentle rasp against my skin. His warm breath ghosts over my lips, a silent plea, a whispered command. "Come with me, Chele."

His thumb finds its way back to my clit, a knowing caress, and the world dissolves. My orgasm explodes, leaving me shattered, breathless, adrift in a sea of ecstatic sensation. His answering grunt follows, a low rumble in his chest as he spills into the condom. Our chests are pressed tight together, skin on skin, hearts hammering against each other in a frantic, primal rhythm, a single, shared heartbeat echoing in the silent night air. Soft lips drop against my own in a tender kiss. "You're mine, Wildflower. All mine." The words hang in the air, a promise, a threat, a declaration that binds us together.

ethan

Days of the week have never meant much to me. As a firefighter, I work in rotating shifts throughout the week. And with wildfires, well, they don't burn during normal business hours. But until Reynolds leaves, I'm working a weekday schedule, and I'm not mad about it. This is something I'll enjoy getting used to.

After a Monday morning check-in with Reynolds, I met with the local wildland crew. They walked me through their training and equipment, and we discussed their concerns in the upcoming fire season. I left feeling empowered and honored that so many opened up to me so easily. They seem like a great group who want to put in the work, get home safely, and not play in the politics of it all. It's the best a leader can ask for.

They have a training session scheduled on Wednesday for the newest recruits, hoping to get them ready for the start of wildfire season in July. I promised to be part of the training. There's value in leaders doing the grunt work every now and then. Showing your team you worked your way from the bottom, and value each position that works tirelessly to keep our forest and firefighters safe.

On top of that, there's a SAR training Thoren is going to help me lead this weekend, and a controlled burn that my team is going to be working on next week. My mind needs to be focused and learning as much as I can in this transition.

Yet here I am, daydreaming about each dip and curve on Michele's body. The way my chest gets tight and my ears burn red every time her beautiful face crosses my mind. There are still conversations we need to have. Not only about why I left, but how she feels about my career. I may be one step further removed from directly fighting the fires, but that doesn't make it a safe, stable, or easy career. I'll have to go at the drop of a hat, and I still plan to be as hands-on as I'm allowed.

That's not easy for a partner to take on. She'll be giving up her security, the surety she's been begging for from me. I've reassured her that I'm here to stay, but I can't ensure my safety. I can't promise that I won't die out in these woods. It's a dangerous job. Unpredictable. Unreliable. All the things Michele has removed from her life.

She says she's in this with me, but I need to know she truly understands the risk she's allowing to impinge on the perfect life she's created. I'll likely miss holidays, events, and meals. When duty calls, I have to go. Seeing it with my dad is different than being the one experiencing it. And he wasn't even gone as much as I likely will be.

Thoren mentioned that, while most are complete in a matter of hours, some SAR cases can last days, and I know fighting wildfires can lead to weeks away. Last wildfire season, there were no casualties, but that's not always the case. In this life, death is a real possibility. It's a conversation I need to have with the guys as much as with Michele. I need to know she'll always have a place to go. That they will make a place for her on the holidays I miss. To know they will be a phone call away in emergencies when I'm in the forest with no service.

Leaning back at my desk, I examine the calendar on the wall that's quickly filling up, and it all hits home. This is the dream I've been working so hard for. I've achieved it. I'm living it. Every lonely night, every hard call, every blazing fire, was worth it to get here. Back in the place I love, fighting for the woman who owns my soul.

I thought I would feel complete. More settled. Something is missing, and I can't quite put my finger on it. Maybe I need more time in the position, or maybe I need to go through my first fire or rescue mission. Whatever it is, it leaves me feeling uneasy.

The shrill ring of my office phone scares me so bad I tip over in the chair and crash into the wall behind me. I rub at my shoulder and half crawl over the toppled chair to grab the old phone.

"Hello?" I ask in a grumble, using the desk to stand.

"Hellooooo," comes a voice on the other line, in a truly awful Mrs. Doubtfire impression.

"River?"

His laughter is so boisterous, I can still hear it when I set the phone on the desk to pick up my chair. In doing so, I notice the two cracks in the drywall, one from the chair and one from my shoulder. *Fuck.*

I grab the phone in time to hear River's whine. "Oh, come on, that was funny."

"How did you get this number? I didn't even know this phone worked. You scared me so bad I fell out of my chair and put a hole in my damn office wall, jackass."

"Rude," he huffs. "Can't I call my best friend. Thoren gave me the number, obviously. I'll have to come check out your digs when I'm there next week, but I'm not helping you fix the wall."

"I never asked," I mumble under my breath, rubbing at my shoulder again. "Wait. You're visiting next week?"

"Yeah, man. My contractor's been getting annoyed with all

the video calls, and I have a few days off. It sounded like the perfect time to come home and check on things."

My shoulders slump in relief. I need my best friend here. "Is Vanessa joining?"

"Not this time." His tone is clipped. Resigned.

I hate that for him, but I won't push it when he clearly doesn't want to address it. We talk for another twenty minutes, catching up on how the new job is and how his team is doing. He officially announced his retirement and has been met with very mixed responses. In true River fashion, he's handling it all with kindness and a smile. By the time we hang up, my shoulder is throbbing, and I'm ready to go home.

Michele told me she was swamped with work this week, so I promised not to show up every day again. It works out because I have just as much to do. While these woods used to be like a second home to me, I'm not as well-versed in the area as I once was. I need to map out the hiking trails, the biggest fire hazard locations, and where the fires have been over the last ten years, and whether there are repeat or overlapping locations.

Stopping to grab a quick dinner sounds enticing, but I avoid it and drive straight home. The welcome home sign greets me when I step from the truck. I have never deserved Michele. Not back in high school, and certainly not now. It's not going to stop me from pursuing her with everything I have.

After heating up one of my prepped dinners, I settle into my office chair behind the new desk Jake made. I dive into the research, only stopping when I have every major hiking trail listed in a spreadsheet and marked off on a map by coordinating numbers. I'm determined to memorize where everything is to be the best leader possible in both roles.

With the busy week ahead, I really should go to bed early, but the peace of finally being in a place I love is calling me. I grab a beer from my fridge and some nuts from the pantry, and step onto the back patio, sitting in one of the rocking chairs out here. The sliver of moon doesn't offer much light, but the stars make up for it. It's been so long since I last sat outside in silence and gazed at the night sky lit up like this. There's something about it that makes me feel small and insignificant in this big world. One single drop in the ocean, meaningless in my own right. Yet, sometimes all it takes is one drop in the right place at the right time to change everything.

The beer is cold as it slides down my throat. My squirrel neighbor, who should be asleep, is skittering down his tree to sit in the silence with me. It's become a routine for us, listening to the evening bugs come alive while the rest of the world sleeps. I toss him nuts that he quickly scampers over to and stuffs in his cheeks.

This is nice, peaceful, but still, I'm unsettled. It's lonely. Arguably lonelier than I was in the city, because at least then I was surrounded by people. I'm isolated out here, and even though this is the space I asked for, I thought I would have this with someone. With *her*.

My phone pings in my pocket, so I slide it out. I let my feet rock the chair while I take another sip and read the message on the lock screen.

UNKNOWN:

I miss you, Ethan.

I can't hold back the scoff. Of course she does. We used to talk all the time. Back before I found out the truth she was hiding from me. I miss her, too, obviously, but I need time to figure things out here before I approach that again.

After slipping my phone back in my pocket, I lean my head back and get lost in the vast expanse of the stars. This is my life now, and maybe one day, that chair next to me won't be empty.

michele

Spring is a busy time for me, as most homebuyers start looking at this time. Add to that the abundance of flowers blooming, and my schedule is packed. I wouldn't trade it for the world, but sometimes, I wish I didn't have to do it all alone. This is the time of year I want to be in my garden for hours, arranging bouquets for the house, and keeping it all pristine. It's perfect weather to open the windows, bake treats for my friends, and drink coffee on my porch.

Instead, I'm spending half my days driving clients around, preparing homes for showings, and managing listings. To top it off, Anna has been trying to convince me to expand our bee and flower operation. There's a market for it, but I'm not sure I can add anything else to my plate. If she had asked me a few months ago, I would have jumped on the idea. Now, though, I want to hoard my free time and give it to Ethan.

He's been texting me every chance he gets. Everything from "good morning" to "my new squirrel friend ate the nuts I left out for him" to my all-time favorite, "I want my cock to be molded to fit in your pussy." Those walls I had up are crumbling fast. I'm still hurt, maybe a little bitter. But you never fully get over your first love, and Ethan is my first, and my only. A broken heart can't love again, at least not in my experience. It needs to mend and heal before it can let something new grow. I've never given it a chance.

Speak of the devil, my dashboard lights up with an incoming text.

ETHAN:

Dinner tonight? I'll cook.

MICHELE:

I have a few showings this evening. I won't be home until 7.

ETHAN:

Perfect, I'll have dinner ready and waiting.
Where's your spare key?

I shake my head at his antics. I still haven't told him I know the security system is from him. That's something I should share with him. I'm still kind of mad about it. As sweet as it is, where does he get off thinking he has the right to care about my safety now?

Driving up to my next showing, I shoot off one last message, telling him where it is, before putting on my bright realtor smile and hopping out of the car.

Five hours later, and I'm beyond ready for this day to end. It's almost 7:30 by the time I pull into my driveway. Ethan's on the front porch, gently rocking on one of my chairs, beer in hand. His smile is soft when he lifts his bottle to me. As much as I want to tell him I'm too tired and to just head home, I can't. The light in his eyes when he sees me makes the butterflies in my stomach take flight.

I grab all my things before climbing out of the car and slowly making my way to the porch. I dump everything at my feet and slump into the rocker next to him. The smile on his face grows as he stares at me.

"What?"

"You're being messy."

After kicking off my heels, I wiggle my toes and lean back, before rolling my head to the side and eyeing him. "And?"

"Nothing." He chuckles. Bending down, he grabs a glass of wine from next to him and hands it to me. I take it gratefully, swallowing a few large gulps. We sit in silence, listening to the crickets and the subtle creak of the porch under our chairs as they rock.

Ethan gets up, dropping a kiss to my forehead, before grabbing my purse and bag and heading into the house. I turn and stare at his retreating form as he places them on my entry table and disappears from view. It's a warm feeling that he feels so at home here. Like this is his place as much as it is mine. It was always meant to be our place. The home we dreamed of building together one day.

My toes press into the wooden boards to keep the chair rocking, and I notice how smooth it is. I lean forward to check it out when Ethan clears his throat and hands me a plate of food. "I swept and pressure-washed it today," he comments, nonchalant, taking a seat beside me again with his own plate.

"You did what? When?"

He digs into the casserole on his plate, but doesn't take a bite. "I only had to work an hour this morning since I have some training sessions coming up. So I, uh, I tried to help out." He takes a bite, shaking his head as he chews. "You know, you really make it hard to help when you do everything yourself all the time."

"Who else is supposed to do it?"

"Me, Michele. I want to be the one who does these things for you. It always should have been me."

"Yes, it should have," I snap. "I shouldn't have had to do any of this alone. But you left me. You left me, Ethan, and I had to do it all by myself. I still do it all by myself."

My eyes turn hazy as my stupid tears gather along the lashes. This always happens when I'm upset, but he doesn't get to see me cry over this. I'm working on forgiving him, even though it still hurts. He walked away and never looked back. I deserved more than that. I *deserve* more than that.

"Michele, I—"

"No. It's in the past, and you've already apologized. I did it on my own because I had to. And you don't get to come back and worry about me now. Not when you didn't worry about me for the last fifteen years." The first tear falls, and I quickly swipe it away. "And while we're at it, you don't get to worry about my safety. I've been living here for over ten years just fine without you watching over me."

He reels back, that light in his eyes going dim. I'm being harsh, I know that, but it's the truth. Needing a moment to recenter myself, I take a bite of the casserole and immediately melt. It's incredible. Cheesy, saucy, rice goodness, and exactly what I needed after this long, exhausting day. All of this is. The wine, the quiet time on the freshly washed porch. I let the frustration out with some deep breaths in between bites, while Ethan eats silently next to me.

"I'm sorry."

"You don't need to apologize. Everything you said was true."

"I didn't mean to take my bad day out on you. We already talked about this, but it still hurts, though. I don't want to seem ungrateful for you caring about me. Thank you for the security system, and for worrying about me." I take another bite before continuing, "And this delicious meal. I see all that you're doing, and I appreciate it. I asked for effort, and actions, and you're showing them."

Ethan sets his empty plate on the porch railing, then sits back in the chair, looking contemplative.

"The girl I grew up with was brave and fierce. She knew exactly who she was and what she wanted, and she made it happen. There wasn't any concern for what others thought of her. That girl gave parts of herself to others and wore her heart on her sleeve. She also never turned down help."

I open my mouth to protest, but he shakes his head and carries on, "I've been focusing on the girl I used to know, not the woman you are now. The Michele who doesn't need a man to come in and do things for her, because she takes care of all of it herself. The Michele who wants a partner, because she has worked her ass off to give herself everything. The woman who was so hurt by me leaving that she made sure to never wear her heart on her sleeve again. Who hid what she thought were the ugly or broken pieces of herself so no one would have a reason to leave."

His assessment sits heavily in my throat. I can't deny it. Not a single word.

"You took all that hurt, and you made yourself stronger. I'm so damn proud of you, but it breaks my fucking heart, Michele. My actions changed the way you show yourself to the world, and that's a damn shame. Every bit of you is stunning. The messy, the kind, the frazzled, the provider… all of it makes up the most incredible woman I know. I hope one day you will see that it was never you. You weren't the reason I left, but you're the reason I fought so hard to come back."

My empty plate sits in my lap as I stare at him. His green eyes piercing me, relaying every word he spoke. The slight stubble on his cheeks makes him look rugged and a little more handsome. Not that he needs help in that department.

I watch with rapt attention as he tentatively leans over and takes my plate, stacking it on top of his. Then he grabs my chair and scoots it closer to his, angling us toward each other. I still haven't moved, unsure what to do or say.

Ethan grips my thighs, running his hands down until they reach my calves, and pulls them up into his lap. His strong fingers grip my feet, digging into the arch. The groan that leaves my lips is unholy, and he tries to hide his smile.

We sit in silence, me finishing my wine while Ethan rubs my feet, and we look over my front yard. While it's not the flower oasis my backyard is, it's equally peaceful. The quiet critters singing their nightly song, lit up by the stars.

"Thank you."

"I'd do this every night if you let me, baby."

I chuckle, raising a brow at him. "Don't tempt me, a girl could get used to this," I say, wiggling my toes. "But I meant all of this. Dinner, the porch, your concern for my safety." I take another sip of my wine. "You really like it when I'm a mess?"

"It's my favorite, Wildflower. Let me see my messy girl, and let me help clean her up."

"You just made that sexual." I laugh, digging my toes into his ribs.

He grasps my ankle tighter and brings it up to his lips, tenderly kissing the tips of my toes. "I mean in all ways. I'll do your dishes, hide your bodies, and lick our cum from your perfect little cunt. Let me be there for it all."

Heat creeps over my chest at the look in his eyes and his filthy words. I'm in so much trouble with this version of Ethan. The one who's done playing by my rules, and is taking exactly what he wants.

After helping me clean up dinner, he kisses me good night and promises to drop off dessert tomorrow after his controlled burn. When I make my way upstairs and start stripping off my dress pants, I notice the vase of flowers on my bathroom counter.

Flowers that he definitely went back to my nursery to get, since I only deliver two of those pink roses to the florist every week.

It's a dangerous game he's playing, a slow burn that's captivating me. Every glance, every laugh, every brush of his hand against mine chips away at the foundation of my carefully constructed composure. The way he looks at me, like I'm the only person in the room, is enough to send shivers racing down my spine. I'm falling, losing my grip on the sensible, rational woman I try to be. He's a wildfire, and I'm the dry grass, ready to ignite.

CHAPTER TWENTY-SEVEN

ethan

There's a mental mindfuck that all wildland firefighters go through. Our job security depends on natural disasters occurring. So, while we're working tooth and nail to put out these devastating fires, a small part of us is sometimes also screaming, "burn, baby, burn."

For me, it makes things like prescribed burns that much more impactful. We get to work, we get to do the thing we love, and we are, hopefully, preventing something later that may become out of control. This burn was planned out by the Forest Service, but it will be part of my job for the park in the future. The map I've been studying helps identify the high-risk locations to work with. While my team usually only participates in ones for our national park, we don't have them often. The Forest Service crew is kindly letting us parkies tag along to get some hands-on experience.

While it's not in my job description to participate, I'm desperate to. I want to get to know the team better; it's been too long since I've worked hands-on. This job is my dream, but I'll miss being boots on the ground during each fire.

Our location today is about ninety minutes down the mountain, in a drier area. The team is already in place by the time I get there, yellow shirts dotted all over the landscape. I take my helmet from the front seat and grab my gear from the back, including my lucky Pulaski.

I know it's stupid, but this thing has been with me from the beginning. Michele bought it for me as a high school graduation gift, and I've had it ever since. It's not department-issued, but it's the same quality and style, so I've gotten away with using it all these years. I make sure it's sharpened after every fire, and I have yet to get hurt on the job.

A few of the guys wave when they see me, but most keep to their assigned groups. I made it right on time for the talk the prescribed fire manager is giving. He lays out the parameters, makes sure every leader knows their roles, and sets us off. His boots crunch over the dried grass as he makes his way over to me, and I understand immediately why this location was chosen.

"Hey, it's Ethan, right?" he asks with an outstretched hand. He's younger, like me, maybe mid-to-late thirties, which is good to see. "Michael. I'm glad you decided to join us. It's nice to put a face to the name."

I shake his hand as the crew bosses gather their teams and get into position. "Nice to meet you. I really appreciate you letting us work in tandem today. The prescribed burns in Colorado were limited, and I only participated in a few. That's why I wanted to be here today."

He chuckles and slaps me on the back. "Besides us being better," he ribs me, "we're all in this together. I know most of these are your local guys. They'll put you to work. Espinoza's team has a few rookies completing their training, if you want to jump in there and help him out." He nods over to one group with eight members, so I make my way over there.

Espinoza introduces me to his crew before handing the floor to me. This is the part of the job I've been focusing on for the last few years. Monitoring the weather, the winds, and the fire patterns. Together, we spend ten minutes reiterating what they all should have read up on by this point, then we get to work.

Our task today is ignition of one section, and of course, monitoring. Carley, who is the newest recruit, sets the fire with the drip torch, igniting all the same spots I would have. Espinoza gives me an impressed look as we watch the rest of the crew spread out and monitor the fire line. These tend to be pretty low-key, if all safety protocols are followed. It's not unheard of for fire to jump the line, especially in conditions like this, with some of the area's grass reaching two to three feet tall. However, each and every member has been trained on how to react if that happens. We almost want it to happen in this setting so we can assess response time and whether the proper procedure is followed.

I flank to the east with some of the crew, while Espinoza flanks in the opposite direction. The vegetation is a little heavier over here, and my team seems rigid on watching for embers. To keep them on their toes, I ask as many training questions as I can. It could be seen as distracting, but it relates to real-life scenarios. They need to be able to do their job while also keeping an eye on their surroundings and fellow firefighters for any hazards or change in conditions.

The area we're working on is being burned from the outside in. That won't help with the spread today, though, as the winds that were supposed to stay mild start picking up and changing direction. My group of four seems vigilant and spots when an ember sparks outside of the fire line, instantly catching onto the dry grass floor.

The first kid, Aaron, does the one thing we train them not to do and loses his cool. "Fire!" he shouts, pointing at the small patch of earth covered in flames. The next thing he does is equally stupid, dropping his tools to run over. Thankfully, Carley grabs his discarded shovel before running over to help.

I was intending to stand back and evaluate, but it's quickly going downhill. Aaron is actively trying to kick dirt on the fire, which I can understand the thought behind, but he ends up kicking up ash and burning clumps of grass.

To my horror, some flies under Carley's helmet and into her eye as she bends to shovel dirt on the spreading flames. The chaos that ensues happens too quickly for me to stop it. Her scream of pain sears through me as she stumbles backward, straight into another firefighter, and the Pulaski he's holding.

It's like I'm running in slow motion, watching the two fall to the ground. The minute he hits, Carley's body follows, the back end of the axe, the mattock, embedding in her shoulder. My radio is in my hand in an instant, calling in the incident and requesting a medical team and backup for the spreading fire.

Thankfully, the other member yells at Aaron to help him smother the fire with dirt, *with his shovel*, while I try to get a handle on the scene.

"Don't move," I instruct the two on the ground. When I brush the ash from Carley's face first, I notice the burn forming there. Her skin is red and mottled, tears streaking down her cheeks. "Can you see out of both eyes?"

"It's a little blurry," she manages to force out between gritted teeth.

"It's okay to show pain, you have nothing to prove here." My hand reaches around her back, trying to keep it supported. "How are you doing, Kenny? Anything hurt?"

His wide eyes are frantic as he squeaks out, "No. I'm so sorry, Carley."

The shouts of people running over to help become louder as I assess the wound. Kenny is one lucky bastard, the head of his Pulaski blade missing his shoulder by mere inches. I'm not entirely sure of the protocol here. Moving them at all could move or dislodge the mattock, and I have nothing but my dirty shirt to stanch the bleeding.

"You're both doing great. Help is on the way, Carley. Tell me what else hurts."

She takes some shaky breaths before answering, her lip quivering the whole time, "No problems breathing, I'm afraid to wiggle my fingers, and the pain is radiating down my arm." Her tear-filled eyes meet mine. "It all hurts. Am I going to be okay?"

Knees hit the ground next to me, and I look over at Michael, who is now evaluating the situation. With backup here, I finally check on the fire that jumped the line, but it seems under control and is almost put out.

"Medical is right behind me," Michael states, in clear control. On Carley and Kenny's other side, an EMT drops down, and I move to let them assess. "As soon as she's in a rig, want to tell me what happened?"

Five hours later, I find myself in the waiting room of an unfamiliar hospital with flowers, a book, and all the snacks I could wrangle. After a long talk with Michael, and a promise to fill out the necessary paperwork by the end of the week, I helped with the rest of the burn. Aaron asked to leave, and we all agreed he's not the right fit for such a high-pressure role.

I've never heard of something like this happening, especially at a prescribed burn, so it sits heavy on my chest that it happened on my watch. Even though Michael assured me I did everything right. The nurse at the station points me in the direction of Carley's room, and off I go to apologize.

michele

With an afternoon free, I'm spending it organizing my greenhouse in the backyard. There are whole rows of summer vegetables that will be ready to transfer to the beds next week. This greenhouse has seen better days. The top windows are in decent shape, but the ones on the sides are covered in splattered dirt, rain streaks on the outside, and the floor is littered with soil and leaves, no matter how often I sweep it out.

Still, this little glass and wooden box feels like my second home. It's where, with a little love and dedication, I make magic happen. The endorphins I get from playing in the soil and seeing little sprouts pop up keep away the dull ache I feel otherwise.

I have a life that provides everything I should need. A beautiful home, a rewarding and successful career, and amazing friends. Yet the bitter loneliness hits way too often. This greenhouse filled with all my little plant and vegetable babies cures some of that. It brings me joy that few understand.

My phone vibrates on the table in the center with a text, so I wipe my hands on my shorts and grab it. Ethan's name pops up on the notifications, and a smile crosses my lips. That is, until I read the message.

ETHAN:

> I'm so sorry, baby, I won't be able to bring you dessert tonight. Rain check?

I'm responding before I can think it through. I know where he is today, and there's only one reason he wouldn't come over. Something went wrong.

MICHELE:

> Are you okay? What happened?

The thumping in my chest is echoed in my ears as I watch those three little dots appear and disappear again. If he's taking this long, it can't be good. His job is dangerous, I know that, but this is one of the safer activities. In fact, most of his new role is made up of safer situations.

We used to talk about this when we were kids. He's always wanted to follow in his dad's footsteps, and the life of a firefighter means long hours and dangerous scenarios. I talked to his mom about it at that time, and she always said firefighters weren't meant to have wives and families. It used to make me so angry how she always harped on like that while actively living out that life and encouraging her son to follow that path. Even if I understood it. You're signing yourself up for a life full of worry, missed occasions, last-minute calls, and, if what she shared was true, a high chance of infidelity.

I didn't care then, and I don't care now. All of those scenarios are worth it for Ethan. Growing impatient with the flashing dots, I hit the call button.

Ethan answers on the first ring. "I'm fine."

The breath I was holding releases on a whoosh. "There are a lot of ways to be fine without being fine."

"One of our crew got hurt today. She had to have surgery and might lose sight in one eye." There's a pause on the other end.

"Michele," he says, sounding utterly defeated. "It happened on my watch."

"Tell me everything."

We spend fifteen minutes discussing his day and the events that occurred. No matter how many times I tell him this isn't his fault, I can feel his guilt from here. Plus, he's still at a hospital almost two hours away because Carley's stuck there overnight, and Ethan doesn't want her to have to spend the whole time alone.

He's a good man, a selfless man, and the perfect match for me. I can't fault him for his actions; I would have done the same. In fact, I hop in the car to run to the store for supplies so I can fill Carley's freezer with some prepped meals. I'm channeling my inner Evelyn and helping in the only way I can. By the time I've batch-cooked six different dinners and dropped them off with Carley's roommate, per Ethan's instructions, I'm beat, but my greenhouse is still calling my name. I need to do something with this frantic energy, even if it's late in the evening now.

I change back into my gardening clothes and head out back, turning on the twinkly fairy lights when I enter. My brother laughed when I sent him a picture, telling me outdoor spaces don't need charm, but it makes it feel cozy, and adds a touch of feminine flair. It was that or a chandelier, which seemed too over the top.

All the plants were watered, clipped, and dead leaves removed earlier, so I dive into repotting the ones that have grown too large, and organizing the sprouts by which garden bed I'm going to plant them in.

When it's all complete, I rinse off my hands and wipe down the worktable. I debate not sweeping up the floor, just this once, but I can't get myself to do it. I'm in the back corner when I hear footsteps behind me.

"Wildflower," Ethan calls, with a scolding tone. "You know outdoor spaces are meant to get messy, right?"

Without turning so he won't catch my grin, I answer, "Technically, this is inside."

"Sweet girl, I really wish you hadn't said that."

Before I can ask what he means, he grabs me by the hip, spins me, and pulls me into his body. Soft lips land on mine as he tugs me tighter to him. The kiss is gentle, warm, and I sink into it. My butt hits the table, and he uses his hips to cage me into place. One hand disappears, and one spears into my hair, tugging just enough to angle my head back. Ethan kisses down my neck, finally leaning back to smile at me.

It's then that I realize his other hand is in the bag of soil at the edge of the table. "Ethan, don't you dare," I warn.

"Don't do what, baby?" He takes out a small handful and drops it on the ground, immediately scooping up another. "I thought I told you that you don't have to be perfect all the time. It's okay to be messy."

With one hand still holding me in place by the nape of the neck, he lets his knuckles travel across my chest from collarbone to collarbone, dropping dirt as he goes. His smile grows when he flattens his hand against my arm and rubs the dirt over my heated skin.

"Ethan," I warn again, but he only chuckles at my stern tone. He flips me around, pressing me between the table and his hips. His large chest pushes against my back, slightly bending over the table. His smoky and minty scent surrounds me when he puts his lips to my ear.

"What do you say? Want to get messy with me?"

Goosebumps travel from my neck through my body, followed by a shiver that runs down my spine. His hard cock rocks against me, and I can't hold back my whimper. For a moment today, I thought he was hurt. It may have been short, but it didn't stop the nervous energy from flooding my body. A fear that, after finally getting him back, I was at risk of losing him again.

Feeling him against me, safe and in one piece, helps quell that panic, and like a drug, I want more of it. Arching my back, I angle my ass to rub harder against him. His sharp intake of breath gives me all the encouragement I need to continue. He lets me rub against him twice more before stilling my hips with his own.

"I need you. Now."

"I'm yours."

There's a shuffle behind me as he wipes his hands down his pants, then undoes them and shoves them down his legs. Quick fingers reach around, undo my shorts, and pull them and my panties down to my feet.

"Step out." I do, and he toes them to the side. Using his boot, he kicks my legs further apart before bending me over the table until I'm flat against it. His clean hand rubs a circle on my ass before one finger trails from my tailbone down to my pussy. "So wet and ready for me. Maybe there's hope for my messy girl after all."

He shoves two fingers into me, scissoring them to stretch me out. With how wet I am, he could probably get away without this, but his cock is thick, and it's probably better I don't get split in half. I must mumble that, because he chuckles behind me and immediately removes his fingers, slamming into me in one hard thrust.

I cry out, the perfect mix of pleasure and pain. Ethan stills his hips, letting me adjust, while rubbing his hands up and down my back.

"Please."

"Please what, baby?"

"Fuck me, Ethan."

He slides his cock out to the tip, then slowly pushes back in, torturing me. It's when I let out a frustrated groan that his sinister laugh slips out and he fucks me in earnest. He pounds me into the table. The bag of soil tips and spills to the ground, but Ethan doesn't slow. My hips slam against the edge with every thrust, and I know there will be bruises tomorrow. This is exactly what I needed from him. To feel him alive and well. *Safe.*

It hits me then again, how even this safer role in his career can turn dangerous. How his life could be constantly put on the line. He must feel the change in me, because he stops immediately, pulling out and spinning me to face him.

"What's wrong? Did I hurt you?" His thumbs brush over my cheeks, searching my eyes for the answer.

I don't even care that there's probably dirt now streaked across my face. All I focus on is the love and devotion twinkling in his eyes.

"No, and don't you dare stop. I just need to be able to touch you. Feel you. Know that you're here, safe with me."

His eyes soften, traveling over my face. Strong arms wrap around my thighs and lift me, setting me on the edge of the table. He wraps a hand around the nape of my neck, pulling our foreheads together. We watch as he lines himself up and pushes into me again. Our exhales mingle in the space between us. I let my fingers tickle from his shoulders to his elbows, gripping him there.

"I'm right here," he breathes, thrusting again. "Safe." *Thrust.* "Feel me." *Thrust.* "Hear me." *Thrust.* "I'm yours."

Ethan fucks me slowly. Intentionally. Letting me feel every inch of him as his hands roam over every inch of me. I thought last time was magical. The location, the views, and all of him. This time feels just as significant. With every rock of his hips, he's burrowing himself under my skin. Like the smoky scent that never seems to leave him, that smoke travels through my veins, smothering my heart with his love.

He angles my hips, holding me tighter so I don't fall. The added pressure drives my sensations higher, breathy moans leaving my parted lips. His mouth captures mine in a searing kiss.

I open, letting his tongue explore my mouth, tasting everything, including the tiniest hint of dirt. There's a slight sting when he bites my lip before kissing and nipping his way down my neck.

I turn my head to the side to give him better access, and that's when I see it. Our reflection in the glass windows behind him. It's distorted, only lit by the twinkling lights above. Streaks of dirt cover us, both in the reflected image and from the glass itself.

It's messy, it's raw, it's perfectly imperfect, and it might be the most beautiful image I've ever seen. His powerful glutes rutting into me, my thighs spread around him. There are no flaws to be seen, my stomach rolls hidden behind his broad back, yet I wouldn't hate them if they weren't.

He makes me feel seen for exactly who I am. I can let him in. I can give him my heart. He doesn't try to fix me; he simply accepts me. He sees my messy parts, the insecurities I try to hide, and he loves them, too. It's a love that feels safe, a love that feels earned, and a love that I want to return without reservation. Every time I look in his eyes, I fall for him a little deeper, rediscovering the reasons I fell in love with him in the first place. The effortless transition, the seamless flow between affection and adoration, is a testament to the deep connection we share. Time with him feels like coming home, like finally exhaling after holding my breath for so long.

"Eyes on me," he grunts, pulling my face back to his. We lock gazes, and I'm once again mesmerized by his vibrant green. The deep forest outside reflected beautifully.

With his thumb on my clit, he tips me over the edge, following me immediately. Streams of his cum fill me as I clench around him. The look on his face is pure adoration, and I know it's reflected in my own.

His forehead slowly slumps to rest against mine while we try to quell our ragged breaths. "My messy girl," he whispers. "My perfect messy girl."

CHAPTER TWENTY-NINE

ethan

Michele sits on the edge of the tub, waiting for it to fill with warm water. I carried her up here bridal style, and she only protested once, which is a win in my book. As if I can't carry her up a flight of stairs. As if I haven't trained with structural firefighters and hotshots alike. Her curves not only feels light, but turns me on instantly.

She lets her fingers flow through the water, popping some of the bubbles forming before turning to look at me.

"Oh, God. Is that what I look like?" she asks in horror, seeing her reflection in the mirror. There's dirt streaked across her face, down her neck, and covering her chest. Her hair is a tangled mess from the number of times I ran my hands through it, also spreading soil in there. The best part is, she's only wearing a shirt and bra, her panties and shorts still outside.

I turn to look at myself, and I'm not much better. My hair is sticking up in random places. My shirt and pants were already covered in ash and dirt, only compounded from our tryst in the greenhouse. I like the look, though. The raw desire we shared to have our hands on each other. The need to be close to one another, to feel her skin heat under my touch.

"You look beautiful, baby." I shut off the water, then let my fingers trail from her shoulders to the hem of her shirt, and I lift it off. Her bra follows, putting those pretty pierced nipples on display for me.

Holding my hand out to help her in the bath, she takes it, then freezes. "I don't want to sit in our filth."

In true Michele fashion, she turns on her shower to rinse off first. Chuckling, I move to the sink and splash water on my face and over my hair, getting most of the dirt off. After scrubbing at her face and chest, Michele turns off the shower and tiptoes over to the tub, sinking into the bubbles. I strip out of my clothes, putting them and hers into the hamper like I know she wants me to, before coming back.

My girl watches with hungry eyes as my cock bobs with each step. "Lean forward."

I slide in behind her, loving how her silky smooth skin feels against mine. "We don't fit," she grumbles when my legs have to squeeze to bracket hers.

"Oh, I'll always make it fit," I retort with a pinch to her nipple. She scoffs, but doesn't push me away as my hands explore, kneading her perfect tits, rubbing her luscious thighs, and digging my thumbs into the knots in her shoulder.

When she's putty beneath my strong fingers, I grab her shampoo and squirt some into my hands, working it into her scalp. "I'm sorry if I scared you today. Thank you for doing that for Carley."

"It's a fearful thing, opening your heart to someone. Putting yourself in a vulnerable position, knowing you might be hurt. I've known your job is dangerous since we were kids, and I thought I was prepared for it. But it's kind of been this out of sight, out of mind thing. The dangers don't feel so real when I don't know whether you're on a call or not. When I can be blissfully unaware, thinking you're safe at home. This was the first time that I felt true fear about your career, and loving someone that can hurt you, simply by getting hurt… that's terrifying."

Tilting her head back, I rinse out the shampoo and drop a kiss to her forehead before grabbing a washcloth and filling it with soap. I start at her neck and rub it delicately over her skin.

"I know that it's scary. You know, for a long time, I didn't feel fear on jobs, only a rush. Today, though, even though I wasn't the one hurt, I was scared. That tells me, for the first time, I finally have something to lose. I can't promise that I'll always be safe, or that I'll make it home from every fire. I can't tell you if the fear will lessen over time. All I know is that having someone to fight to come home to every time makes everything worth it."

The washcloth trails over every inch of her skin. She squirms when I run it over her pussy, but I don't play, focusing on washing her. "This life is hard. Being the partner of a firefighter, especially a hotshot, is hard. But take a look around you. Look at the home you built. The life you built. You can do hard things, Michele. You've been doing them for years."

I have to lean over her to reach below her knees. Michele sucks in a sharp breath, halting my arm in its path, and pulls it further forward. This moment was a long time coming. I'm not entirely sure how she hasn't seen it until this point. I've done my best to hide it, but it pokes out from my sleeve, and I've been shirtless around her a few times.

"What's this?" she whispers, tracing her fingers over the tattoo inside my left bicep.

"A tattoo."

Michele dips her fingers into the tub and flicks the water over her shoulder at my face. "I know that, dumbass. When did you get it?"

Her touch, as she skates over the petals of the bunch of forget-me-nots, sends shivers through me. "The day you left Colorado."

"What?!" Her voice pitches, and water splashes over the edge of the tub when she abruptly sits up and tries to turn and face me. "Why?"

"For you, Wildflower. I knew then that I still had a chance with you. I vowed from that day forward to do everything I could to come back to you the right way. And if you were still willing to give me a shot when that day came, I wouldn't mess it up again. This tattoo is my reminder that it will all be worth it if, in the end, it's you by my side."

My heart cracks wide open when I watch the tears gather on her lashes and begin to fall. Her bottom lip quivers when she speaks. "It's really all been for me?"

"*Every* decision, *every* job, *every* move. It's all been part of paving the path back to you. I'm yours, Michele. You're the breath in my lungs, the calm shore to my restless waters. I want to be the embers that help spark your flame. Always near, always present. I choose you, every day, in every lifetime."

Her lips crash into mine; hungry, demanding, and warm. We spend the rest of the night wrapped up in each other, whispering the words that don't feel as scary when said in the dark. Words that explain how right this still feels, how we won't let fear hold us back, and promises to see this through.

When I wake up to my alarm, the bed is empty. Michele's side is made up, and my disoriented mind locks in on the fact that she let me stay. My dirty clothes from last night are clean and folded on the bathroom counter with a note on top.

Since you like to make a mess, I have a date idea for this weekend - Michele

I'm definitely winning my girl back.

michele

I couldn't sleep with Ethan in my bed. My mind was racing, and my body wouldn't sit still. So, I got up, did the laundry, cleaned the rest of the greenhouse, even though I knew Ethan was planning to do it, and as soon as the sun started to rise, I was at the nursery.

Watching the sun peak through the trees, and seeing the steam rise from the morning dew evaporating from the flowers, was everything I needed. I spent a few hours out there, weeding and clipping back the dying plants. After, I filled some buckets with clippings for the florists in town, and a few extra for my stop this morning.

When I was sure Ethan would be gone, so I wouldn't have to tell him why I ran, I made my way back home to shower and change for the day. The florists were my first stop, before driving over to the James's. Thoren and River's parents have always been the ones all of us kids turn to. They have an open invitation for Sunday dinners, though not nearly enough of us show up. I haven't had the heart to ask if they still do it now that chemo and treatments have taken over their lives.

A beautiful woman in scrubs opens the door, and even though

I've yet to meet her, I know who she is. Her short, dark brown hair sits perfectly straight against her head, and she dons a professional expression. "Hi, can I help you?"

"Yeah, you must be Ivy. I'm Michele, Lily's best friend. Is Evelyn up for visitors today?"

"Of course I am," Evelyn calls from the living room. Ivy rolls her eyes and chuckles before stepping out of the way to let me pass.

"How's she doing today?" I ask under my breath.

"She's putting on a brave face, but she's in pain."

When I step into the living room, Everlyn is propped up on the couch and wrapped in blankets, despite the warmth of the house. Her skin is pale, and there's a knitted cap covering what I know is a head of peach-fuzz hair. Ivy nods to the bouquet in my hands. "Want me to put those in water?"

"That would be great, thank you."

Evelyn smiles when I sit next to her and take her hand in mine. "I've missed you. The only reason I haven't rioted over my flowers not showing up the last two weeks is because I know who is back in town."

"I'm so sorry. I should have made the time to come over. How're you feeling?"

"Oh, no. This isn't about me. This round of chemo was a doozy, but you know what will make me feel better? Hearing about you and Ethan." She half-heartedly waggles her eyebrows before complaining. "Since someone wouldn't bring her sweet Vivi along, I have to get my joy from somewhere."

Ivy places the vase of flowers on the coffee table, then crosses her arms. "She would have been all over your lap and demanding you play Barbies. You need to rest. Plus, I pay for daycare, it's a waste not to use it."

"Spoilsport. I told you she can come with you every time."

"You're not my only patient. I'm going to make you a smoothie, then I'll be back this afternoon for another check."

Evelyn speaks loudly enough to ensure Ivy can hear her from where she's walking to the kitchen. "She's a grumpy gus, but we love her. And she has the cutest little girl. Do you and Ethan want kids?"

I stall, my answer stuck on my tongue. "I don't know. I think I'd be okay being the fun aunt."

"Really?"

"You sound surprised. I don't know if I have the maternal instinct. I love kids and babies, but with Ethan's job and my busy schedule, it doesn't seem ideal. I don't know how he feels. When we were kids, he definitely wanted a big family." I run my hands through my hair, flustered. This isn't something we've talked about, and I'm not sure we're on the same page about it either, and that's scary. It's not a small hurdle to be talked out.

Evelyn hums thoughtfully, considering. She takes her time before responding. "I think you'd make an incredible mother. Now, tell me everything before David gets home."

My shoulders slump, and I take a deep breath. "You know our history."

"I do. Watching that boy chase you around, with eyes only for you, was a highlight of those crazy times."

A smile crosses my face because she's not wrong. Since Ethan and River were best friends, we hung out here after school sometimes. Well, a lot of times, actually. No one ever minded that Ethan insisted I tag along, and I ended up spending time with Evelyn here and there. She's the reason I'm a decent cook. I'd often help her in the kitchen so the boys could play video games. "So you know how much it broke me when he left. Having him back is everything I want. I'm just struggling with completely opening my heart again. That and… the dangers of his job."

Evelyn nods, patting my hand. I knew she would understand

since her husband spent his entire career in the police force. "I won't lie and tell you it gets easier. Every day David went into work, I worried it would be the last day we would see him. It doesn't matter how safe this town is, or how pulled back from the fight their position is; it's still a risk. What helped me was realizing that bad things happen every day to any person. You can't live your life scared. Choose to be grateful for every day you have."

I instantly feel like a bitch because this brave woman is fighting for her life, which cancer is trying to strip away, and I'm complaining about the fear of the unknown. She shakes her head at me, scolding, "Don't you go there. Tell me what's been going on since he's been back. And don't leave anything out, Lily's been stingy on the details."

Ivy's laugh startles us when she walks back into the living room with a smoothie in tow. She places it on the side table next to Evelyn with a straw. "Drink all of this, please. You need your strength. David was supposed to be home by now. Do you mind staying until he's here?" she asks me. When I agree, she starts walking to the front door, turning at the last minute. "It was nice to meet you, and don't believe a word she says. I've heard her asking Lily and Thoren, and even on the phone with her other son, asking for details and all have given them."

"Ivy!" Evelyn yells after her. Ivy's chuckle echoes through the entryway before the front door slams shut. She turns back to me, a little more pink flushing her cheeks. "Tell me it all anyway."

"What if he hurts me again? What if it doesn't work out in the end, and I've been holding out hope for a love that doesn't exist the way it once did?"

"Oh, sweetheart. There's no shame in knowing what your heart needs and holding out for it. Some of us get it right away, some of us have to wade through the rubble to find it, and some even find it at the worst possible time. You didn't waste your time; you didn't pass up on Mr. Right because you still had Ethan in your heart. If someone else were Mr. Right, Ethan wouldn't have even been a factor. There's a reason you both have held out on love. You know what true love is, and you refused to settle for anything less. That's admirable."

She takes a sip of her smoothie and cringes. "And the best part of it all is that your love doesn't exist in the same way. It's evolved. Grown. Risen to the challenge and stood the test of time. Your love is brighter, bolder; a conscious choice by two people who are willing to fight for it."

"So, basically, you're telling me to buck up and appreciate what I have?"

"I said it much nicer than that."

"Yeah, yeah. I'll tell you about his groveling efforts while you drink your smoothie. Deal?"

For the next thirty minutes, we discuss the things Ethan has done for me over the last couple of weeks. She's not surprised about him sleeping in his truck and wipes under her eyes when I tell her about the little gifts he left me. I tell her about my plans for our date next weekend, and she loves the idea. She mentions that David has heard grumblings of the bonfires the high schoolers have up there, so she suggests bringing trash bags to clean up, too.

When David gets home, he apologizes for being so late and immediately asks what he can do. He's always been a good man. A man who loves his wife and family. A man who would do anything to protect them and keep them happy. It's what I aspire to have, what I felt like I had with Ethan, and what is so clearly still there.

I stay and chat for a few more minutes before heading out. There's another busy weekend ahead, but I'll embrace it. Less time for me to worry about the SAR training Ethan's leading. Talking with Evelyn helped, but it makes me wish I had taken the time before she got sick to be more involved. I let the pain of losing Ethan let me pull back from her and David. Being at their house without him brought on an ache I couldn't bear. Watching her suffer through rounds of chemo and good news, always followed by bad, has been so hard on our group of friends.

I rummage through my purse to find my phone and shoot off a group text.

Besties and the Boys 2 group chat

MICHELE:

Saw Evelyn this morning. Rough day. Might not hurt to have more visitors this week.

LILY:

Griffin is running a fever, so I can't bring him over.

RIVER:

I'm included again? This is the greatest day.

JAKE:

You don't live here yet. Don't push your luck. My parents, Amber, and I are bringing over food for Sunday dinner.

THOREN:

I'll bring Shadow over after work tomorrow.

RIVER:

I'll be there next week to spend a few days with her. I request a friends' dinner invite.

ETHAN:

I'll stop by Saturday morning before the SAR training.

MICHELE:

I'll host friends' dinner next week. I think it's my turn anyway.

ETHAN:

I'll help cook.

AMBER:

Sooo… does this mean you're a couple again.

RIVER:

Leave them be.

RIVER:

Sooo… is that a yes?

ethan

Time used to fly by in a blur. When you have nothing to look forward to in life, it kind of passes you by. There was an ease to that, simply doing your job and enjoying the little pleasures when you can. The problem is, it's not really living.

I would get rushes from fighting fires, from saving lives, and from acing a new training session, but they were my highlights. My life was empty. *Dull.* Filled with shades of black and white, in the monotony of my routine. The only color in my life was from the little flowers I collected. The ones that made me think of her.

Michelle is color. She is everything that embodies it. Her mind, her spirit, her light. She brings joy to the world around her. The vibrant colors of the wildflowers we love have nothing on her. Her bold personality shines with an array of pink, her smile the brightest shade of yellow, rivaling the sun. Even when she's sad I can see bold streaks of blue, and the deepest reds when you stand in the presence of her love. It's why I love getting her flowers with an abundance of color. They may look chaotic, but I see the different facets of her in each and every petal.

Before going to see Evelyn on Saturday morning, I stop off at Hidden Meadow Nursery again. No one is there, but Anna gave me her phone number last time I was here. She told me to take what I want, but I left some money in the greenhouse. I realize they only do wholesale, but I love getting it directly from them.

It's when I drop them off with Evelyn, and she comments on how Michele brings similar flowers every time, that I realize my original thought was correct. The name of the nursery, the location, the flowers, even the honey that Michele left out for me one day. Remembering the story that Anna told me about the owner. It's Michele's nursery. It has to be.

Before our date on Sunday, I stop by again, picking a very strategic mix of flowers, and leaving money again. As I look over this second business she's built from the ground up, a business revolving around something we loved, I can't help but feel overwhelmed. Completely overcome by awe and amazement for my girl.

When I convinced Michele to tell me her messy date idea, I immediately latched on to the plan. I even added a few surprises for her. Every day, I find out something new about her that makes me fall that much harder.

The fact that she wants to clean up our meadow and restore it to the way it used to look when we were kids tells me everything I need to know. This isn't just about nostalgia; it's a shared future. She's not just reminiscing, she's actively working toward it with me. Planning a life together, while accepting the past. She understands the importance of preserving memories and creating new ones. This project, this shared dream, confirms everything I've ever felt. We're a team, bound not just by love, but by a desire to build something beautiful and lasting. This meadow, this act of restoration, is a testament to our commitment to each other and to the life we want to build.

My truck bed is filled with an abundance of supplies when I park in front of Michele's place. It's no surprise at all that she has piles of buckets, gardening supplies, and plants waiting on her porch. By the time I'm out and have the tailgate down, she's already bringing things over. I had to do some digging to ensure we could plant these in the meadow. As it turns out, it's private land, which I had no idea of all this time. It's only the forest surrounding it that's owned by the national park. The owners were very nonchalant about it and had no problem with our plan when I reached out.

"Wow! You came prepared, too. Did you make sure they're all native plants?"

"Of course I did. This is our meadow. I love this idea, by the way. I can't decide whether this is you showing your willingness to get messy, or trying to make one more thing around you perfect."

She scoffs, grabbing another tray of flowers. "I garden all the time; this is a type of mess I thrive in. Plus, I think I showed you just how dirty I can get."

I grab her waist, nuzzling into her hair. "Mmm, that you did, baby." After dropping a kiss to her forehead, I move around her to grab the bouquet from the back seat. "Want to put these in water before we go?"

Deciphering Michele's facial expressions and movements used to be a specialty of mine. I don't need that skill now; her face is as readable as they come. She knows these flowers, I know she does. Her hands delicately wrap around the stems I tied with twine I borrowed from her greenhouse, and her eyes move from the flowers to meet mine. There's a question in her gaze, but I neither confirm nor deny.

"Thank you, Ethan. They're beautiful."

While she puts them inside, I finish loading up the truck bed, and then wait by the passenger side door. The spandex shorts she's wearing hug her thighs, showing off every perfect curve. I want to sink my teeth into this woman, mark her in a way only we know.

She thanks me as she slides into the passenger seat, the earthy floral scent of her lingering when I shut the door. On the drive over, she explains her plan for the day, because, of course, she planned out how she wants to pick up trash and spread some seeds. I smile, knowing I'll do anything she asks of me. Eventually, she grows quiet and plays with the edge of her shorts.

"Spit it out."

"Where'd you get those flowers from?"

Ah, I knew she wouldn't be able to resist asking. I know the nursery is hers, it has to be, so I decide to have a little fun with it. "You know that nursery I told you about? Hidden Meadow?" She nods, a small smile on her lips. "Well, there's almost never anyone there, so I've been stealing flowers."

"You what?" she screeches.

"I've been stealing them." I shrug. "I thought about leaving money, but there are so many flowers, I doubt they notice a few random ones missing."

"Ethan. What in the actual hell?"

"I know, it's crazy. But they clearly do well. It's kind of incredible the sheer amount and different varieties they've grown there. I looked it up because I was curious, and most nurseries have specialties. They only grow certain varieties and have them in bulk. But not at Hidden Meadow. The owner must put so much love and attention to detail into that place."

"Yet you're stealing from them?" Her voice is filled with accusation, arms crossed tight over her chest as she angles her body toward me.

I can't hold back my chuckle. "Wildflower, the only thing I

plan on stealing is your heart. I've been leaving her money. But now I'm questioning if she's been getting it."

"What makes you say that?"

"Have you? Been getting my money?" I can't look over to see her reaction, focusing on pulling off the main road into our meadow.

The atmosphere in the truck changes. Gone is the light tension, an air of relief filling the space. Her voice is whisper-soft when she responds, "How'd you know?"

I put the truck in park, leaning over the steering wheel to check that my plan is already being put in place. Finally, I glance over at her. "I should have figured it out sooner. The name should have been the first clue. Then Anna said something that had me thinking. It wasn't until I brought a bouquet to Evelyn and she mentioned the ones you bring that really verified it."

I take her hand in mine, rubbing over the back of it. "I see you. Every day, I'm seeing more of you, and every day I'm falling more irrevocably in love with you. I never stopped loving you. Not for a single day. But my heart has been incomplete, desolate, and gray without you. Every little thing I learn about who you have become and what you have accomplished on your own has brought color and joy back into my life. I'm so proud of you, baby. Beyond amazed with what you have created. I'm assuming no one else knows about the nursery?"

She shakes her head, her glassy eyes blinking rapidly.

"I don't know why you're afraid to tell people how hard you work. They would feel the same sense of pride and awe that I do. For now, can you not be upset that I invited them to crash our date?"

"What?"

I use my finger to tip her chin to look out the windshield at the cars parked on the other side of the meadow. "Our friends are going to help us, and then I thought we could have a picnic. I've been reconciling the old version of you with the woman you are now, and I thought it might be nice to mix some of our past with our present."

She unbuckles and leans over, pressing her lips to mine. "Thank you, Ethan."

I pull her back to me and deepen the kiss.

michele

"How'd you learn so much about flowers?" Lily asks from her spot in a camping chair. She helped for a while, but we all forced her to sit and rest.

I can feel Ethan's eyes on me, so I focus on the hole I'm digging for Amber to put my starters in. "When Ethan and I were kids, we used to look up information about what we found in this field. I loved it and slowly taught myself how to garden when I graduated. A lot of trial and error, some phone calls with Evelyn, but I have the hang of it now."

"I would say you more than 'have the hang of it.' Your yard is to die for," Amber chimes in.

"I can't wait to see what's in bloom next weekend for friends' dinner. It's been too long, but I don't want Griffin to destroy your hard work."

"Speaking of, where is our son?" Thoren pipes up from where he's helping Ethan plant some seeds.

"Jake is treating him like a dog with Shadow." Everyone's head whips over to Amber, and she shrugs like she doesn't see the problem. "He's playing fetch with them."

Sure enough, on the other side of the meadow, Jake is tossing a ball that Griff and Shadow are chasing. Shadow is the best big sister, staying near Griff's side everywhere he goes, and herding him when he tries to run into the woods.

"I love them," Lily claims wistfully, rubbing her baby bump. "He can play fetch with him all day if it means he'll go to sleep easily tonight."

Their help has made this go so quickly. We had the trash picked up in less than thirty minutes and have been working together to dig and plant ever since. Ethan and I are trying to be strategic about where we plant so they won't get trampled, but will still bring some of the meadow back to life.

The symbolism isn't lost on me. We're honoring the roots we have dug deep, and planting something new alongside them. To have a garden bursting with life at all stages. Seeing the beauty in the rings on an oak tree's trunk, a testament to enduring strength and the passage of time, and the delicate sprouts of the future, reaching for the sun with unbridled optimism. We're not just preserving memories; we're cultivating new ones. It's a deliberate act of remembrance and renewal. We are tending to the soil of our past, enriching it with new experiences, shared friendship, and the vibrant growth of tomorrow. The old and the new, intertwined and inseparable, a symphony of growth, resilience, and the promise of a love that lasts.

The starters I brought from my greenhouse were going to be planted at the nursery, but I love the idea of seeing them here. I can always plant more, and they don't always sell as well. They're more for the butterflies and bees, and to make my heart happy.

"How do you feel about rose bushes? I don't bring roses to Jana's grave as often anymore, but I thought about planting my own so I don't have to keep going to the florist's downtown." Amber grabs the last flat of starters to plant, careful not to look me in the eye. "It was the weirdest thing, though. When I told the florist that I was thinking about it, she mentioned that her whole-saler specifically asks for one pink rose to be set aside for me every time. It took me by surprise, until I really thought about it."

I spin to glare at Ethan, who raises his hands in defense.

"I knew it! What the hell, Michele? How long have you been doing that? And why does *he* know before us?"

"Hey, hey, now, why'd you say it like that?" Ethan interjects. "Plus, I figured it out on my own."

"Wait, what's happening?" Lily asks, looking between all of us. Of course, Jake chooses this time to walk over, carrying a squealing Griffin under his arm as Shadow chases them, her tail wagging and nose booping him every other step.

I suppose it's as good a time as any. I'm not entirely sure why I've kept Hidden Meadow to myself all this time. It was nice to have something that was mine and mine alone. A place that was created out of heartbreak and my love for the man staring at me with a look of absolute pride. That nursery is a labor of love. The place I poured myself into so I would be too exhausted at night to cry over the man who promised he would be sharing my bed and wasn't. I've turned it into a profitable business. A business people in town rely on, but have no idea is mine.

I played it close to the chest because admitting why I had the business would be admitting how broken I was. I'm not that girl anymore. I'm healing, and I see the possibility of each bloom, not the roots that don't take hold. The nursery is no longer a symbol of the heartbreak over a love I missed, but the strength I showed in tending to that love, even when it was hard. For that, I'm proud, and I'm finally ready to share.

"I own a nursery." I blurt out, then take a steadying breath. "I started it about ten years ago, as a way to heal my heart." My eyes find his, an apology written in both our gazes. "It's grown a bit. I also have bees and sell local honey. When I found out about the pink roses you left for Jana, I planted some bushes for you. I've been supplying them ever since. I didn't know how to help you through your grief, but I could do that one small thing. So I did."

It's quiet, only the sound of Griffin's giggle running off again, chased by Shadow. Surprisingly, it's Jake who breaks the silence. "So first you don't tell us about the piercings, and then we find out you have a whole double life? What's next, Michele? You and Ethan are getting hitched this weekend?"

"That's not a bad idea," Ethan mutters, sending a wink my way.

I would say something snarky, but my focus is on Amber. The woman who hates crying in front of others has tears streaming down her face.

"You did help me through my grief, though. Michele, without you, I would probably still have my head in the sand about loving my now-husband. You gave me the tough love I needed to face it, and now I find out you've been supporting me quietly with my grief, too." She takes a moment to wipe her cheeks angrily. "You're too good. Too good for us."

She gets up and wraps me in a hug. Lily is sniffling behind her back, while the boys step away to chase Griffin and give us a moment.

"Not you, too. Why are you crying?"

"I'm pregnant, I'm allowed to cry. And I am so proud of you. I ran from my past, Amber turned a blind eye to hers, and here you were, turning your past into something beautiful. Something full of hope that benefits everyone else. It's everything you are, yet it's so bittersweet."

Lily joins us on the grass, completing our group hug. It's the perfect moment, until Shadow comes bounding over, trying to join the huddle.

"If you ever keep anything this big from us again, I'm removing you as godmother."

"Harsh," Amber chides.

"I mean it, Michele. You're the glue. You kept those boys in line and together until we came along. You connected us all. But you don't have to hold it all in place anymore. We're here with tape."

"And rope," Amber adds.

Lily flicks her, then continues, "You're not alone. You haven't been for a while now. Heartbreak, fear, celebrations. You've been by our side through them all. It's time to let us do the same for you."

I grip them tighter before letting go. This meadow has always held special memories, and admitting the last of my secrets to my best friends here will be one of them.

"Enough sappy, I worked, and now I need food."

We all turn to Jake, who absolutely did the least amount of work, judgment clear on our faces. "What? I made a picnic. That was my contribution." He walks to his truck, pulling a cooler from the bed, and brings it back over.

As we all sit there eating, laughing, and watching Griff and Shadow chase butterflies, I realize how much this place has changed in the most beautiful of ways. The love cultivated here is different now, but it's just as special, and exactly what I need in my life.

CHAPTER THIRTY-THREE

ethan

I've been looking forward to River's visit since he called last week. Knowing he's so close to being here, living permanently in the same place, makes me impatient. I love Thoren and Jake, but having River around, the man who *really* knows me, is a game-changer. He's spending most of his time with his mom. I guess it works out because her home health nurse had an unexpected week off. Still, he made sure to find time to show me the progress on his house.

The gate to his property is inlaid with an insignia of a large metal J made from a baseball bat, and the circle around it is made of baseballs. He's not usually one to brag about his career, so it's nice to see him embracing it a little.

The driveway is paved and winds through the woods until opening to a clearing. The sprawling house is incredible. There's a three-car garage to the side, and a large front porch covered in stone. It almost puts Michele's wraparound porch to shame with the regal style and size. My phone vibrates in the cupholder, and the message shows up on my screen.

UNKNOWN NUMBER:

Please call me back.

With a heavy sigh, I park next to the line of cars and trucks as River comes bounding out of the house.

"Hey, man!" He slaps my back and brings me in for a hug, a wide smile splitting his face. "What do you think so far?"

"All I've seen is the gate, driveway, and front of the house, but it's very fitting. I love the gate."

"That was all your girl, she had it designed when I bought the property. She said to just wait and see what her housewarming gift will be. I'm not sure whose will be better, hers or Jake's. It's a rough problem to have."

Of course Michele did something thoughtful for him. It's who she is down to her very core. River leads me into the home where the drywall is being hung, and the kitchen cabinets are being installed.

"It's coming together nicely. I think in another month I can start moving things in. I haven't decided on landscaping out back yet. I might have to hire someone for that."

River leads me up a grand staircase, showing off the rooms upstairs and the views from each one. The back of the property has been cleared about three acres back and is surrounded by forest. Hints of a creek flowing through are dotted between the trees, and the mountain peaks can be seen from every room.

"There's a lot of bedrooms in here. Do you have plans to fill them all?"

"Every single one if I can. A house full of love and laughter. I want this to be a gathering place. I want to host Sunday dinners so my mom can rest. I want to have kids running through the kitchen when I'm trying to cook. Hell, maybe I'll finally get that dog I've been wanting for years. You and Michele want kids?"

"I do." My response is so instant it shocks me. I've always

wanted kids, but we haven't discussed it. What if she doesn't want them? I never even considered asking, until this moment. I didn't realize how badly I want them until he asked. This is a major life-changing admission, and I have no idea where my girl stands. My hands get clammy at the realization, so I move the subject along.

"How are things with Vanessa?"

"I just got off a video call with her. She loves the place and said she'll start looking at paint samples. I guess that means she's planning on moving."

"You guess? She hasn't explicitly said?" He stares at me, and I read the pointed look well. He needs time to think this one through on his own. "How's your mom doing?"

"She was chatty as ever. All I heard about was Ivy this and Ivy that. If she's so great, why is she suddenly off during a chemo week? Why couldn't she wait until her next break?" He runs his hand through his hair, shaking off his rant. "Sorry, I'm just worried about her. She looks so fragile." He takes a deep breath, trying to shake off his worry, but it's etched over every feature of his face. Slapping my back, he heads toward the stairs. "Come on, I'll show you my initial thoughts for outside."

By the time I leave his house, I feel out of sorts. That's how my life should have gone. Would have gone if I hadn't left. If I had stayed, and built Michele a home we could fill with kids.

My beautiful girl should resent me, and instead, she forgave me so easily. Accepted me back into her life, and into her heart. I've never deserved her, but that disparity feels extra now. What do I have to offer her that she doesn't have already? I feel like less of a man, unable to provide for her the way I wanted to at seventeen. The way I still do.

The funny part is, if Michele knew about these thoughts going through my head, she would yell at me for my toxic masculinity bullshit. She would tell me how a woman could have it all on her own, and that a relationship should only add to her life. I want to provide for and add to her life in any way that she will let me.

Starting with this friends' dinner. It's the first one I get to be a part of, and River assured me they are the greatest. He's basing that off the one time they allowed him to participate. I'm starting to understand the dynamic—River's the fall guy. The one they all pick on and make seem like a goofball. He's been playing that role since we were kids. It makes me question if anyone has seen the man behind the mask he wears. The man who protects his people, who fights for what's right, who hides his pain to bring joy to others. I hear it every time we talk. I see it when he talks about where his life is versus where he wants it to be. As his friend, I worry that he's never going to get what he wants and deserves.

The gravel crunches under my tires as I navigate Michele's driveway. Even though she said it's her turn to host and loves cooking for her friends, there's no way I'm letting her do it on her own. I know she's making baked ziti, so I told her I would take care of everything else.

Carrying the bags full of salad fixings, garlic bread ingredients, and a pie from the local bakery, I knock on her front door. When Michele pulls it open, my breath hitches at the sight of her. A blue summer dress skates along her curves like a second skin, accentuating her ample cleavage. Her hair is up in a bun, a few wavy strands framing her face. There's a small apron tied around her waist that clings to her hips. She's back to her perfectionist self, and I can't even be mad.

"Close your mouth," she mocks, the cutest blush on her cheeks. She takes the pie from my hands, bumping the door closed behind me. I'm careful to line my shoes up when I slip them off before following her into the kitchen.

"I need to prep the salad and get the garlic bread in the oven, but then I'm here to help, so put me to work."

She leans against the counter, watching me pull out all the ingredients with a soft smile. That smile turns to surprise when she sees the butter, garlic cloves, and parsley.

"Ethan Hill, are you making garlic bread from scratch?"

I reach around her to grab a cutting board and serrated knife to cut open the bread, using that as an excuse to hide my grin. "I am."

"You know, I thought the groveling stage was almost over, but now I'm not so sure. I think you have some more work to do."

After setting everything down, I pull her into my arms. "I know that, baby. But I will always do the extra work for you. Because you deserve it. You're worth it. I want to make you happy and show you how much you mean to me through every action. Every word. Every touch."

I run one hand up her back to grip her neck, the other down to squeeze her ass, before taking her mouth. When I pull back slightly, I whisper against her lips, "Especially with every touch." Letting her go, I spank her ass, hard. "I need a mixing bowl and sea salt. Get to it. This dinner isn't going to make itself."

"When I finally fuck that perfect ass of yours, I'm going to make you pay for that."

"A man can dream." I wink over my shoulder at her while adjusting my quickly hardening dick. I love it when she talks like that.

michele

This is the biggest group we've had yet, and I love it. It's also the first time I'm not solo. I never brought any of the guys I was dating. It's not like there were many, or they were ever serious enough. Jake and Thoren would have put on their big brother act, even though they're younger, but it's not like I dated losers. Everyone would have gotten along fine. It just never felt right.

This group here… feels right. And I'm not only saying that because River can make it and isn't bringing his twit of a girl-friend. I've only met her twice, and she was a stuck-up brat both times. Jake and Amber are helping Ethan set the table when River comes through the door. He walks right past the dining room and straight into the kitchen to give me a hug.

I try to wipe my hands off on my apron, but he squeezes me tighter and grabs one of my arms to wrap it around his back. Chuckling, I give up and hug him back.

"What's this for?" I mumble into his chest, where he has my face smooshed.

"I'm so happy for you two. Thank you for giving him another chance. I promise he won't squander it."

"You know I love this place, but it's never quite felt like home since he moved away. It feels complete now."

He squeezes me again and drops a kiss on my head. His hold loosens, then tightens again. The front door opens again, and Griff's little voice squeals, "down, down."

"Want to let go of my girl?" Ethan asks. *So that's why he grabbed me again.*

"Mmmm." I still can't see anything, but I can feel River's laugh.

"Not this again," Thoren gripes from somewhere close. I can't help but join in the laughter. River loves to stir the pot, but he does it in a way that pushes us all closer together. He's always been sneaky in that way.

The sweetest "Uncky Wiv" finally gets him to let me go and immediately scoop up Griffin. He takes him to the dining room, where Lily is setting up his highchair. The first time Thoren hosted us all at his house, I watched him step back and take it all in. I understood fully, and now that it's my turn to experience it, I'm a little overwhelmed.

It's my house that is filled with love and laughter. My house that has the man I dreamed of doing this with standing right beside me. My house that now truly feels like a home. As if he can sense my thoughts, Thoren squeezes my shoulder as he walks past, a knowing look in his eye.

"Can we eat? I'm starving, and it smells amazing."

"You were the late jackass we were waiting on," River scolds his brother.

"You showed up five minutes before him, dick," Jake adds, taking a seat.

"Dick," Griffin repeats. Everyone stops dead in their tracks and looks to Lily, who is managing to give us all a mom glare.

Thoren is trying to hide his laugh behind his hand, but fails miserably. Amber finally caves first and bursts into hysterics, followed by the rest of us.

"If everyone doesn't watch their mouths and give me food immediately, I'm going to riot," Lily says, plopping into the chair next to Griffin and whispering to him.

We all immediately find a seat and start dishing up. Thoren beams at his wife, proud as hell. "She's so sexy when she's bossy and pregnant. I think I'm going to keep her knocked up forever."

It's then that it really hits me: Ethan and I haven't talked about kids at all. I'm neutral on the idea and always have been. He used to want a house full of them, and I have no idea if that's still the case. Watching Griffin grow and seeing Lily waddle around pregnant again, I don't think I'd be opposed to having one. Ethan would make an incredible dad, but him being gone for fires would be difficult. Nothing we couldn't work through, though, if that's what we decide.

He reaches under the table and grabs my thigh, giving me his brightest smile. "This is better than I imagined," he whispers while the conversation continues around us. "I'm glad you've had them all this time."

When dinner is done, Ethan demands that I stay seated while he cleans up. Griffin's eyes start getting heavy as he picks at his piece of garlic bread.

"I set up the pack-n-play in the guest room in case you want to put him down," I tell Thoren and Lily.

"Thank you," Thoren says, picking his son up from the high-chair. "Say goodnight to everybody, bud."

"Night night," he says, blowing kisses. "Night night, dick."

"Jake, you better fix that," Lily says, pointing her fork at him.

"Why me? River swore first!"

"You're the one who said dick!"

Ethan walks back into the dining room, fresh plates and a pie in hand, halting the catfight between the two men who act more like children than Griffin some days.

As he makes the first slice into the pie, River cackles. "Please tell me I'm not the only one who remembers Jake's murder madness pie."

Ethan looks confused until Amber and Lily explain the monstrosity of the bloody face pie Jake made for the Fourth of July a few years ago.

"I hate you all. It was one time. I've learned my lesson."

The laughter dies down, and Thoren joins us again, and everyone starts digging in. It's been a great night. I've missed the laughter and joy that is so prevalent when we all get together. It's lighter with Ethan by my side. Having these dinners for the last few years has been wonderful, but it has always accentuated how lonely I was.

River puts his fork down, a serious look on his face. "I've decided what to name my dick."

"Oh God, not this again," Jake groans.

"It's only fair. You guys have names, why can't mine? He's worthy of a name."

Ethan looks between Jake and River, then to the rest of us. "What the hell?"

"This all started when they came back from college. Thor's hammer, Jacob's ladder, and now..." I look questioningly at River.

"Slugger. I'm naming mine Slugger."

"Love the baseball reference," Lily chimes in.

"Don't encourage him, baby." Thoren shakes his head, but there's clear amusement there. "Just because you play baseball doesn't mean it's a good name."

River scoffs, then flashes his brightest smile. "It obviously fits because I always hit a home run."

Jake looks at Lily. "Look what you've done now."

"Me? That was all Thor."

Ethan's gaze has been ping-ponging between everyone this whole time. He looks beyond amused, taking it all in. "Well, now I clearly need to name mine."

"Good luck with that. It's taken me years to pick one. This isn't a rash decision."

"Already have it. It's my axe."

Amber snorts into her drink. "Do firefighters really use those?"

"Wildland firefighters do," Ethan replies, giving my body a slow once-over. "And I'm known to split people in half."

Jake's deep laugh echoes through the room, and my cheeks heat. The girls give me impressed looks, but I try to hide the smile that's trying to break free. It's not like he's wrong. Ethan reaches for my hand, bringing it to his lips for a tender kiss that's too endearing for the comment he just made.

"Damn it, that's actually a good name." River pouts. "I'd slug you right now for upstaging me if I wasn't so happy for you two idiots."

I can't help myself. "Would you use your slugger to do it?"

I'm met with a round of groans and Lily's loud "Ew, Michele!"

"Oh, come on. I know you're dying to write a gay romcom next. I'm giving you some good material here. Best friends turned lovers, everyone loves to see it."

River leans over me, winking at Ethan. "What do you say, pretty boy?"

"Enough, please. I'm begging you." Thoren rolls his eyes at our antics.

The table stays rowdy as we finish our dessert and talk about life. Things have changed drastically from when Thoren, Jake, and I started these. It's the sweetest change I could have hoped for. This group has had such a major impact on my life. They support me and have my back, no matter what I choose with Ethan, and that means so much. Them accepting him so quickly, despite the bitter feelings I know Thoren and Jake still have toward him, shows how incredible our bond is.

Everyone stays for another two hours, and by the time they are shuffling out the door, my heart is full. Griffin is sleeping soundly on Thoren's shoulder as I hug them goodbye. With them all gone, I close and lock the door, slumping against it with my eyes shut.

I peek one eye open when I hear footsteps coming to a stop. Ethan's leaning against the doorframe to the kitchen, a dish towel slung over his shoulder, arms crossed. "You happy, baby?"

"Very happy."

"Good," he replies, throwing the towel behind him and stalking toward me. He picks me up bridal style and makes a beeline for the stairs. "Now I'm taking my girl to bed."

CHAPTER THIRTY-FIVE

michele

My morning was spent signing closing papers with one of my clients, and I felt like celebrating. I usually take myself out to lunch after closing on a property, but today I realized I don't have to do that alone anymore. There is someone who will be equally thrilled for me, and who I want to eat my lunch with.

I don't think Ethan has been back to the infamous Munchen Garten, so I stopped to pick up some brats for us. This is my first time visiting him at his office, and I'm excited to see the work he's doing. There might be a few small things in my bag to add to his desk as well, so I hope he has room for them. Thoren ensured that Ethan would be here all day, so I get to surprise him.

There's a directory in the front, which is already updated with his name. The building isn't huge, but since it is shared by so many different entities, it can be confusing. Following the small layout, I make my way down the hall, hands full of goodies.

The door to his office is ajar, but I stop a few feet shy of it when I hear Ethan's voice. He must be on the phone, because there are pauses between each time he speaks. I don't want to interrupt, so I remain in the hall until he's done. With the door open, I can hear every word he's saying clearly, and one sentence catches my attention.

"Of course I remember her… A year… We were never really together… Yes, I do."

No.

No.

I'm seventeen all over again, and as fragile as a glass doll. A crack reopens on my porcelain skin, a spiderweb fracturing the smooth, pristine surface of my composure. My heart pounds a frantic beat against my ribs as I lean closer to the door. Each word is a dagger, piercing through my carefully constructed frame. This isn't a conversation I should be hearing like this, when Ethan doesn't know I'm here. I need to make my presence known or turn and flee. And yet, my feet, seemingly made of lead, stay rooted to the spot. "Fight," my head yells. "Flight," my heart responds.

The conversation gets continuously worse, the words becoming more pointed, the implications more devastating, each sentence a blow that shatters another piece of me. The color drains from my face, the world tilting precariously on its axis, and all I can do is stand here, listening to the unraveling of everything I thought I knew.

"What's the salary?" There's a really long pause this time. "It sounds like a good position. Anyone would be lucky to be offered it."

The crack spreads, rupturing the glue of time and healing I painted over it. This can't be happening again. People always leave. My heart is in my stomach, a sickening squeeze of pain following. *Hold it together, Michele.* Tears gather on my lashes, my hands tremble, and still, I stand there. Frozen in time, the dropped porcelain doll, waiting for impact with the cold, hard floor of reality.

"Colorado did have its charms… When do they need to hear by…? I hear exactly what you're saying. You're offering a new job and a new girlfriend."

My hold on time stops, and every broken piece of me shatters. He's leaving. Every insecurity, every imperfection comes rushing back to the surface, mocking me. I told myself I'd remember the pain, so I wouldn't allow it to break me again. But here I am, broken.

I can't listen a moment longer. Turning, I rush down the hall, but run into Thoren and River halfway to the front door. River grabs my shoulder, his eyes softening when he sees the tears on my cheeks.

"What's going on? Thor said you were bringing lunch, so we were going to crash your date." He holds up the take-out bag.

My lower lip trembles as I try to speak. How do I tell them I feel like the same girl I was at seventeen, having her future ripped from her hands? What can I say to make them understand that I was shattered then, and the cracks are starting to form again?

"I have to go. Give him this?" I thrust the bag of food and my gift into Thoren's chest and step around them, running for the door. They call out after me, but I'm long gone. Out the door and in my car, heading home.

This was my biggest fear. Ethan's been chasing fires and adventure for years. He said it was paving his path back to me, but was it really? The life of a wildland firefighter is unpredictable, and the dangerous aspect brings a sort of thrill to those who seek action and adventure in their lives. I never thought that was why Ethan was in the career field. His career path says something completely different.

He hasn't even been here two whole months, and now he's already talking about going back to Colorado. And the woman… I'm choosing not to think about that part of the conversation. I didn't hear the other side of the call.

Why won't these tears stop falling? It's going to be fine. Everything is going to be fine.

CHAPTER THIRTY-SIX

ethan

I slam the phone down and run my hands through my hair, beyond frustrated. I should have shut my dad out of my life completely. I've had multiple grounds to. For some reason, his betrayal never felt as bad as my mom's. I expected it from him. Yet, I answered that call and immediately regretted it.

The same manipulation tactics he's always used came out to play again. A large part of me wanted to give him a piece of my mind and hang up, but I let him ramble on, thinking I was interested. I'm not, but I have someone in mind that may be.

Trying to entice me with Claire shows how out of touch with me he is. Still trying to push his agendas and have my life play out the way he wanted his to. Claire was a mistake, one who pursued me for over a year. One date with her, and she wanted more, but she didn't really want it with me. She just wanted someone to take care of her.

If my father is so concerned about her being the assistant for the open position, he should take it. She's exactly his type, pretty and wanting to be loved. There's nothing wrong with that, except if you end up falling for narcissistic men like my father. In fact, I wouldn't be surprised if she got the job by sleeping with him.

He's been using his position of power to aid in his infidelity for years.

He knows my plan has always been to come back here, and Michele is the reason why. I'll never forgive him for making me his puppet all those years ago.

I lean back in my chair and run my hands down my face. All I want is to see Michele. Getting to hold her and feel her soft body in my arms makes everything better. Maybe I'll pop by her place on my way home tonight and see if she's there.

"Ethan!" Thoren yells as he comes stomping into my office with River on his heels. Both of them look upset. Thoren dumps two bags on my desk, slamming his hands down. "What did you do?"

"What are you talking about?"

"Why did Michele just run out of here crying?" He's leaned over my desk, a hard look on his face.

What? "Michele was here?"

River shakes his head and takes the free chair in my office, setting another bag on my desk. I'm so confused about what's happening. When was Michele here, and why didn't she come see me?

"Grab a chair, Thor."

Thoren huffs, his gaze full of disappointment, then he walks into the hall, coming back with a chair in hand, while River opens the bags and takes out some to-go containers. When they're both seated across the desk from me, and my patience is wearing thin, River talks.

"You didn't see Michele today?"

"No. When was she here?"

"Only a minute ago," Thoren answers. "She texted me earlier, making sure you were in the office today." He slides over a container, and I open it, seeing two brats and two soft pretzels.

"She was bringing you lunch. So why the fuck did she throw these bags at me and run out of here crying?"

"I don't know! I didn't see her. I just got off the phone with my dad."

"What did that bastard want?" River asks, then takes a bite of his sub sandwich.

I'm still so very lost. "Why are you guys here? And why didn't you stop her and ask her what was going on?"

River rolls his eyes. "Catch up. Michele was bringing you lunch, so we got our own lunch to crash your date and hang out with you. On our way in, she was running out. All she said was she had to go. Now we're here asking what you did wrong, and what your asshole father said."

My father. *Oh fuck, my father.* She must have overheard my conversation. Did I say anything bad? Even if I didn't, it might have sounded bad. I was too nice, letting him keep talking about the job, because I wanted the specifics. If he thinks I'm interested, he will keep the submissions open for a few more days, and then I can recommend Brent for the job.

I snag one of the brats and take a bite, taking my time to chew. "My dad's trying to get me to take a position in Colorado. It'll look good for him and give him a boost to get the local fire chief position he's gunning for. He listed everything possible to make it enticing."

"Like what?"

"Double the salary I'm making now. And he found a girl I went on one date with and promised to make her my assistant if I take the job. Basically offered her up on a silver platter." I toss the food back into the container, disgusted. "He treats women like shit, and I'm so fucking tired of it. As if either of those things would get me to leave here or Michele."

I say that, but doubling my salary could provide Michele with a better lifestyle than what I can offer here. She wouldn't have to work so hard. She could open another nursery and solely do that or not work at all.

"Wait, your parents aren't together anymore?" Thoren asks.

"Oh, they are. Dear Old Dad just steps out like it's his second job, and my mom turns a blind eye. I need to tell Michele the whole truth."

"Wow, what an asshole. Of course, man. I'm sorry to hear that. You think Michele overheard the conversation?"

"She must have, that's the only explanation." I let my head thump onto the desk, no longer hungry. "I can't even sneak out to explain things to her. I have a meeting in an hour, and this is not an over-the-phone conversation."

"Send her a text. Tell her you'll explain in person. And thank her for the lunch that you better eat because she left hers, too."

I feel like a jackass. My girl is hurting because of me, and here I am with the meal that she bought for us to share. After sliding out my phone, I send her a quick text, and eat the rest of the food because I know she ordered this special for me.

ETHAN:

It wasn't what it sounded like, I promise. Please come over tonight and let me explain.

Our conversation flows to River's season, Evelyn's health, and then the SAR team that Thoren still volunteers for and helps with when able. When we've finished eating, Thoren peeks into the brown paper bag left sitting on my desk.

"Man, you really fucked up," he says after letting out a low whistle.

I look inside the bag. First, I pull out the plant that's taking up most of the space. I don't recognize what it is, so I pull out my phone to look it up because, knowing Michele, this has a deeper meaning. Sure enough, the jade plant is supposed to bring luck and prosperity. I set it on the side of my desk that gets a little sunlight, then pull out the next item. It's a photo of Michele and me from one of our high school dates in the meadow. The frame looks hand-painted with little axes and boots, which is extra funny if she made this after our dick naming conversation with everyone.

Last in the bag is a glass paperweight with forget-me-nots in the center. It's personal and thoughtful, and makes me fall even harder for her. River knows the significance and leans forward to flick my forehead. "Idiot," he mutters. "Never should have answered that call."

"I know. But she's pretty incredible, isn't she?"

They both nod, and a slow smile breaks out across River's face. "Forgot to tell you, I have that contact you asked for." He slides his phone out and sends me a text with a wink and a knock on my desk. Standing, he grabs all the trash and kicks the leg of Thor's chair. "Let's go. He has work to do."

My office is too quiet with them gone, so I focus on getting myself prepared for the meetings this afternoon. I have them back-to-back. Yet, my mind keeps straying to the phone call with my dad. I know what he's doing and why he wants me to take the job.

Why did I have to answer?

michele

I'm parked outside Lily's house before I fully register where I was heading. Shadow, her and Thoren's dog, comes bounding out from the back of the house to greet me. I run my fingers through her soft black fur, reveling in the way she sticks to my side. She's always been a very emotionally intuitive dog.

I follow her around the back of the house to find Lily sitting on the back porch, laptop open in front of her, and a baby monitor perched on the table next to it. She glances at me before focusing back on her laptop, finishing typing. My favorite author, always working so hard.

"I was wondering who was here," she says, still plunking away at the keyboard. "Want to join me for lunch?"

I take a seat across the table from her, trying to gather my thoughts. "I think I need five minutes of truth," I admit, my voice breaking on the last word.

Lily's eyes fly from the screen to meet mine, as the tears I had under control start to gather on my lashes again. In an instant, she's standing and rounds the table, wrapping her arms around my shoulders with her baby bump pressing against my back.

"Is this a me and you moment, or should I tell Amber to get her butt over here?"

"If she's not at work."

"She'd leave work in a heartbeat for you, but I think she's doing inventory today." She snatches her phone from the table and sends a text. "Have you had lunch yet?"

I shake my head, and Lily jumps into mom mode. "I'll make food while we wait for Amber. You relax and tell me if you hear Griff wake up." Before going inside, she gives me one more hug. "We've got you."

I've been friends with Lily and Amber for almost three years, and they've never let me down. Since Ethan moved back, I've opened up and relied on them more than ever before. I was scared of being too much, but they've shown over and over that they'll be by my side through it all. The thing is, I thought Ethan had me, too. He told me he wasn't going anywhere; his home was here. That *I* was his home. Who wouldn't want to settle down here? Cedar Ridge has everything you could need. It has charm, all four seasons, stunning views, and every outdoor activity you could want.

Shadow comes bounding up the back deck and drops a ball in my lap. Her tongue lolls out to the side, and I can't deny her sweet face. I wipe my eyes and sit on the steps of the deck. Shadow runs into the yard, anticipating the ball, barking when I don't throw it fast enough.

"Okay, okay," I gripe, tossing it out past her, and into the edge of the woods.

I love my backyard, but Thoren and Lily's is equally peaceful. They have lilac bushes lining the edges of the deck, and planters laid out on the steps next to me. Herbs and flowers spill out of them, bringing such a sweet smell, mixing with the pine and cedar trees in the woods. There's a sense of tranquility in the silence of the mountains that can't be replicated.

The sun warms my face as Shadow and I play fetch, her excited barks echoing around the space. I've worked so hard to build the life that I have, but there's longing when I sit here thinking about the lives of my friends. They have significant others, families, and pets. In comparison, my life is empty. If Ethan takes that job and leaves me again, I don't think I can put my heart through any more loss. Is solitude my destiny?

Lily comes out the back door with a tray in hand. "Amber should be here any minute. I made sandwiches and fruit. Is this a wine conversation? I'm sure I have some for you girls."

"No, I just have to say this out loud."

Lily sets the tray down and hands over a water bottle before taking a seat on the grass and spreading out. Shadow immediately runs over and lies on her spread legs, her furry snout pointed right at Lily's baby bump. She runs her hand through her dog's fur, smiling. "She's the best big sister. Loves these little nuggets from the moment she realizes they're in my belly. Have you thought about having kids?"

Funny she should ask, because it's been on my mind since my talk with Evelyn. "I've gone back and forth. You know I love Griff, and I'm going to love this sweet girl, too. They bring so much joy to your home. I'm not sure they're in the cards for me, though."

"You're still in your prime, there's plenty of time if you decide."

"Damn right I am," I chuckle. "Some days I feel so old. I'm thirty-three, I have my whole life ahead of me still. Why am I holding myself back so much?"

"I don't know," Amber chimes in, walking around the side of the cabin and plopping down in the grass across from Lily. She kicks her sandals off and wiggles her toes, leaning back and letting the sun hit her face. "When I met you, you were fearless, outspoken, and unapologetically yourself. Hell, you pierced your tits simply because you could. You've gotten more cautious since then."

Lily kicks her foot, but Amber shrugs. "Chele has been the outspoken one so many times, giving me the tough love that I need. It's my turn." She looks at me with a sympathetic smile. "You've always been this mythical unicorn to me. Everything you touch is successful and beautiful. You're always put together, organized, brave, and kind. But we worry about you."

"Why?"

"What part of it is *for you*?" Lily asks. "The piercing was for you, and we were so proud of you when you got them done. But the more we learn about your past with Ethan, the more we see how much of yourself you give."

"Your house is a replica of what you and Ethan used to talk about. Your flower business was built out of a love for him. You give up your time and money to make things special and perfect for everyone around you. Your bold personality makes people respect and appreciate you. But that bravery has been quieter lately."

I understand what they're saying. It's the same thing Ethan said. There's no denying their words when they're true. My bravery is quieter lately, but not because it's gone. I'm showing it in ways that not everyone sees.

"I'm ready for my five minutes of truth, but this time I need your thoughts after." Two sets of eyes bore into me, and I swallow down my nerves. "I stopped by Ethan's office to bring him lunch and overheard a phone call. He mentioned a woman and a job in Colorado."

My hands tremble in my lap, so I intertwine my fingers. "I didn't catch it all, but he seemed pretty interested in the position, and I have no idea about the woman. I, uh, I've been quiet in my bravery, but I've been overcoming hurdles that no one sees. When

Ethan left all those years ago, it shattered me. I felt abandoned. Inadequate. Not enough."

I bite the inside of my cheek to stop the quiver. "I felt like if I had been better somehow, it would have been enough to make him stay. It's something I've struggled with since. People always leave. My brother, my parents, Ethan. Every relationship I've ever been in. I have been trying to make sure there's no reason to make anyone leave ever since. If all the aspects of my life are in order, if every hair on my head is perfectly styled, and my outfits are put together, what excuse do they have to go?"

"Oh, Michele," Lily says with tears sliding down her cheeks.

"I still don't know why Ethan left. What it was that drove him off, or what I was missing to make him stay. But I've been facing those thoughts head-on since he came back. With a quiet ferocity, I've been fighting to let him in. To let him see all of me, even the parts that aren't always pretty. He begged me to let him in that way. So I have. Every day, I face my fears and let him in. Let him past my barriers, and in turn, I fell so blindly in love with him. Despite my fears that he could leave again."

Amber's eyes hold a sadness that I haven't seen there in years. "Do you really think he's going to take a new job and leave?"

"I didn't know. He texted me when I was driving over here and told me that it wasn't what it sounded like, and that he would explain when he got off work. I want to trust that. To trust in the love we have. The effort he's been showing, the words he's been saying. But we've been here before."

"I'll kick his ass if he leaves again," Amber grumbles.

"I don't have the fight left in me if he does. He showed me I can be loved for exactly who I am, not who I want the world to see. I don't want to go back. I want to be the woman you girls think I am. The one who is unapologetically herself. Not the tailored version."

"I'm so proud of you. We want to see all of you, Michele.

Show us the dark, scared, and frazzled sides of you. Let us love them just as much. You've been by our side through the good, bad, and ugly. You have been the first in our corner through it all. Let us do the same for you. If he doesn't stay, we will be here to pick up the pieces. If he does, we will continue to remind you that you're worthy exactly as you are." Lily sits up, and a second later, Griffin starts talking through the baby monitor. "Mom intuition," she jokes, taking her time getting up off the ground. "Talk to him. Let him explain what you heard and go from there. I've seen the way he looks at you, and I truly believe it has to be a misunderstanding. Dig in, I'll be back with Griff in a moment."

Amber hops up and holds out a hand to pull me up off the steps. She wraps me in a hug, holding me tight. "It's our imperfections that make us who we are. Show the world all that is Michele, and I promise they will be even more amazed by the incredible woman you are. And I really will nut punch him if he leaves again."

I fucking love this girl.

CHAPTER THIRTY-EIGHT

michele

After my afternoon with the girls, I'm feeling confident that, no matter the outcome of this conversation, I'll have the support I need to make it through. I told Ethan he could come for dinner and we would talk, but he insisted we do it at his place. Wanting a calm before the storm, I call my brother on the drive over.

Surprisingly, Austin's voice comes through the car speakers after the first ring. "What's up, sis?"

"Not too much. I closed a sale today, and now I'm heading to Ethan's for dinner."

"Of course you did because you're the shit. Now tell me how that's going? Do I need to come beat his ass yet?"

I laugh, but it's a little watery. "No, things are fine."

"They don't sound fine." There's a gruff protectiveness in his voice.

"I overheard a phone call. It sounded like he was making plans to leave again, but I'm going to give him a chance to explain." I take a deep, steadying breath. "What if he leaves me again?"

"Then you'll hurt for a little while, but then you'll build yourself back stronger. Just like you did the first two times. You're older, wiser, and you have friends and family who love you. You'll be okay… but he'll be in the hospital after I break his face."

That draws a laugh from me, before we both fall into silence again. "I don't think he's leaving. It's going to be okay. Thanks for always having my back."

"Of course, you're my baby sis. You'll let me know how it goes?"

"Yeah, I'm almost there now. I'll text you later. Love you." I hit the end button on the dash and flip on my blinker for Ethan's. The gravel entrance is weed-free when I drive up, and the front looks even better than when I came to drop off the flowers.

I haven't been back here since then, so I haven't seen the inside at all. We've spent all our time at my place, and I never questioned it since this place is a little run-down. However, this house looks like night and day since I was here last. There are pretty wooden shutters around the windows, and the front door is newly painted. Ethan's put in a lot of work into a temporary home.

He's doing it anyway, like he has been with me and our friends. He's been putting in effort and time to make roots here, to build his life here. That isn't something he's done before. River said he's seen the places he's lived on video calls and that he's never painted, put up pictures, or even spent money on decent furniture. He never bothered to put down roots, knowing he had no plans to stay.

Things have to be different now, right? He's making a home for himself. His front door opens, and he leans against the frame with his arms crossed, staring at me with a smirk on his face. How long have I been sitting in my car, too nervous to go in? He chuckles and shakes his head before crooking a finger at me.

Like a dog with a bone, I get out of the car and follow his

command. When I get to the top step, he pulls me into him and lets out a heavy sigh. "Come on," he says into my hair. "I bought some wine."

With an arm around my shoulder, he leads me into the house. There's a small couch, coffee table, and TV stand in the living room that fit the space well and look inviting. In the kitchen, I recognize one of Jake's tables, with a bottle and two wine glasses waiting on it.

"Have a seat," He motions to the bistro table and pours two hefty glasses. He hands me one, then leans against the counter across from me. I take a healthy sip, and he laughs. "I guess now's the time for our talk?"

"I guess so."

I'm ready for this. From the day he left, I've been ready for this. But now that it's here, and the explanation I've been waiting years for is within reach, I'm petrified. Will he break my heart? Repair it? Do I even want to know anymore? What if it alters my perception of everything that's happened?

The glass spins between my fingertips, each turn tugging a string tighter around my chest.

"When you came to surprise me today, I think you overheard my phone call with my father." There's a pause as I watch him take a few gulps of his wine. "He has a job in Colorado that he wants me to take. It's a good position, double the pay, and the most important part… it would make him look good to have me as his 'successful hero son who loves working with him.'" He air quotes that last part, rolling his eyes.

"I'm not taking the job. I was *never* taking the job, but I have someone I used to work with who I think would be a great fit for the role, so I was trying to get more information about it."

My shoulders slump with relief, but there's still a heavy feeling in my stomach. "Did you consider it?"

"For a second, but only a second. And it would have only

been a possibility if you had come with me. I told you I'm not leaving you again. Michele, I would never ask you to move away from your home. I couldn't ask you fifteen years ago, and I certainly can't now, seeing everything you've built."

"And the woman?"

He throws back the rest of the glass of wine, slamming it on the counter, then runs his hands through his hair. "My dad's been trying to manipulate and control my life. He's been doing it for far longer than I realized, but there was a time he tried using women as pawns. When we were both working in Colorado, he would send women to the fire station to see me. He'd tell them I was single, dependable, looking to settle, and that I just needed 'a little push.' So they would show up in droves, asking for a tour with me."

His gaze is haunted, miserable. "They were nice, sure, but there was a woman who had my heart. Someone my dad sent would never replace her. I wouldn't even let them try." He moves to the table to pour another glass of wine and tops mine off.

"Anyway, there was one woman I kind of hit it off with. She asked me out for drinks that weekend, and I went. It went okay, but I realized she wasn't someone I wanted to spend time with. For the next year, though, she tried pursuing me. Showed up at the firehouse often. She wouldn't take the hint. My dad hired her as the personal assistant for the position he wanted me to take."

I try to hide my hurt with another sip. I know that woman wasn't the reason he considered that job, but the feelings still sting. My body doesn't look like those other women. I have curves and rolls, and I jiggle when I walk. I'm not the type of woman his dad would approve of. He never liked me back then, he certainly wouldn't be my biggest fan now. I was too opinion-ated, too stubborn, and too loud for his meek-and-mild-mannered tastes.

Ethan used to look up to his dad. He wanted to be like him,

follow in his footsteps. Clearly something has changed with the way he said his name, it was laced with such vitriol and disgust. Still, he's entertaining the idea of leaving for his dad's sake. Would he leave me to please him?

"So you're not going to leave? You're staying for real this time, no matter what offer your dad, or anyone else, throws at you?"

He steps over and cups my face, his green eyes looking deep into mine. "I'm staying here. I promise. There is nowhere I'd rather be. No one I would rather be with. You're it for me, Michele. Until my last dying breath."

I'm immediately taken back. The first time he said that to me we were lying on the bed of his truck, parked in our meadow. He's said it a few times since, but the last time I heard it was in Colorado, and I'm not entirely sure I didn't dream it up.

"Thank you for being my person again and choosing me. It couldn't have been easy, turning down a big position like that."

"That's the thing, Wildflower. It was the easiest decision I've ever made. I've been working my way back to you for half my lifetime. I'm not going to throw that away for a few dollars. I choose you. I will always choose you."

CHAPTER THIRTY-NINE

ethan

9 years ago
Colorado

I've been counting down the hours for the last three weeks. There's been a hole in my life since the day I left Cedar Ridge, and nothing seems to fill it. Except Michele. Always her. She's always made me feel complete. Steady. Sure.

How I've managed to go this long without seeing her, I'll never know. I've wanted to get her out here for a while now. Years, honestly. But I've been too busy to give her the time she deserves. There was also the fear she would say no. Aside from the flowers I've sent every year on her birthday, we haven't talked since I left.

With me transferring from the fire house to the wildland team, I took two weeks off in between to recenter and get my girl here. I thought about flying out to surprise her, but I'm not ready to go back to Cedar Ridge yet. If I do, I'll never leave.

When I called her, she was hesitant at first, but she reluctantly agreed to come and stay with me for a week. There's a chance, or more so a guarantee, I'll feel the same way about her being here.

I'll never want her to leave. I'm willing to deal with the pain of the goodbye simply to see her. To hold her in my arms and have everything feel right in my world, no matter how fleeting the moment.

The crowd parts, and there she is. Looking as beautiful as ever, Michele slings her purse over her shoulder, strutting through the airport doors. Her dress is too nice for a flight, but I appreciate the effort. Looking down at my plain T-shirt and jeans, I scold myself as I hop from the truck and wave.

A smile instantly forms when we lock eyes, and my heart beats out of my rib cage. *She's really here.* I rush over to her, wrapping her in an embrace and spinning her around, causing her to drop her bags. I bury my nose in her neck, inhaling her warm and sweet vanilla scent. Goosebumps skitter down my arms, and my chest flushes. Her heart races against mine, two matching flutters, overwhelmed by each other. She spears her nails into my hair, and her shaky inhale tilts my world on its axis. Years apart, and it all feels gone in an instant.

"I missed you."

She wraps herself tighter around me, pulling me close enough so there's not a breath of space between us. Not a care for the world passing by around us. "I missed you, too."

We spend the next few days exploring. Michele and I hike all my favorite local trails. We go biking, kayaking, and visit a few too many breweries. She lets me hold her hand in public and kiss her in private. There are no barriers, no feelings of lost time. Our conversations flow, and our hearts mend. This was everything I needed, and for the first time in years, there's a genuine spark in my eyes when I look in the mirror.

I don't want her to leave. I don't want her to go home. Her

home should be with me, the way it was always meant to be. Every fiber of my being wants to beg her to stay with me. To be able to feel this happiness and contentment all the time. Then I remember the reason I never asked her to come with me in the first place.

Michele was meant for Cedar Ridge. For the people. I couldn't ask her to leave them all behind. I know how much her brother signing up for the military hurt her. How much she talked about him being in a dangerous job and how she had nightmares over it. Between that and what my mom said, I couldn't ask her to follow me. It would have been selfish and only hurt her in the end. She deserves more.

In the evenings, I get to hold her close and dream of our future when this will be my reality every night. We make love, and it's even better than I remembered. Tracing her curves, licking every inch of her perfect body, hearing her whimper when I pinch her clit. Her eyes always coming back to mine, needing the connection. Needing to be grounded in the moment together, expressing everything words can't capture.

On the last night, she falls asleep early, exhausted from our week of adventures. With her head on my chest, arm wrapped around me, I realize this is my favorite time of day. The time when she is comfortable and protected in my arms. Where there's peace in her features, and I run my fingers through her hair, feeling her heart beat against me.

We never got to experience this before. There was a time or two we fell asleep in the bed of my truck together while studying, but this week has been the first time I've held her through the night. To wake up to her smiling face and kiss her, despite her protest of morning breath. I can't let her go tomorrow, yet I can't selfishly ask her to stay. My heart is torn in two, indecision warring for doing what we want, versus doing what is right.

After dealing with the way I left, and my absence for so long,

Michele deserves what is right. She deserves to have a man who can give her everything, and I'm not able to do that yet.

I let my fingers trail from her hair, down her back, letting the warmth seep through me. She doesn't stir, so I whisper the truth I'm too scared to say in the light. "I'm coming back for you, Wildflower. I know I have no right to ask anything of you, but if you wait for me... I'm coming for you. I promise. It's you, Michele. Until my last dying breath."

MICHELE

I was surprised when Ethan called out of the blue and asked me to come visit him. There was a definite hesitation on my part, but I couldn't deny my heart. I've loved this man for most of my life. Getting the chance to see him again, to see whether things still feel the same between us, isn't an opportunity I can pass up. He purchased the plane tickets the moment I said yes, as eager for this trip as me.

When I saw his handsome face waiting for me at the airport, I thought my heart might burst out of my body. Everything felt right, everything felt whole. It's been the most incredible trip so far, catching up on life, exploring local scenery, and collecting a few wildflowers on our hikes. It's been perfect, except I leave tomorrow, and we haven't talked about the future. About what this trip means, and if anything will change.

I thought he might ask me to move. Maybe tell me his wildland position is actually in Washington, not here in Colorado. Instead, there hasn't been a single word uttered about either. I'm too afraid to ask. My heart can't handle the disappointment.

"This was my fire station," he says, driving past on our way to breakfast. "It was a good crew, and I'll miss them, but I'm ready to get back to wildland firefighting. That's where my heart really lies. I don't want to go back after this, I want to stay in wildland for the rest of my career."

"Can we bring them coffee and donuts on the way back?"

He looks over at me with his signature smile. "Of course we can."

That's how we find ourselves walking through the fire house two hours later, coffee and donuts in hand. Ethan dumps them in the kitchen before showing me around. He introduces me to the crew, all of them warm and welcoming, telling him he's missed already. It's nice to see that he's not completely alone out here. He has people looking out for him.

One man comes and asks to steal him away for a moment, and he checks that it's okay with me first. I nod and make my way back to the kitchen to wait for him when a firefighter approaches me.

"Hello, beautiful, can I help you with anything?"

"No, thanks," I respond. If I did need something from a first responder, that's not the way I would want to be approached.

"Are you here with someone?" he asks casually, looking over the picked-through box of donuts.

"Ethan."

He pauses, his gaze raking over me, before he casually replies, "You're not his usual type."

"Excuse me?"

"That's his move. Bringing the blonde bombshells on a tour here before undoubtedly taking them home. Cut your losses now; he'll never be serious about anyone. The same one has never been around twice."

The sting of his words hits instantly. I'm baffled at the careless way he delivers them and how he smirks as he walks away. I know I'm not a size two, but I'm comfortable in my skin and happy with my health. Ethan hasn't said anything about the pounds I've put on. If anything, he's celebrated and worshipped my body for exactly how it is.

Is this really Ethan's go-to move to get women? I'm the one who suggested we come here, not him. We haven't talked about what's happened while apart, and honestly, I don't want to know. I just want to be his again. The woman he seeks comfort in. The place where he can let down his guard and share his burdens. The one who will cherish every moment because any fire could be his last.

Soon after, Ethan finds me, taking my hand as he leads me back to his truck. I know we need to have this conversation now, no matter how much it's going to hurt.

"What does this trip mean?" I ask, buckling myself in.

"What do you mean?"

"For us. What does this mean for us? Where do we go from here?"

The defeated look in his eyes sends chills down my over-heated skin.

It's happening.

Again.

An elephant sits on my chest as I try to keep my breathing calm. Nothing is changing. He's staying in Colorado, I'm still going to be alone in Washington, and the love of my life is too scared to tell me.

I'm not even sure I would want to move to Colorado, but for him, I'd consider it. There is very little I wouldn't do for Ethan. Isn't that the most pathetic thing? After this man broke me then walked away without a single look back. I could be brave and tell him I would move for him. I don't have a shy bone in my body, but I need more. The way he left me means I need to hear the words coming out of his mouth. He can't expect me to chase him. *He* left *me,* not the other way around. Inviting me to visit is not the same as telling me he still loves me, he can't live without me, and he's sorry for the hurt he caused.

"You don't have to say it. We don't have to talk about it. I leave tomorrow, let's just enjoy our time together." The words taste like shit coming out of my mouth. It's not the way I feel. I can hold it together for twenty-four hours and break down tomorrow when I'm home. The shards of the porcelain doll feel pressurized again, ready to shatter the moment I stop holding them together. Only then will I let the weight of him rejecting me twice take me out at the knees.

michele

The memories still haunt me. Not in a "meet me in my dreams" sort of way, but in an ache that lives dormant in my body. Some days, I forget it's even there, then I see the perfect sunset, or a young couple holding hands walking down the street. That's when it hits like a shot to the heart, and the ache would spread, crippling every ounce of security I had built. I'd see the way his green eyes would shine in the sunlight. How his smile would light up a room the moment he saw me. The whispered words we'd share, and the way his hand always found mine.

"You can check out the changes I made around the place while I cook, or you can hang out here with me."

His voice breaks me out of the haunting hold my memories have on me. I need to do something with my hands, unable to sit with my thoughts a moment longer. "Actually, can I help?"

He stares at me for a tense moment. "Are you going to try to take over?"

"No," I grin. "Promise."

"All right," he concedes, and starts taking out ingredients and explaining the brown sugar glaze he's making for the salmon and the squash he bought for the side. "Want to start with chopping?"

He sets me up with everything I need and pulls a beer bottle from the fridge. The lid plinks on the counter where he drops it. I peek at him out of the corner of my eye. "Need liquid courage for something?"

"Yes." His long fingers swipe over the growing condensation as I try to focus on my cutting. "I want to talk about something else. Can I tell you a story?"

Without meeting his gaze, I know exactly what he's going to tell me. I'm not sure I'm ready to hear it, but my conversation with Austin earlier plays in my head, so I nod. Turning around, I pour out what I need to glaze the salmon. Even after promising not to take over, I know he needs the space to focus on his words. Behind me, his breath is loud before he clears his throat.

"There once was a young boy who cherished his mom and looked up to his dad," he begins. My breath hitches, not prepared, but he keeps going, "The young boy was also madly in love with his best friend. They were inseparable, always off on one adventure or another. Their love was special, filled with shared firsts and promised lasts. He saw his whole life every time he looked in her eyes."

He takes a sip of his beer as I refill my wine. Pouring it a little too high in the glass, I gulp half of it down before putting the salmon in the oven.

"One day, his dad sat him down and talked to him about his future. He told him the family was moving, and if he wanted to follow in his footsteps, going with them was the best way. He laid out the reality of trying to survive on his own, working during the fire season, and leaving for weeks at a time at the drop of a hat to fight wildland fires. They talked about the pay, and how low it was, the exhaustion, the long hours, and how that impacted relationships. He told him that working at both a firehouse and with wildfires is the best place to start his career and that Cedar Ridge is too small to do that."

He picks up the beer and chugs the rest down, looking anywhere in the kitchen but at me. I didn't realize he had talked to his dad about all this. As far as I knew, his dad had always known Ethan's dreams of being a local firefighter and supported him. Of course, he would have preferred him to follow in his *exact* footsteps. Ethan never mentioned that his dad brought it up again.

"The next week, his mom sits him down to talk. She tells him that not everything is how it looks from the outside. She shatters into a shell of who she is and admits that this life is hard. The fear, the anxiety, the loneliness. His heart breaks as his mom tells him that she hasn't been happy in years, that being the wife of a firefighter is hard, and that if he loves his girlfriend the way he claims to, he needs to let her go. That a girl as bright and kind and happy as her deserves a man who will come home to her every night, and will put her before his career. She tells him that young love is great, but it's not meant to last, and the hurt will fade."

His words tear through me like a snag in tights that spreads with every step. While none of our parents were amazing, they weren't bad. They were just kind of... *there*. Yet they felt like they had the right to influence his future. Why? He chose them over me for what? Because for once in their lives, they decided to have an honest conversation with him? *It was me.* I wasn't enough to make him stay. The first tear slips down my cheek.

"That young boy is scared out of his mind that he'll make the wrong decision. He debates it, cries over it, and stresses over it. Then one day, he takes that beautiful girl he loves out to their favorite field and tells her he loves her, like he always does. In that moment, he sees it all so clearly. Their struggles as he tries to make enough to support them. Their first, tiny apartment with an air mattress on the floor and ramen dinners. But it's filled with happiness and love. His decision is made."

I stall what I'm doing, finally turning to look at him, tears slowly sliding down his face. My knees feel weak, ready to crumble when he admits I wasn't enough for him. It has to be his explanation, and the heartbroken teenager is screaming in my heart that she was right. That was the future I saw with him at seventeen. There were no illusions on my part that things wouldn't be tough for us for a while. It is for most young kids moving out on their own. The problem is, this was obviously not the choice he made.

Ethan looks up from where he's picking at the bottle label, looking as devastated as he did the day he left me. "When he went home that evening to tell his parents his choice was made, he found out there was never a choice to be made. His father assumed he would move with them, controlling his future. He was enraged that his son had 'chosen wrong' so he made some calls and had him black-walled from the local departments. It left that young boy unable to pursue his dreams and have a way to support himself, let alone his girlfriend, when she graduated."

"Oh, Ethan," I whisper, feeling his pain to my very bones. How wrong I was. Here I am feeling sorry for myself when he had the rug ripped out from under him by the people he trusted.

I get it. I *truly* get it. He would've had to give up his passion, his career goals, to stay with me. Not only that, he would have lost the support of his family and the ability to provide for himself. It was an impossible decision for a scared eighteen-year-old boy.

I don't blame him for the choice he made. I never did, but understanding the circumstances behind it changes everything. It makes me irrevocably angry that he was manipulated like that. This should never have been a decision put on him, and he shouldn't have been treated the way he was by his own family.

Emotion sits heavy in my throat as I watch his Adam's apple bob and his eyes turn glassy, and I realize there's more. "And when he goes to his mom years later and tells her that the hurt never stops, and the love never fades, she admits that she said that because she couldn't bear to watch me break your heart the way my dad broke hers. How he cheated on her repeatedly, and she stayed anyway. That she wouldn't let that happen to you." He scoffs, but it's bitter and filled with heartbreak. "Like she didn't raise me to be a better man than him. Like I could ever look at another woman when I knew I had you to come back to."

The first tear slips down his cheek, and suddenly dinner's forgotten behind me as I launch myself at him. He catches me easily, holding me close. His face nuzzles into my neck as he tightens his hold. "I wish things could have been different. That I could have been the man to stay for you. It's what you deserved."

I'm not even focused on that part. "You've really loved me all this time?"

The smoke alarm in the kitchen starts blaring, and we pull apart to see the veggies burning in the pan. With tears streaking down my face, I can't hold back the laughter. Ethan rushes to move the pan from the stove and turns off the burner, then opens the window. "It's not funny," he barks, cracking a smile. "I'll never live it down if I have a fire in my house."

Using a hand towel, he wafts the smoke away from the smoke alarm, mock glaring at me as I cackle. When the blaring stops, he spins the towel and snaps it at me, swatting me in the thigh. "Jerk," he mumbles, lightheartedly.

"While I try to salvage dinner, I need you to go look at the walls in my bedroom. And with each frame, I want you to take them off and look at the back."

"We aren't done with this conversation."

"I know, baby. Just please go do that for me."

Cautious, but excited, I make my way down the hall to his bedroom.

ethan

My hands shake as I plate up the salmon and *crispy* vegetables. It's smaller portions than I would have liked since we burned half of it, but that just means more room for dessert. Michele has been in my bedroom, and I haven't heard a peep from her. There's a lot for her to read, but still, I'm terrified.

Was it too much to show her? Too much to admit to? Those frames have been sitting in boxes for years, but it felt like it was time to have them on display. I make my way to the bedroom and find Michele sitting on the edge of my bed, silent, as she reads the back of one of over thirty picture frames.

Not wanting to disturb her, I lean against the door and wait. My hands are sweating, so I wipe them on my jeans and stick them into my pockets. The one she has in her hands is from the middle of the wall, but I didn't put them in order of date; I simply hung them all around the room. Each one is filled with dried and preserved flowers. Some that I picked, some I bought, and some I found by accident. Each and every one of them made me think of her. On the back, I wrote where they came from and why they reminded me of her. Why I missed her, and why I wanted to keep this little memento to remind myself of how she would always be my girl.

Finally, she gently sets the frame down next to her and looks up at me. The tears from earlier are back, tracing down her pink cheeks. She looks stunned, but I can't read her emotions besides that.

"When did you start?"

"Collecting them?"

"Yes."

"About a year after I left, I found the first ones on a run. It's the black-eyed-susans in the corner." I point to the frame on the opposite wall from her. "The yellow was so bright it stopped me in my tracks. It reminded me of the time you painted your toes that color, thinking it would be cute, and then you realized it looked like you were diseased." I can't help the smile that comes to my face, both from remembering that moment and the flowers that started it all.

After stepping further into the room, I point at another. "These little pink ones are called filaree, and I found them on a hike. They're the exact shade of the pink you wore on your sixteenth birthday. Oh, and those over there." I motion to the one directly over my headboard. The picture frame is filled from edge to edge. "That was my last day on a wildfire. It was a hard one, almost a month fighting it, and a lot of injuries. I had a couple of close calls that I felt I'd gotten lucky. On the drive home, we passed a meadow, and I made the crew I was riding with stop. I felt like you were there with me on that mountain. They all made fun of me as I picked as many different kinds of wildflowers as I could find. When I got home that night, I wept. I cried so hard for you and the love I still felt for you."

Michele scoots over so I can sit on the bed next to her. My

thumb rubs over her cheek, collecting her tears, when I cup her face. "I never stopped loving you. Never forgot about you. I promised you, Wildflower. Until my last dying breath."

She lets her forehead drop onto mine, and her hands cover mine. We stay like that, breathing each other in. Connected and centered with each other.

"I love you," I whisper against her lips, before placing an achingly soft kiss on them.

Her voice is watery with a reverence I haven't yet heard. "I've never stopped either. Not for one second."

"I know, baby. Let's go eat dinner."

"Can I read the rest after?"

Chuckling, I take her hand and lead her back to the kitchen. "Of course."

Michele sits at my small table while I do the dishes, still pouting that I won't let her help. "Can I ask a question?"

"You can always ask me anything."

"How'd you get this job if you were black-walled?"

After drying the last plate, I place it in the cabinet. "That's the kicker of this whole story." I wring the towel out and hang my head. I'm still furious about it. "I never was. My dad lied. He never did a thing. It wasn't until four years ago that I found out when he drunkenly admitted it to me." I sling the dish towel over my shoulder and lean against the counter, my fingers gripping the edge to keep my anger in check. "This whole time, I thought that in order to get you back, I would have to either ask you to move, or get a job hours away and commute on the weekends. I hated both options. I couldn't ask either of you. You don't just deserve more, you deserve *everything*."

When I found that out, the first thing I wanted to do was call Michele. It didn't matter that she hadn't seen me in five years; she was the only thought in my head. I wanted to confess it all to her. Why I left, and how it felt after finding out it was a lie. She was the one I wanted to commiserate with, but I'd lost that right. I was bitter for so long. At my parents, at myself, hell, I even let myself be angry with Michele for letting me go.

It wasn't until I met up with River when he was playing in the area that my attitude changed. He said I was acting like a miserable prick, so I spilled everything to him. Finally, having someone know the truth felt good, even if he was pissed that I still hadn't admitted everything to Michele.

"I deserved the truth."

"I know, but at that point it felt self-serving. You called me selfish the first day I showed up here, and you were right to. I asked you to come to Colorado because I couldn't stand another day without you in it. There was no consideration of your feelings or how hard that would be. I was an asshole, not thinking about that. I broke your heart again for my own selfish gain. I couldn't call and say 'hey, turns out I never had to leave. Oh, and I still don't have a job so I can't come back to you?' You would have never forgiven me."

"You were an asshole for that."

A watery smile crosses my lips. There's my girl. "I know. Until that point, I was trying to climb the ladder, so to speak, as fast as possible. I thought if I could outrank him, he couldn't keep me from getting certain jobs. After I found out he had lied, I've been doing everything possible to come back here so you would never have to make an impossible decision like I did."

"I would have made either of those choices for you."

"You say that, but you wouldn't resent me being gone constantly, only seeing me a day or two a week. Or moving away from this town and all your friends, and your businesses?"

"You didn't even give me a chance to make that decision." Her brows are furrowed, and there's a scowl on her face. She has a right to be angry. I didn't ever tell her those options. I didn't ask her to stay when she came to Colorado. How could I though? How could I put two impossible options in front of her when I know how it feels to have the weight of your entire future put on one. I'll protect Michele at all costs, and in my head, that meant protecting her from having to choose.

"No, and now you don't have to. I knew there was a risk of you moving on, but I know we are meant to be. And I knew, if I could make it back to you, things would work out. Here we are, and now we can move forward."

"I really hate your dad."

"You and River both."

"Why do you still talk to him?"

"I guess inside, I'm still that scared young boy, hoping one day his dad will tell him he's proud of him."

"I'll be proud enough for both of us."

She beams at me, and I can't help but smile back. Fuck, I love this girl. I toss the towel onto the counter and pick her up.

She kicks her feet but wraps her arms around my neck nonetheless. "Put me down! You've proven you can carry me already."

"Baby I'll carry you everywhere, every day, for the rest of my life if you let me. I love the way my cock rubs against your ass with every step." I grin and wink at her.

She slaps my chest but giggles, wiggling her thick ass, making me groan. When we get to my room, I kick the door shut behind me and toss her on the bed. "What do you think you're doing?" she asks with the cutest mock-horror expression.

I pull my shirt off and throw it in the hamper. "Getting ready for bed. You're staying the night. And before you protest, I don't care that you don't have your things. You can sleep in one of my shirts, and I have a new toothbrush under the sink. Plus, you have more picture frames to read."

"Demanding tonight, aren't you?" she jokes. "You're lucky I'm into it."

Mmm, my little wildflower has no idea.

CHAPTER FORTY-TWO

ethan

Michele spends another hour reading all the frames before getting ready for bed with me. Even having her back in my life, and earning her love and trust, there's been a rope around my lungs. Never able to take a deep breath because she wasn't truly mine until she knew the whole truth. This day has been fifteen years in the making. I can breathe easy for the first time, and my God, what a feeling it is.

The bathroom light shuts off, and there she is. My stunning girl with her hair flowing around her shoulders and not a scrap of clothing on. She is absolute perfection, the sway of her hips mesmerizing, and the jiggle when she walks makes me want to take a bite of her. To each their own, but I love a curvy girl. More to grab on to, more cushion to be rough with. Fuck, she turns me on.

She does a tiptoe run to the bed, and rushes to get under the blankets, covering herself immediately. That just won't do. I yank them back, exposing her to me again. "I know you love your nice outfits, and you look so pretty in them, but you should always be naked. No clothes allowed. Who would cover up beauty like this? It's truly such a shame."

"Oh shut up." She giggles, and tries to pull the blankets back up. "Ethan," she whines when she realizes I'm not letting them go. "I'm cold."

"Why didn't you say so, baby? I'll warm you up."

I sit up and yank the blankets down even further, pulling her ankles apart so I can fit myself between them. Lying on my belly, I spread her thighs wider and salivate at the sight. "Pretty girl, I am going to spend years worshipping this pussy."

She shudders when I place open mouthed kisses on the inside of her thigh. I suck, and kiss, lick and bite, marking her as mine and causing her to squirm beneath me.

"Please," she begs. "Taste me, Ethan."

I use my thumbs to spread her pussy lips and blow before licking. Her little whimper sends a thrill through me. I run my tongue along her slit again and again, savoring her flavor. I spear into her pussy, fucking her deep with my tongue. I'm rewarded with more of her taste, my senses overwhelmed with her. Her smell, her flavor, the way her legs shake when my tongue circles her clit.

There isn't a single part of her I don't want my mouth on. Gripping under her thighs, I spread her wider and lift her slightly. It positions her ass for me to try something we've never done.

I start with a kiss, and a gentle nip. Michele trembles in my hands, but I hold her in place. "Do you like that, Wildflower?" My tongue rims her hole, causing an immediate loud moan. *Perfection.* "Do you like that I can't get enough of you? Of your body? That I want to own, mark, and worship every inch of it?"

I spend my time exploring her, tasting her, and figuring out what makes her whimper and what makes her moan. She's a soaked mess, shaking and crying out for me, but I hold her firm and don't let her come. I want her begging, so spent that she struggles to walk tomorrow. Skittering on Bambi legs after I'm done with her, so I know I've done my job well.

"Please, Ethan, let me come," she begs when I suck her clit again.

I drop her thighs and curl two fingers into her to stroke her sweet spot. With my other hand, I press lightly on her belly and flick my tongue over her clit. I've only been able to make her squirt once, but damn, I want to do it again. I add pressure everywhere as I continue. Her breath hitches, and her hands spear into my hair. Her nails dig into my scalp as she arches into my touch, and then she screams.

Her body convulses, and she lets go as the rush of liquid covers my face. Her thighs are quivering around me, her chest gasping. I will never get over how much joy it brings me to give her pleasure. Michele slumps back, her body satiated, but I'm nowhere near done. I lift my head and smile, wiping over my chin. "So good for me, baby."

"Is this you still groveling? Because please never stop," she says sleepily and wholly satisfied.

"I don't plan to," I mutter before licking her pussy from ass to clit. Fuck, I need to make her come again. The sheets are already wet; might as well make a mess of them. Spreading her pussy again, I focus my efforts on her swollen, pink clit.

"Fuuuuck."

"That's my girl. One more, then I'll fuck you." I swirl my tongue around her again. "I'll be gentle," another flick over the nerves, "take it slow."

And I do. I lavish her pussy. Edge her to the brink of tears, and back, before finally letting her come again. When she trembles beneath me and her quiet cry of relief hits my ears, I give her clit a soft kiss and crawl up her body.

My sheets are messy, her thighs and my face are covered in her release, my jaw is on fire, and I've never been happier.

My cock is aching, throbbing, and leaking. The fact he's held on this long is a miracle. I lay over Michele, her vibrant eyes puffy from all the tears she's shed. She smiles at me and leans up to place a soft kiss on my lips. I deepen it, thrilled when she opens for me. Not afraid of sharing her taste, of intertwining us that much more.

"I need to be inside you."

She spreads her legs wider, lifting her thighs despite their trembling. Reaching down, I rub my cock up and down her slit before sliding in with ease. My head lolls back at the feel of her squeezing around me.

I slide my hands into hers, holding them next to her head. "I love you, Michele. I always have, and I always will."

"I love you too, baby. You've always been my forever."

In the inky dark of the room, illuminated only by the faint glow of the stars filtering through the curtains, we find solace in each other. I move with deliberate slowness, savoring the moment, rolling my hips in a sensual dance over her. My hands trace the contours of her body, mapping every curve, every dip. I'm acutely aware of the texture of her skin, the rise and fall of her chest, the subtle vanilla scent of her mingling with the musky aroma of our intertwined bodies. I want to mold myself to her, ensuring she feels every inch of me, every pulse of desire.

We lock eyes, the unspoken language of love passing between us. The world outside ceases to exist. There's only the two of us, our hearts beating as one. We hold each other's gaze, neither of us ever breaking the connection, unwilling to shatter the fragile intimacy. We move in perfect harmony, breath against breath, until the boundaries between us blur and melt away. Without a word, without a sound, we find our release, two souls merging into one.

I've never felt the peace I do when I'm with Michele. I kiss her soft lips, prolonging the moment.

Her eyes flutter shut from the utter exhaustion of the day and the evening I put her through. Quietly, I sneak out of bed, grab a cloth from the closet, and wet it with warm water. Back in the room, I gently roll her to the dry side of the bed and wipe her down. She mutters a halfhearted "I love you" and reaches out to pat me lightly.

She does it so casually. Half asleep. It's perfect, and mundane, and something I hope to experience over and over again for the rest of my life. I could change the sheets, but I hate the idea of waking Michele, so I lay down a blanket and take the other side.

Her butt wiggles when I don't immediately wrap myself around her. I love that she's expressing her emotions and desires to me more, even in these little ways. We've come so far. I thought I wanted the love we had as teens again, but I was wrong. This right here is what I wanted. This mature, raw, intrinsic desire that we have. A love that sees past the airs we put on, that grounds us to the core, yet shakes up everything we've been doing. It's the type of love that has grown and molded with us, that is steadfast and ready to stand the test of time.

This is the love I will cherish and pursue for the rest of my life.

CHAPTER FORTY-THREE

Triple Threat Group Chat

MICHELE:

I'm so fucked.

AMBER:

Like literally or…?

MICHELE:

Well, yes.

MICHELE:

But. He has flowers… walls of picture frames filled with flowers that he's picked over the years, and on the back of them, he wrote why those flowers reminded him of me.

LILY:

HOLY FUCK

AMBER:

Lily cussed, I'm telling mom.

AMBER:

How long has he been collecting them?

MICHELE:

Since he was 19.

AMBER:

HOLY FUCK!

LILY:

Marry him.

LILY:

Right now.

LILY:

Today.

MICHELE:

I think I'm going to ask him to move in…

AMBER:

YES!

LILY:

Can we have a girls' day to discuss all this?

AMBER:

Yeah, I'm still wrapping my head around the flowers. I second Lily, screw moving in. Marry the man,

MICHELE:

I love you guys.

I thought I had walls up. I was proud of having them and not caving to his sexy, sweet groveling. Turns out, walls are for chumps. Walls are built out of self-preservation, but also out of fear. Fear of being hurt again. Fear of falling so utterly hard for someone, you lose a part of yourself. Fear that you will pour everything into someone, and they will simply open a well and take more and more until you have nothing left. Fear that every dark and damaged part of you will be brought into the light, and still not be seen.

Everyone seems so scared of allowing themselves to become dependent on someone else. Of losing sight of who they are by allowing someone else to shape parts of their heart. Those were some of my fears. I see the other side of it now, though.

All of those are possibilities, and even probabilities, with the wrong person. But with the right one… with the right person, all of those fears are irrelevant. They will take that part of you and make sure it's never lost. They will be the guiding light, reminding you exactly who you are. They will open that well, not to take more, but to pour part of themselves back. They will meet your dark and damaged parts with tape and glue and find the right way to heal them.

That's what Ethan does for me. So fuck the fear. Fuck holding back from something that I know in my heart is right for me. Fuck not taking life head-on and asking for exactly what I want. Ethan is who I want, and living together in our dream home is what I want.

He's tending to the proverbial garden in his rental, and I hate it. Every action shows he wants to put in the effort. He wants to test the soil and water the seeds, and he intends to stick around to watch the flowers blossom. Why wouldn't I want him to do that here with me every day?

Like Amber said, if I never turn to face it, I'll never see what becomes of that garden. I'm ready to face it head-on.

When I call Ethan that afternoon and ask him to come over tonight, his response is an instant "I'll be there," followed by an "I'm staying the night."

I can't wipe the smile off my face, because I hope he'll be staying a lot longer than that. This is a huge next step for us. Even though I'm ninety-nine percent sure I know his answer, I'm still a little nervous. He's been showing me that he's here for me, and he's confessed everything from our past. It's time for me to return that. It's time for me to tell him that I'm in this as much as he is.

Deciding on the best way to ask him, I make a few quick stops in town, one of them being to Jake's shop. "Hey, Sonja." I wave to his mom as I pop my head into his store. "Is Jake out back?"

"He's there or next door. You'd think those two would get over their obsession with each other already." She rolls her eyes, then winks at me. We've all loved watching the relationship between Jake and Amber grow and flourish. Who knew Jake would turn into putty for his girl, and Amber would turn into a badass who now rides a motorcycle? "You doing okay?" she asks when I give her a quick hug.

"Yes, ma'am. More than. Just need a quick thing making if he has a moment."

"He always does for you."

I walk through the back door and into the alley, immediately spotting him. The bay doors of the shop are open, and he's arguing with Colby, his employee. "It doesn't count," Jake states, arms crossed.

"Yes, it does." Colby gestures. "It totally counts!"

"What are you guys bickering over?"

Both heads turn to me, and Jake smiles widely. "Perfect timing, Chele. Colby turns twenty-one this weekend and thinks having a beer bought by his girlfriend at home counts as his first legal drink. Please set him straight."

"Why would I buy beer that she already has at the house? It will be my first legal drink, I'll be drinking it while of legal age. It counts."

"I feel like I have to side with Jake on this one because I'm about to ask a huge favor, but under normal circumstances, I would agree with Colby."

"Told ya!" Colby shouts as Jake turns to glare at me.

"Traitor. What do you need?"

"I was hoping you could make something for me. I want a key holder for the entrance. Maybe something with three hooks, saying something like yours, mine, and ours? I can pick up the hooks at the hardware store. I just need it today." I bat my lashes, and he shoves my shoulder.

"Get out of here with that. Let me see what kind of wood I have lying around. And Colby here has been working on his wood burning, so he would love to do the words for you." He turns to the young kid, raising a brow at him. "Don't fuck it up."

"Sooo," Jake starts when I follow him to the storage room on the side of his workshop. "Does this mean what I think it does?"

"Do you think it means I'm asking Ethan to move in with me tonight?"

He pauses, turning slowly. He stares at me… and then stares some more. "Michele?"

"Yes…?"

Jake picks me up and spins me around before setting me down, but doesn't let me go. "This is it. You're finally getting the happily-ever-after you deserve. I'm so damn happy for you."

It feels good to hear those words out loud. I've been watching my friends find their once-in-a-lifetime love for years. All while knowing mine had already come and gone. Now it's finally my turn. I get to live out my love story, and I'm not letting my fears get in the way.

CHAPTER FORTY-FOUR

michele

The dinner I picked up in town is sitting in the oven to stay warm, and the table is set. I don't want to make a big deal out of this, but at the same time, I know this is a huge step for us. In my head, this is the last step before marriage, which seems a little crazy to think, but I'm ready for it. I just hope he feels the same.

I called my brother while at the hardware store earlier and told him my plan. Twenty minutes after our talk, he sent me an article with the divorce statistics of firefighters. I know he's just looking out for me, but that one stung a bit. He followed it up with, "Don't look up the mortality rate."

So to say my hands are trembling and my heart is beating out of my rib cage while I'm waiting for Ethan to get here is an understatement. I hear his footsteps on the porch before his keys jingle and he opens the door, walking in like he already lives here.

"Excuse me, sir. Just because I told you where the spare key was doesn't mean you can use it whenever."

He kicks off his boots by the door and drops his keys onto the entry table before joining me on the couch. "Good thing that's not the spare. I made myself a copy," he says, totally nonchalant, before kissing my cheek and pulling me into his side. "How was your day?"

I turn and gape at him. "You did what?"

"Made myself a copy." He shrugs. "I plan on being here a lot. As much as you'll let me, really. And while I enjoy leaving you things on the porch, I would like to leave you things on the counter instead. What if my new squirrel friend follows me here and snags your breakfast? Then I'll have to get mad at him, and he's too cute to be mad at."

Can I really be upset at that answer? I'm a little peeved that I made him another copy today, and he already has one. Do I really need four house keys? *Whatever.* "I'm going to choose to ignore this conversation ever happened. My day was wonderful. How was yours?"

"Pretty great as well. New equipment came in, and I received my official uniform for this crew. Might have customized my helmet if you want to see it later. And, of course, the best part is I get to spend the evening with you." His smile is so bright, and suddenly my heart is racing for a totally different reason.

"You're laying it on thick for a guy who stole my house key," I joke, pulling him off the couch with me. "I have take-out Chinese, are you hungry?"

"Starved," he replies, grabbing a handful of my ass.

My once-quiet evenings alone are now anything but. They're filled with conversations over dinner, someone to share my struggles and meals with, and an absolute menace who keeps me on my toes. The goofy lovestruck boy of my teens is now the goofy lovestruck man in our thirties, and I can picture us in another fifteen years still giggling over stupid things while making dinner.

Ethan fills water glasses for us while I pull the take-out boxes from the oven. He waits for me to sit across from him before taking his seat. He pops open the boxes and uses his fork to scoop some fried rice onto my plate. "Still prefer General Tso's?"

My smile is small, but won't leave. He remembers the little things. It's sweet he's checking, too. Tastes and people change, and he's always showing me that he still knows who I was, but he wants to know who I am now, too. "Yes, please."

He adds that to my plate before filling his own. He starts to eat, and I marvel again at how comfortable he is here. How natural it is to be sharing dinner with him in my home. How it already feels like this home is his. I can't wait any longer.

"I have something for you." I move to the side table where I have the small bag sitting. "You kind of ruined it, but… Well, just open it."

He tears the paper from the gift bag and flings it behind him with a wink. "Don't worry, I'll pick it up." When he reaches into the bag, he looks up at me with a confused expression, then slowly pulls out the wooden sign.

Jake ran to the hardware store with me, and we picked out the perfect hooks to match the cherry wood backing. Colby did a surprisingly good job on the burnt lettering. His handwriting might be even better than mine. The two outside hooks are empty, but the middle one is labeled 'ours' and has a little bow with the house key on it.

"I wanted to give you a key to this house and ask you to move in with me. This place was always meant to be ours. And with you here, it truly feels like home. So, Ethan, even though you already have a key… Will you move in with me?"

Ethan puts the gift down and runs his fingers over it, lightly plucking the key off. He doesn't look excited, or even happy. His eyes stay glued onto that key for so long, I think he's going to tell me no, when he finally lets those forest green eyes meet mine.

"I always had this idea in my head when we were kids. We would get the dinky apartment and struggle for a few years. Then I would buy us the perfect piece of land, and propose to you there, promising to build you the house we dreamed of. We would get married and live out this beautiful life we had pictured."

His Adam's apple bobs as he swallows, and he leans forward to take my hand. "I know I've apologized several times already, but I will never stop being sorry for missing all that time with you. And I will never stop being so proud of you for doing it all on your own. I would love to move in with you, Michele. Nothing would make me happier than spending every moment I can by your side. Things may be a little out of order, but our future starts now."

He gets up and rounds the table, pulling me into him, and kissing me hard. "I love you, baby." Ethan giggles, full-on giggles, and picks me up to kiss me again. "I love you, I love you, I love you," he repeats between kisses. "Our home. It's really going to be our home."

"It's always been ours. It was just waiting for you to come home."

"Michele, I—" His words are cut off by his phone ringing. He slides it from his pocket, pausing when he sees the number. "Sorry, it's work."

He lets me go and answers. I try not to listen, but his face turns from shock to anger, then fear, as the person on the other end continues to talk. "Are we officially called in?" He pauses again. "I'm on my way, but call everyone. They're going to need extra hands, and this is our specialty." Our eyes lock, and my stomach sinks. Whatever it is, it's not good. "See you soon."

"Just say it."

There's sympathy in his gaze. "Our meadow's on fire. Sounds like a bonfire party got out of control. Kids are missing, and it's spreading fast," he says as he walks to the entry, slips on his boots, and starts tying them.

"I'm coming with."

"No, baby. I need you here, safe. I'll do my best to preserve our place, but I need to make sure all those kids are out first. I need to know you're nowhere near to focus on my job." He kisses my forehead, lingering for only a moment. "I love you. I'll call you when I can."

With that, he's out the door and running to his truck. My heart's racing, and there's a squeezing in my chest. I know this is his job. It's what I'll have to deal with and face, going forward, but I wasn't ready for this. I didn't expect the first fire to be so close, and to be our special place.

I slump against the door, holding my chest and trying to calm my breathing. Everything is going to be just fine. Our future starts now.

A phone lights up and vibrates on my entry table. When I reach for it, I realize it's Ethan's and he must have set it there when he put his boots on. There's a text message from an unknown number sitting on the screen, and it sets off my panic all over again.

UNKNOWN:

Please just talk to me, Ethan. I love you.

CHAPTER FORTY-FIVE

ethan

The entire drive to the meadow, my body is rioting. My hands are clammy, slick with a nervous sweat that makes the steering wheel hot under my grip. My heart is racing, a frantic drum against my ribs, echoing the insistent thrum of the engine. A cold sweat has formed over my chest, plastering my thin cotton shirt to my skin and sending a shiver down my spine, despite the warmth of the evening. This panic, this suffocating anxiety, is not what I should be feeling.

With the sun sinking toward the horizon, the heavy smoke from the distant wildfire is visible, rising above the skeletal silhouettes of the trees and creating a hazy gray veil over the vibrant orange and yellow hues of the sunset. It casts an eerie, almost ominous blanket over the landscape. I pull to the side of the road to let an ambulance pass, its siren amplifying my already frayed nerves. As soon as it's gone, I hit the gas, determined to reach the meadow faster.

The turn-off is filled with cars. Firetrucks, ambulances, and police alike are parked along the entrance and in front. I can't see exactly where the fire is or where it was started, but based on the kids filing out as best as possible, it's spreading fast.

Luckily, I have my new uniform in my truck, so I recline my seat and swap to my fire-retardant shirt and pants, then grab my helmet and pack. I clip my radio and belt on as I jog to the captain, who's barking orders.

"Maddox." I shake his hand when I reach him. "My crew is being called in. Where do you need us?"

He takes my hand and shakes it and his head. "This is a fucking nightmare. They don't have an accurate headcount, but some kids are saying that when the fire started spreading, people scrambled in all directions, including into the woods. I have my team working on getting the bonfire under control and searching the woods. Our two brush trucks are here, but it's spreading fast. It's been an unseasonably dry spring."

"How'd the bonfire spread?"

"Some idiot kid threw a gas can into the fire. There are a couple of burn victims who will need transport. If your team can work on controlling the spread, I think we can get a handle on this. When we got the call, they said a small fire. With the spread to the national park and forest, your team should have been called in sooner. You running this?"

"Yes, sir. I have my radio on, I'll keep the lines open to update you. And, Maddox? This place means something to me. I'm not sitting on the sidelines."

He nods, understanding. "Stay safe, Ethan."

It's then that I realize I don't have my phone on me to check in with Reynolds. He's the one who called and was putting in the call to the team. It's either in my other pants in the truck or still at Michele's. Either way, I'll have to work without it.

I take out my Kestrel weather meter to track the wind speed and direction. Since the department hasn't called this in as an official job yet, I only expect a few guys to show, and I'm not expecting much. If we can get a line dug to stop the spread, I'll be happy with that.

Reynolds pulls up two minutes later, and together we scour the map where Maddox's men are calling in the edges of the fire, and assess the Kestrel readings to make a plan of attack. To my utter surprise, fifteen of my men are here and ready, with local hotshots from the Forest Service on their way as well to volunteer.

"This place is our home. We can't sit back while it burns," Evans, one of my crew bosses, says, slinging his Pulaski over his shoulder. "You lead, and we follow."

It's dark now, the sun completely hidden behind the trees and the wall of smoke. I take a moment to look up, but the smoke is covering the stars. Still, I send up a prayer that we can stop this fire in its tracks tonight. My heartbreak over all our hard work and memories being ablaze needs to take a back seat. This is my team, and I'm not letting them tackle this alone.

"Keep the line of communication open, Reynolds."

My team and I head to the west, having deemed that's where the wind will take the fire. It's the best place to choke off its supply. We hike out about half a mile and start digging a line. While the fire is spreading, we have the firehouse crews working on the other side to douse the flames. Together with them and my crew cleaning debris and cutting off its path, we should be able to have this under control by the morning.

I hop in with them, clearing debris and keeping an ear out for the calls coming through. It sounds like there are three kids still missing, but they've sent the rest of my crew who showed up southwest of us to set up a fire line there.

"Ethan." My radio crackles again with Reynolds's voice. "Winds are changing."

I walk further down the line, away from my saw team, and lean my Pulaski on a tree to respond, doing a mental check-in on my team. It's starting to get really smoky, and even with our flashlights, visibility isn't great. I cough and choke on the thick, ash-laden air. "All right, what's the plan?"

"This is your team, and your position. I'm here as support, but this needs to be your call."

Damn it. This is the downfall of being hands-on. Focusing on my guys, their safety, what I'm doing, and trying to stay on top of the changing elements and location of the fire is too much.

I know this is what I signed up for when taking this position. Stepping back from the operations to help run things. I was ready for that, until it was this field and forest that were affected. My mind can't stop replaying all the memories I have here. From the first time Michele and I stumbled upon the meadow on a drive, to last weekend with our friends.

"Ethan," Patrick calls, pulling me from my thoughts. "I've got the team. You make the calls. You have to be present. You have to be here."

He's the newest superintendent, but he already has the leadership skills honed. Knowing I can rely on him to do his job, and do it well, I pull out the Kestrel again to check the readings. The humidity has dropped, and the wind speed has increased by two knots. Reynolds was right to send the rest of the crew south with the slight change in direction.

If we can get this line dug fast enough, we can try a back burn to stifle the flames and meet it. Grabbing the radio, I inform Reynolds we're going to keep digging the line southwest to reach the rest of the team. He reports that a firefighter will bring in the drip torches for us to start the back burn when it's ready.

Normally, things would be more organized, and I'm making notes of things I need to have accounted for with larger fires. This is a rare occurrence, being called in for a fire like this without actually making the call to get our team in. Some are up to three hours away, and by the time they get here, we'll hopefully have things under control. After relaying the information to my three superintendents, I pick up my Pulaski and get back to work.

We work tirelessly for another two hours. The smoke is thick and heavy, invading our lungs. The fire is becoming visible in the distance by the time we link up with the rest of the team to finish the last of the line. I'm confident this will work, and we can burn this out, relying on the back burn until the helitack crew can dump retardant from overhead.

The rest of our crew has the drip torches, so we send them to strategic points to ignite. When the line is complete and dug down to the mineral soil, I make the call over the radio, and we set the fire.

My team is spread out along the line to watch for backdraft and any fire that may jump the line. This is where we see our hard work put into action. It's brutal, watching this forest ablaze, even though the goal is to burn this one part to meet the main fire head-on and starve it, saving the rest of the forest in turn.

I walk along the line, checking on my team and ensuring everything is running smoothly. If only I had my phone to let Michele know things are okay. I don't want her to worry. This is going to devastate her when she sees how much is burned.

My boot catches against a root sticking out, almost taking me out. It's that root that causes me to catch sight of the small bunch of blue forget-me-nots on the ground. I pluck them up, running my gloved fingers over them before sticking them in my pocket. It may be the tiniest gesture, but they make me feel safe. I know Michele will cherish them when I add them to my collection on the wall.

"Ethan!"

I turn to see one of my men, Gerald, waving his arm and yelling at me. I jog over, and he points frantically toward the fire. "I think I heard people yelling."

"What do you mean?"

"I swear I heard voices." We both quiet, trying to listen through the crackling fire and breaking of branches, and sure enough, I faintly hear it, too.

Grabbing my radio, I ask Reynolds, "Did they find the last three kids?"

His crackled voice comes through. "No, three girls are still missing."

ethan

Fuck.

FUCK.

I look at Gerald, who stares back at me. "I didn't light my spot yet. We have maybe five minutes to get in there, find them, and get back out before we're trapped."

"All right." I tighten the straps on my pack. It won't do much, but it has a fire-retardant blanket for a worst-case scenario. I radio Reynolds and let him know what's going on, and where we are.

"I'll send backup and call the helitack team. See if they can get here any faster and start the drop there."

Gerald and I rush past the line together, calling out to the voices, trying to locate them. The smoke is thick, and the trees and woods are dense. This isn't a place we can run through on a good day, and with the lack of visibility and ash and smoke burning our lungs, this isn't a good day.

We continue to call out, tracking their shouts until, miraculously, we find the girls. None of them looks in great shape, with dirty clothes and soot-covered faces. They can't be older than seventeen, with wide, frightened eyes and red cheeks. They're huddled together, the one in the middle limping and bloody.

Gerald assesses them quickly while I radio to inform Reynolds that we found them, and they'll need medical attention quickly.

"She fell," one of the girls says on a wheeze between coughs. "We left her shoe back there because her ankle is swollen and her arm is all cut up."

"We've been trying to take breaks," the other girl hacks out. "The fire keeps getting closer, and we can't find our way out."

Gerald hands them bottles of water from his pack after loosely wrapping the third girl's arm. The fire is entirely too close, the smoke getting thicker by the minute. There are trees popping and groaning around us, and there's embers floating around with the ash. It's spreading quicker than we were anticipating, and we need to move fast.

"You take the two that can walk. I'll carry the third."

Gerald looks at me like he wants to argue, but he doesn't. He's fit, but he's a smaller guy. I'm the best shot she has at getting out of these woods on time.

"Hold each other's hands," he tells the girls who link up with him. "Try to keep up, keep your head down, and breathe as shallow as possible. Pick up your feet, there's lots of hidden branches and roots."

That's the downfall of the beautiful ferns littering the forest floor. They hide the dangers below and create a hazard you may not see until it's too late. "What's your name?" I ask the third girl, whisking her into my arms.

"Kate." She has red-rimmed eyes, and I know she has to be in serious pain. Her pupils are dilated, and I suspect she was drinking tonight. "I'm scared," she admits, her voice sounding wobbly and on the verge of tears. She wraps her good arm around my neck to hold on.

"Well, Kate, I'm Ethan." I spare a glance at her before focusing back on the ground and Gerald ahead of me. "I'll be brave enough for both of us, okay?"

She nods, gripping me tighter. A branch ahead of us catches flame, an ember igniting it, and Kate starts trembling against me, so I attempt to calm her down. "You have some great friends there. Sticking by your side for hours trying to get to safety."

"I put their lives at risk." I take another look at her and watch a tear make a clean streak down her soot-covered face. "They didn't want to come out tonight. I begged them." Her body shudders with sobs. She tucks her face into my chest, and I'm grateful because it might be the one thing to protect her lungs.

Mine are burning, the air so heavy. I adjust Kate in my arms and focus back on my next steps. It's going well until I look up and realize I've lost sight of Gerald and the other two girls. Stopping, I turn in every direction, attempting to see through the hazy night air. All I can see are trees and flames. I cough to the side, hiding my fear, and decide which way to go. I'm not heading for the flames, so I continue the path forward, hoping I reach the line before the flames reach us.

Kate must realize my steps have slowed, and she lifts her head, glancing around. I can feel her gaze on me when she whispers scared words. "You're lost, aren't you?"

"I'll find the way out."

The wind must have picked up; the heat of the fire licking at my skin. My eyes are burning, and everything hurts. Each step is a struggle as it gets harder and harder to breathe. Kate coughs uncontrollably into my chest before getting quiet.

"Ethan?"

"Yeah?" I grunt, stepping over a fallen branch.

"We're going to die, aren't we?" Her tone is quiet. Resigned. Like she already knows the answer.

Glancing around again, flames are on all sides now. There's no clear path. No way out. I gently set her on the ground and slide off the backpack. "You aren't."

I search through until I find the folded-up fire-retardant shelter. It's really only big enough to fit one. We could squeeze under it, but it would make it impossible to fully cover us both, allowing smoke and flames in.

Kate's young. I'm not risking her life like that. I shake out the shelter and ask her to lie flat and small on the ground. The silver material covers her fully, and I stand next to it, kicking away as much brush as I can, talking to her to keep her calm. "You're going to be okay, Kate. They're doing an air drop soon, then my team will rush in here and get you out. It may get hot under there, but do not come out until someone gets you."

"I'm so sorry, Ethan," she cries from under the shelter.

I want to tell her it's okay when it's anything but. Instead, I rely on my training, using the small folded shovel in my pack to dig in the spot beside her. It's the best shot I have at making it out of here. My lungs squeeze and protest, the thick air choking me as I keep pushing, digging out a spot as best as I can to lie in. With shaky arms and fuzzy vision, I finally slump down into the makeshift hole in the dirt.

The static crackles in my ear, so I pull the radio off my shoulder. Here I am, the supposed hero, the protector, altogether helpless. My chest aches, the weight of the day crushing me. I pull the crumpled, wilting flowers from my pocket, their vibrant colors now dulled, mirroring the life draining from me.

My first tear is icy and unwelcome, forging a path down my overheated cheek, a stark contrast to the burning in my chest. Finally, after all this time, the fragments of my existence are aligning. Years of chasing ambitions, of prioritizing my career over everything, and I had her. The love of my life, her hand in mine, and this… this is the cruel joke the universe decides to play.

A wave of self-loathing washes over me, a bitter tide of regret. The hatred I have for the wasted years, for the choices that led me away. I hate myself for ever leaving her, for the pain I caused then, the pain I'm about to inflict on my perfect girl again.

Another round of hacking coughs racks my body as I try to breathe through my shirt. It's useless. I know I'm not making it out of here alive. My nerves are screaming as they heat past the point of comfort, and my skin sears under the encroaching heat and flames. Oh God, what have I done? I spent so long dismantling the walls she'd built around her heart, carefully, painstakingly, burrowing my way back into her soul, only to meet my end here, in the sanctuary of our shared dream. In the place where we first expressed our love and were supposed to grow old together.

She'll never forgive me, and I don't deserve it. I'm shattering her world, and this time, I won't be there to gather the pieces. The image of the pain in her eyes, the echo of my absence in her life, is a fresh, agonizing stab. The world around me spins, so I lie on my stomach and brace for the inevitable darkness.

The radio squawks beside me. "Ethan, where are you?"

Wiping my tears, I rub my thumb over the wilted petals again. "Kate is under the fire shelter. I think she has a broken foot and severe smoke inhalation. As soon as the helitack comes through, you need to come get her out."

"Ethan," Reynolds says, and even through the radio, I can hear his fear as the realization sets in. We've all done the training. I know the reality of my situation, and I've accepted it.

"It's okay. I know. Did Gerald get out?"

"He and the girls are safe."

I breathe a sigh of relief. It was all worth it knowing they are going to live. A branch cracks and falls near me, spreading the fire from the trees to the forest floor. I watch, horror-struck, as the ferns less than a hundred yards from me ignite.

My lungs are on fire, each tight inhale a raspy wheeze. My fingers are trembling as I push down the radio button. "Can you relay a message for me?"

"The helitack crew is only two minutes out."

I ignore that, because two minutes is too long. "Tell Michele,"

I fight against the burn to suck in one more breath, "until my last dying breath."

Black dots crowd my vision as I try to hold on. My body is weak. I lie next to the shelter and pat Kate's back with one hand, clutching the flowers under me with my other. There are too many different noises, the crackle and snap of the fire approaching. Kate is sobbing next to me, and someone's speaking through the radio by my side.

I close my eyes, and all I see is Michele.

Her smile, the way her hazel eyes shine in the moonlight.

Her body fitting so perfectly against mine.

I see her on the first day of school in second grade.

Then, on the day she agreed to be my girlfriend.

In the pretty pink dress on her sixteenth birthday.

The day she landed in Colorado.

And tonight, confidently asking me to move in with her.

She's my life, my entire world, and I've wasted so much of it apart from her.

All I want is her. *All I see is her.*

My Michele.

My messy girl.

My wildflower.

Eventually, it all turns to a fuzzy background noise when my lungs can't suck in any more oxygen. The fight leaves my body, and everything goes black.

michele

The keys slip from my shaky hands on the way to the car. I don't even know where to go. Do I drive up to the meadow and return his phone? Would I even be able to find him? Or look at him without crying? Could I see our meadow burning without breaking further?

My thoughts are a desperate storm, a chaotic jumble of cries for help, swallowed by the crushing weight of the unknown. Tears blur my vision as I think of the meadow, its vibrant colors a painful reminder of what we're losing, the echoes of our love. It's the catalyst to our story. He told me he loved me there for the first time. We lost our virginity there, and he laid himself bare there to make me feel safe in this again. No matter how many times I tell myself it's "just a place," I feel an ache in my lungs. It's a place that means everything to us.

Ethan's phone lights up in my hand again, this time with a group text to his hotshot crew. Sitting at the top of the screen is still the unknown number text. There has to be an explanation for it. I know, but it doesn't mean I'm going to like it. It has to be from an ex-girlfriend. How recent a one is she? He said he never really dated. Not like I did. I'm spiraling. I'm worried about him, the text, the meadow… I don't know what to focus on. Which pain belongs to which feeling. I need something to distract me.

I slip my phone from my purse and trade it with Ethan's. My hands are still trembling when I find the name. Sitting in my car in my driveway, I wait for them to answer.

"Michele?"

"River," I breathe out. I don't need to say anything else; in that one broken word, he already knows.

"Oh, Chele. Tell me what happened."

So I do. I tell him about dinner, and Ethan moving in with me, then about the phone call and the fire in our meadow. Finally, I tell him about the text on his phone that he left. Out of everyone, I knew River was the one to call. He knows Ethan as well as I do. We've always been good friends, but after getting drunk and having a six-hour heart-to-heart two years ago on the Fourth of July, we've been closer than ever.

When I've finished spilling my guts, he asks, "Where are you now?"

"In my driveway."

"Okay, two things. One, there isn't an ex, so I don't know who that message is from. And two, you're going to carefully and slowly drive to Thoren and Lily's. I'll let them know you're on your way. You shouldn't be alone."

"I'm scared, Riv."

"He's going to be okay. I'll check in on everything and give you guys a call."

"Okay." We stay quiet on the phone as I put the key in the ignition and start my car. "Is it going to be like this every time?" I ask quietly.

"No, honey, it's not. And if it is, you'll come to my house for every fire."

"Every one?"

"Every damn one. I'll build a room just for you, and you'll never have to spend a night alone again. You understand?"

This is the River I've grown to see and cherish. The fierce protector and provider. The man behind the goofy persona he loves to wear. "I understand."

"Good. Text me when you get to Thor's."

The lights are all on when I pull into the driveway, and Amber is already on the porch waiting for me. She leaps from the railing the moment my engine is off and yanks open my door. I send the message to River and give her a pathetic watery smile as I climb out.

"I volunteered to greet you because I knew Lily would cry. Hell, she's still probably going to cry. Do you think she'll blame it on pregnancy hormones forever?"

I give a halfhearted laugh, grateful that she's leading with humor and not the dreaded "are you okay" that always sets people off. I've had time to think rationally on the drive here, and I know River's right. It's why he's the one I called. He knows us both so well. Only he could keep a level head about this and tell me not to freak out.

"Come on," she says, linking her arm through mine and leading me into the house. Shadow greets me at the door, and all the voices in the house go quiet except for Griff, who comes running for me.

"Mel!" Griffin squeals at my feet, holding his arms out. I scoop him up and snuggle him close, reveling in the pure love of children.

"Hey, Griffy boy. I missed you." I carry him into the living room where everyone's sitting. Lily's red-rimmed eyes find mine first, but she holds it together.

Before I can take a seat, Griffin stretches his arms out to Jake. "Dick!"

Jake takes him with a wide grin. "No, Griff," Thoren corrects, scrubbing a hand down his face. "Jake."

"Dick!" Griffin exclaims again happily, pointing at Jake.

"Close enough." Jake shrugs.

"You deserve it. You taught him the word." Lily mock glares at him.

This is the distraction I needed. I don't know if it was intentional, but their lighthearted banter is perfect. I've handled so much on my own. Even knowing I had them to lean on, I refused and took it all on myself. Having them here now, without needing to ask, and not having to sit alone in fear, is the greatest gift they could have given.

"You didn't all have to come, but thank you."

"Yeah, we did," Jake adds. "We would have anyway, but Ethan specifically asked us to make sure you never had to be alone during anything again."

My throat tightens, and tears prick at the back of my eyes. Of course he did. He's been looking out for me for far longer than I realized. Thoren brings out cards, and we start a round of Cards Against Humanity. Through it all, I can't shake the feeling that something's wrong. I pray it's simply the knowledge that our meadow is burning.

Thoren's phone buzzes on the table, and we all go quiet as he answers it. I know it's not good when his eyes meet mine across the coffee table and he stands to leave the room.

"Don't."

He hesitates but sits again so we can overhear his side of the conversation.

"You're getting called in?" Lily asks when he hangs up.

"There are three missing girls. Since Ethan's already on site, they asked me to notify the SAR team that they may need to go out once the fire is under control. They may have made it out already, but no one's seen them."

"How bad's the fire?"

Thoren gives me a sympathetic look. "It didn't sound good. The winds are picking up, and it's been a dry season."

I'm on my feet before I can stop myself. "I need to go."

"Michele," Thoren tries to reason with me, but I'm already heading for the door. "Fine, but let me come with. You're not driving."

CHAPTER FORTY-EIGHT

michele

My leg bounces in the passenger seat of Thoren's truck. The smoke is thick and spreading fast, causing a haze for most of the drive. Luckily, the meadow is nowhere near any homes, but the way it's already spreading is worrisome on a number of levels.

"It's going to be okay," Thoren reassures. He parks on the side of the main road, out of the way of emergency vehicles. We both get out, and he leads the way toward the row of fire trucks and ambulances. "They may tell us to leave. You can put your eyes on Ethan, ensure he's safe, and then we can go back to the house, okay?"

"Yeah, all right."

He chuckles, knowing full well if I want to stay, I'm staying. No matter what anyone says. I try to breathe through my nose, but it burns, and inhaling through the mouth tastes like ash. There's a table and pop-up tent set up near one of the fire trucks, and Thoren heads directly for it. I'm overwhelmed by the sheer pandemonium unfolding. Flashing lights break through the haze, competing with the red and gray hues billowing from the forest.

There are voices and radios crackling around us, as I try to assess it all and the utter devastation that's overtaken the meadow.

Two helicopters fly low overhead, and we turn to see them dropping something over the woods. Thoren spots someone he knows and beelines to him. I follow, keeping my eyes peeled for Ethan. There are a lot of men and women in turnout gear, but not a single yellow shirt of the hotshots.

"Reynolds!" Thoren yells. "Have you seen Ethan?"

The man turns around, shaking his head. His face is unnaturally white, and his eyes wide. "Were you called in? We found the girls; you can call off the SAR team."

"I never called them in. I was waiting for word on the state of the fire. I'm here because Michele wouldn't stay away."

"You're Michele?" he asks, now looking a little green. "You need to let Thoren take you home."

My heart stops. It fucking stops right then and there. "Where is he?"

"Please," the man repeats, desperate.

"Where. Is. He?"

No one responds, but several pairs of eyes are on us now.

The blood drains from my face, and everything feels fuzzy. "Where is he?!" I know I'm screaming, but it sounds underwater to me.

Thoren's suddenly by my side, holding onto me. "Michele."

I can't really hear him, though. Can't feel him.

I can't feel anything.

My lungs seize as I try to suck in air.

This can't be happening. It can't be happening.

I've just got him back. He's just agreed to move in with me. This is not how it's supposed to happen. This job was supposed to be safer. He was supposed to be safe.

My legs give out, but Thoren catches me before I hit the

ground. He carries me to the back of an ambulance, and I'm vaguely aware of an EMT talking to me, but I can't respond.

I can't do anything.

He was mine. From that first day in second grade, Ethan was my best friend. I didn't know then that he would consume my life. My future. But I knew he was someone special. He had a way of making me laugh until my stomach hurt, a way of looking at me that made my heart skip a beat. We built forts in the woods, shared secrets under the starry sky, and dreamed of a future filled with adventures. Then came the years of distance, of unspoken words and silent longing.

Life pulled us in different directions, and for a while, the roots we had so carefully nurtured seemed to wither. But through it all, there remained a silent promise of something more. After everything we've been through. All our time apart, I finally had him back. The weight of the years melted away as we fell into each other's arms, the familiarity of his touch igniting a fire within me. For all these years, we had protected the roots, and now our dormant love was ready to bloom. We were ready to have a whole garden, one that flourished each year, a testament to the enduring power of a love that had weathered every storm, a love that was finally ours.

I picture the nights with our friends. Our days full of children's activities. I can imagine my belly round with his child, and his hand in mine as we bring them into this world. His handsome, proud face as he loads us all up to go to the park. His patience as we spend our days in the garden, planting new flowers, and tending to old growth. His green eyes tired and weathered as we rock on the front porch, reminiscing about the day he showed back up here in his backward hat.

I had it all. Right there. It was in my grasp. *Finally.*

I can't catch my breath, but it's not due to smoke or ash. My broken heart is thumping so hard my ribs might crack. *I had it all right there.*

The man who told me to leave is in front of me, and I try my hardest to focus on him. "Michele?"

I nod, not trusting my voice.

"I'm Carl Reynolds. Can you stay calm while I tell you what's going on?"

I nod again, and Thoren slips his hand into mine.

Reynolds runs his hand through his hair. "Ethan wanted to be hands-on for this fire. He said it was important for him to keep this place safe. He went in with the crew, and they did a great job. They had everything dug in a matter of hours and started a back burn. One section was left, but he and another hotshot heard voices, so they ran into the fire to check it out. They found three missing girls."

The relief I feel is instant.

Until he keeps talking.

"He sent two with Gerald, but one of the girls was injured, so he had to carry her out. They fell behind and got trapped. He used the only protection he had to make sure the young girl was safe."

"Oh, fuck," Thoren whispers, squeezing my hand. "Have they…?"

"The helicopters that just flew over dropped fire retardant. We have a crew going in now to look for them." Reynolds rests his hand on my knee. "Over the radio, the last thing he said was 'Tell Michele, until my last dying breath.'"

And with that, I shatter.

ethan

Pain. So much pain.

My mouth is dry. My lungs are on fire, every breath is a fight to take. Prickles of pain shoot across my back. There's a pounding in my head, and an incessant quiet beeping around me. I need to roll over to turn off the alarm, but I can't move. My lungs feel heavy, like they don't want to expand. I want to cough, but there's nothing but stabbing in my throat. Even opening my eyes is a struggle. The beeping has to stop. I turn my head slightly and try to peel my eyes open.

I'm met with a blinding light. When my eyes adjust, it's the most beautiful sight. My Michele. I'd recognize the top of her head anywhere. Her honey-brown hair spilling in every direction. I stare at her sleeping form when the rest of the room starts to register. She's lying by my arm. My arm that's bandaged, resting on a blanket that's not mine.

Reality comes crashing in, and the scene around me becomes clear. The beeping increases, and my heart rate and breathing spike. I try to speak, but I can't form the words. Michele stirs next to me, lifting her head as wide eyes meet my own.

"Ethan?" She sounds panicked, looking from me to the monitors. "Calm down, you're okay." She looks exhausted, scared, and heartbroken. What the hell happened? "You're okay," she repeats as a nurse rushes into the room.

It's so hard to catch my breath. Like my chest won't fully expand. I'm trying to calm down to reassure Michele, but the air won't enter my lungs. I refuse to let my eyes leave hers. I hear the nurse talking, but it's not registering. My whole focus remains on the scared look on my girl's face.

Something warm flushes through my veins, and everything feels heavy again. Dampened. My eyes flutter shut, but I force them open only to see a solo tear drip down Michele's beautiful cheek before everything goes dark again.

There's a knock, and then I hear her voice. "What are you doing here?"

"It's chemo day. Just wanted to come check on our boy first." Evelyn. The woman is a godsend, taking in everyone Thoren and River bring home and treating them like her own.

"He hasn't woken up again." There's heartbreak lacing her words.

"He will. His body just needs more time to heal, and keeping him sedated will help that. The smoke did a lot of damage to his lungs. He's been through so much."

There's a shuffling followed by muffled sobs. I want to open my eyes, but they're still so heavy, so I let sleep drag me under.

A bang causes me to flinch, and my eyes shoot open. The room is bright, and there's a squeak as two nurses push a cart inside.

"Good morning, Michele," one says. My eyes shoot around

the room until they find her, slumped on a recliner in the corner. "Sorry if we woke you. We're here for a dressing change."

I scour over her body, but I don't see any visible bandages. My gaze tracks down, and I realize they're talking about me. My arms are covered in white gauze. It's all a blur. Why I'm here. What happened.

What happened?

"We have eyes," someone says, and I turn to the nurse. "Hey, Ethan, I'm Eloise, one of your nurses today. How are you feeling?"

There's another crash as Michele jumps from her chair and rushes to my side. "Ethan?"

"Wildflower." My voice is scratchy and painful, but I'd say a million more words if it meant Michele would forever look at me the way she is right now.

Tears are streaming down her face as she laughs and cries together. Her whole body is shuddering with fierce, joyful sobs. I wince at the pain when I lift my arm to wipe her cheek.

"How dare you try to die on me?" she chokes out while sobbing harder. The nurses let us have our moment, pretending to arrange things on their cart, while glancing over every couple of seconds. Michele leans forward, placing a gentle kiss on my lips. "You can't do that again."

"Okay, baby," I croak. It causes a coughing fit that feels like my body is trying to expel a lung, until Eloise holds out a cup of water with a straw.

"Maybe she can tell you what happened while we check your burns? Even with the pain medication, it's going to be painful. The distraction will probably be welcome."

So that's exactly what happens. The nurses roll me onto my side to carefully replace the gauze on my back and arms while Michele talks. I focus on the way her lips move and the emotions that cross her features. She sends me empathetic glances every time I wince, no matter how hard I fight against the pain. Michele tells me that as soon as the helitack crew dropped the fire suppressant, my crew rushed in for me. Kate made it with some first-degree burns, some smoke inhalation, and a broken ankle.

I, on the other hand, was found barely breathing and covered in burns. When passing out, I must have slipped my helmet over my head, because that's how I was found. My face suffered first-degree burns, and my hair is definitely singed at the edges, while my arms and back were covered in second-degree burns, and some spots were bordering third degree. My legs came out relatively unscathed, and my hands were protected under me. The worst was my neck, where there was talk of potentially needing skin grafts in some areas below my hairline.

Michele explains it all. How this is day five in the hospital. The first three days, I was sedated on a vent to help me breathe and let my lungs heal. When I started breathing on my own again, they lowered the sedation, which led to my lucid moments.

My doctor comes in when the nurses are almost done applying a salve to my blistered skin. "Good to see you're awake. How are you feeling?"

"Some pain." It isn't entirely a lie, but there's more than 'some' pain. Every breath hurts, and my skin still feels like it's on fire.

"There are some burns in your mouth and esophagus, along with damage to your lungs. Those are painful injuries that, aside from some bronchodilators, we can't really treat. They will heal on their own in time. You have to take it easy, and you need to minimize future risk, which means considering a change in careers." He flips through my chart when I stare blankly at him, and Michele gives my hand a gentle squeeze.

"We're going to keep you for another few days. Monitor your breathing and the progress of your lungs, as well as your burns. We'll have you working on an incentive spirometer while you're here, and you'll be having a lot more pulmonary check-ups in your future. Your back is healing nicely, but your neck is a cause for concern. Rest, take it easy, and use your voice as little as possible."

I nod, and he knocks on the bottom of the bed. "I'll be around again this evening to check on your neck."

When the room empties out again, Michele drags the chair over to my side and grabs my hand again. "Are you really okay?"

I nod again. I'm not, though. The top half of my body is blistered and swollen, my lungs are damaged, and I know the statistics on that. My chances of lung-related illness and disease just skyrocketed. Without thinking about the future, recovery from this alone could be weeks, if not months. I already felt like I wasn't enough for Michele. Like I had nothing of value to add to her life. Now she's signing up to care for me.

I'm a burden.

To top it all off, I might have to change my career. The one thing I've been working toward. The whole reason I left Michele in the first place. All of it for nothing. All of it to have even less to offer her.

So no, I'm not okay.

"I'm sorry," I croak out.

"Don't," she warns. "Don't you dare do that." Her expression changes from sad and scared to angry, and I know she can read my emotions. "I let you do this once before. Take on the weight of tough decisions on your own. You don't get to do that anymore. You promised you were here for me, and that means I get to be here for you, too. That means I get to help you face those hard decisions. Don't you dare try to cut me out again, Ethan."

The dam behind my eyes threatens to break. "Michele."

CHAPTER FIFTY

michele

"No." I take a deep breath, centering myself so I don't smack the big lovable idiot on his burned skin. "Do you know how they found you?"

He delicately shakes his head. I lean over to the side table and grab my purse. His gaze follows, and he watches me pull the crumpled flowers from inside. A few have melted edges, but they're mostly intact.

"You were clutching these under your chest. Our flowers. In the middle of a wildfire, you found our flowers and kept them safe." I place them back on the table and get up to move to the large table in the corner. There's a bag with his boots and helmet, the only two things on him they could salvage since they had to cut his clothes off.

I pick up the soot-and-char-covered helmet and show him the inside. "Then they told me that this shouldn't have protected your head as well as it did. That while the helitack team dropped on your area before you were burned alive, the heat of the flames and the burn marks around you all pointed to the fact that your face should look worse than your back, and you shouldn't be alive."

My lip quivers, and the damn tears come back. "But you see,

there's this photo hidden in here." I pull out the old picture tucked in the front. The photo of us on my front porch on my sixteenth birthday. "They said you were lucky, but I think the luck was all mine. Life knew I needed you by my side. That my love was enough."

I hand him the lightly charred photograph, and he runs his thumb over our printed faces. A myriad of emotions flash over his features. His eyes rim red, and tears gather on his lashes. "You've always saved me."

Leaning over his bed, careful not to touch him, I place a tender kiss on his lips. "And I always will. Until my last dying breath." Those tears on his lashes fall, and I wipe them with a tissue, which makes him cry harder. "It's okay, baby. I'm just trying to keep your neck clean."

He chuckles through the tears, and, my God, is it a sight.

I thought I lost him. First, when Reynolds told me what Ethan had said, then again when the team radioed they had found the bodies. Again, when he got to the hospital, the doctors were throwing around big words that I didn't understand. I've spent five days terrified I would lose the man I love. And here he is, being more of a man than I have seen yet. One who is human, broken, and vulnerable, and he's sharing it all with me.

"My messy boy."

His green eyes shoot to mine, and I watch a shiver roll through him. Oh, he liked that. I'll tuck that away for when he's all healed.

"I have one more thing I need to talk to you about." This probably isn't the best time. He needs to rest, but I can't keep sitting on these feelings. "You left your phone at home the night of the fire, and after you left, you received a text."

I snag his phone from the table and hold it out for him. He takes it and goes into his messages, a look of understanding crossing his face. "It's my mom."

"What? Why isn't she saved in your phone?"

"She knew. All this time, she knew my dad lied about black-listing me. She knew he was manipulating me. But she was so miserable with him, she thought if she kept me around, it would at least make things easier for her." He takes another sip of water, resting for a minute. "She told me not to marry you. If I really loved you, I would let you go. The life I wanted with my career wasn't for you. She manipulated me just as much, but her betrayal hurt the worst. I expected it from him, you know? Never from her. I'm so sorry I ever fell for it."

"Ethan, it's okay, I've forgiven you. It's okay if you forgive her, too."

This man has been manipulated and lied to by the two people who are supposed to want the best for him. His protectors, his providers, the ones who were supposed to give unconditional love. They clearly didn't teach him a single thing about what it means to be a man, yet here he is. Ethan is the best man I know.

He's filled with compassion, empathy, and kindness. There's not a cruel bone in his body. He's confident in exactly who he is, the definition of masculine, while not being afraid to step outside the traditional meaning. He's emotionally intelligent, demanding, and submissive in the bedroom, and he loves so fiercely.

I see the mess he's always begging me to show him. The pain, the self-doubt, the fear of what the future might hold for him now. It only makes me love him more. His strength is written into his skin. Into the blistered and charred flesh. He's beautiful.

"If you're allowed to love my mess, then I'm allowed to love yours, too. We're in this together, baby. No decisions need to be made now. All that matters is that we have each other."

"Marry me."

"What?"

"I know," he says, then coughs. I hand him the water, and he takes a few sips, trying to clear his throat. "I had a plan. Screw plans."

My heart is racing, pounding beneath my rib cage. Ethan takes some wheezy breaths, then continues, "I don't want to spend another moment without knowing you're mine. It's you, Michele. When the world gets heavy, when things get scary, when all my dreams come true… It's you I want by my side. Marry me."

I laugh, a little in disbelief, but mostly filled with pure love and happiness. "Right now?"

"Fuck no, not right now," River growls, stomping through the door. We both turn to see him looking winded and pissed. "Ethan. You're ruining the plan."

"Plans change." I stare between the two of them, utterly lost. I didn't even know River was coming today. Ethan tenderly reaches for my hand. "What do you say, Wildflower? Will you marry me?"

"Yes," comes my automatic response. "Yes!" I hate that I can't hug him, hold him, and celebrate this moment in that way.

Before I can lean in for a kiss, River pulls me into him. "I'm so glad I got to be here for this! Congratulations, love birds!" He leans in to whisper in my ear, "Finally."

"I hate this," Ethan grumbles. "Give me back my fiancé."

River refuses, sticking out his tongue. "I don't see a ring."

The two glare at each other, and I swear all I can see is them acting exactly like this twenty years ago. Some things never change. Eventually, River lets me go and takes my chair at Ethan's side. "Good to see you, buddy. Gave us a hell of a scare."

I sit carefully on the edge of the bed, Ethan holding his hand out for me. "I made a promise to my girl that I was back for her. I meant that in every scenario, every fire, every day." He runs his thumb over my knuckles. When my eyes meet his, he winks and mouths, 'I love you.'

"So no one calls me when Ethan wakes up, I don't get notified of impromptu engagements… I call horse shit on all of this. Don't make me end our friendship right before I move home."

"You're ruining our moment."

"Bullshit. You ruined your moment by proposing in a hospital without a ring. The wedding better make up for it."

I can't help but laugh, because fuck, I missed the banter between these two. They continue arguing, while I marvel at the fact that I have a fiancé who is very much alive, and all my dreams are coming true.

Finally.

ethan

FIVE WEEKS LATER

The week I left the hospital, Michele and I had a long talk. I wanted to return to work. My career is everything to me, but if she had asked me to step away, I would have. Surprisingly, she told me the opposite. She reminded me that when she said yes to me, it meant in sickness and in health. 'You've wanted to be a firefighter since you were ten, and I've been aware of the risks since then. That hasn't stopped me from loving you, and it never will.'

In that moment, I fell even harder, a feat I didn't realize was possible. She's my perfect match, accepting me exactly as I am. I've struggled with being a burden, but she has shut that down every time those thoughts pop up. I promised to be here for her, and to me, that meant sharing the load. Instead, I had to be cautious of movement, careful not to open the last of the blisters or fragile, healing skin. There was little helping around the house, when dirt and debris could cause infections so easily. The burns in my mouth and throat ached, making eating difficult. I became one more thing for Michele to worry about.

The day I was released, she brought me directly to our home, telling me it was all ready for us. River, Thoren, and Jake had packed up my tiny house and moved everything into Michele's. One more thing I wouldn't have been able to do on my own. There's been an adjustment period because, not only was I still struggling with pain and healing, but Michele also folds my briefs. Now *I* have to fold my briefs. The things we do for love.

There's a knock at the front door, so I shut my laptop to get it. Evelyn's smiling face greets me when I swing the door open. She's holding yet another pan of food, accompanied by a scowling Ivy.

"What a surprise." It's not. Evelyn has been dragging her home health aid over here twice a week for the last month. All under the guise of stocking our freezer, and she just happens to demand that Ivy check on my healing. Evelyn tsks when I take the tin pan from her. "Come on in."

"Thank you," Evelyn says smugly, knowing I would invite them in. Ivy rolls her eyes behind her, but there's love and concern written on her features.

They're sitting on the couch when I come back from placing the food in the fridge. Evelyn looks tired and thin, and my concern ratchets up a notch. She shouldn't be out and about, doing this for me when I'm in better shape than she is.

"Sit, sit," she says, as if this is her house. "How are you feeling?"

"I'm great. I actually had a follow-up this morning, and got the all clear to resume physical activity. I'll be back to office duty at work starting next week. Lung function depending, I could be out on SAR and wildfire calls the month after."

That was the best news ever, because not only did it mean no more working from home three days a week, it also means I can finally be intimate with Michele. It's been so long. Do you know how hard it is to sleep next to your stunning fiancé every night and not dive face-first into her pussy?

"That's great, honey. Does that mean the real proposal is coming?"

Fucking River. Of course he's spilled the beans. "Yes."

"What's the plan? Where's the ring?"

I look between the two ladies. "Are you going to keep your mouths shut?"

Ivy deadpans, "Who am I going to tell?"

She has a point. I slide the box from my pocket and place it in Evelyn's dainty hands. She gasps when she opens it. River's been helping me work with someone in Seattle to design this since the day I moved back. He had it in his pocket when he came to visit me in the hospital. Of course, he refused to give it to me then, because Michele deserved a better proposal than that. There really was a plan in place, but that plan involved our meadow, which is no longer an option.

The bonfire started on the edge of the meadow and spread into the woods. We lost over a thousand acres of forest to the fire. The meadow itself is only partially burned. About half gone, the other half trampled by all the cars, equipment, and people who worked tirelessly to get the fire under control. I haven't had the heart to go see it in person, only seen photos.

I'm not certain I can stomach the realities of it yet. I broke down to Michele two weeks ago, telling her how bad it hurts, knowing we lost all our hard work, and the place we've cherished. My beautiful girl took on my sadness, let me sit with it, and then reminded me that good things can grow again. That time heals all wounds, and in this case, our love can help those flowers bloom again.

Fire doesn't erase memories; it clears space for new ones to grow. It's a cruel irony that destruction often paves the way for creation. The flames consume the tangible remnants of the past, leaving behind only ash and the echoing silence of what once was. Yet, in that void, in the absence of the familiar, something remarkable happens. The mind, unburdened by the weight of nostalgia, becomes fertile ground. New experiences, new perspectives begin to take root. The past transforms into a lesson learned, a foundation upon which a stronger, more resilient future is built. The scent of smoke, a lingering reminder, serves as a catalyst for rebirth. It whispers of resilience, of the human spirit's capacity to adapt and flourish even in the face of devastation, reminding us that even from the ashes, beauty can bloom.

It's with that thought in mind that I go over my plan. I can't keep the smile from my face as I talk about doing things right for my girl. I should have waited to propose, but I couldn't bear to not have her be absolutely certain I'm not going anywhere. Evelyn tears up as I explain, and even Ivy wears a small smile.

They stay for another twenty minutes before Ivy stands and all but drags Evelyn out the door. I appreciate it because I have work to do to pull this off. But first, I have to call my best friend and yell at him.

"Honey, I'm home," Michele singsongs when she walks in later that afternoon. She places her shoes in the basket and hangs her keys on the key hook that's now on the wall. "I'm mad at you. You never told me how your appointment went."

She stops in her tracks when she walks into the kitchen and sees the island. Was this my best choice? Probably not. There's a risk she's going to whip my ass for this. Her eyelid twitches as she takes me in from head to toe. Lying on the counter. Hard as a rock. Naked.

"Ethan."

"Wildflower."

"Does this mean what I think it does?"

"If you think it means I received the all-clear to be touched, scratched, and kissed over every inch of my body…. Then, yes."

Michele's eyes light with glee, and a saccharine smile crosses her lips. "So you thought putting your naked ass on the counter we prepare our food on and eat our meals off was the way to tell me?"

I shrug, because, well, yeah. "I'm offering myself up on a silver platter. But we don't have one of those, so I figured the counter was fine."

"Remember when I said I was going to make you pay when I finally fucked your ass?"

Mmmm, there's my girl. Was a part of me hoping this is where things would lead? Absolutely. I want this, and I need to give Michele all of me. Show her that everything I am is hers. "Yes, baby."

"Good. Get that plump ass upstairs. It's mine."

My cock was already hard in anticipation of her coming home and finding me, but it's leaking now. I jump down, not an ounce of shame, as my axe bobs around. While I want to carry her up the stairs like I used to, I have to acknowledge that my lungs can't handle that right now. Instead, I grab her hand and lead her upstairs.

In the room, I spin on her and grip her dress, sliding it over her head. She's left only in a green lace bra-and-panty set. My mouth instantly waters at the way her hard nipples poke through the flimsy fabric. "Have you had this on all day?"

She shoves me back to land on the bed and instantly looks remorseful. "I'm okay, baby," I assure her. "You can be a little rough, I'm not going to break." Her eyes search mine before she squares her shoulders.

"On your stomach." I follow her command instantly. "Mmm, such a good boy."

Her words skate over me, followed by the tips of her fingers skittering up from my ankle. Goosebumps trail in their wake all the way to my ass. I tense when her fingers slide over the tips of my thighs. A thwack ricochets around the room when she smacks my butt, causing me to clench further.

"Relax, baby. This will only work if you're comfortable." She moves around the bed and rummages in her nightstand before tossing lube, baby oil, and a small dildo next to me. My nerves heighten up a notch, and my heart feels like it's going to pound out of my body.

Still, I force my muscles to unclench, wanting to please Michele. She moves to the end of the bed and climbs on. My cock leaks against the comforter when her thighs straddle me. A bottle cap clicks open and then shuts. I'm practically shivering in anticipation when Michele's warm hands land on my back, spreading oil around. She kneads my aching muscles, taking her time to relax me, careful around the spots on my neck that are in their last stages of healing.

Her hands are strong and don't let up. She rubs down my arms and back up, putting me in a trance with the way her fingers move. They cover my back again, up and down, until I'm putty beneath her. It's only then, when every muscle is loose and I'm melted into the bed, that her hands sink lower. She spreads my cheeks, massaging them, before spreading them.

Michele's fingers slink closer and closer every time she spreads them until they glide over my hole. I hear the cap click open again, and she squirts some between my cheeks. I bite my lip, but when her finger rims me, then pushes in, I can't hold back the whimper.

"Chele," I moan, as she works it in further, fingering my tight ass.

"Yes, baby?" she asks, sweet as ever.

"More."

Her chuckle is soft as she works a second finger in. She presses against my prostate, and I swear I levitate off the bed. There has to be a puddle of precum under me now, and there's no way I'm going to last long if she keeps teasing me.

After a slow, torturous amount of time, she pulls her fingers from me. "Stomach or back?"

Oh God. I want to be bent over for her. To let her truly have her way with me, but I'm equally dying to see her face. "Stomach."

"Good boy."

michele

Ethan squirms beneath me, subtly rocking his hips against the comforter, trying to get some relief. I want his pleasure to come from me and me alone. I slide off the bed, and he turns his head to the side to watch me strip off my lacy negligée.

"Lift your knees."

His green eyes shine in this light, lids lowered with desire. He slides one leg up, and then the other, keeping his cheek against the mattress. I never expected that I would be into this. That *we* would be into this. Yet, with the way my body is tingling and his cock is throbbing, hard, and leaking from the tip, we clearly are.

I climb onto the bed behind him and grab the dildo and lube. He's probably oiled up enough, and the dildo isn't much bigger than my first two fingers, but with this being the first time, I want to make sure he only feels pleasure. After lubing up the head of the toy, I rim his tight ass with it.

He whimpers when I start pushing it in, so I grip his dick and stroke lightly. "Who do you belong to?"

"You. I'm yours, Michele."

"That's right, baby. I'm going to take care of you. Do you

trust me?" I slide the toy in deeper with each thrust, taking my cues from his body on how much he can handle.

"Yes."

I slide it in all the way and am instantly rewarded with more precum covering my hand. "Good. But I'm also going to punish you when it's deserved. Do you deserve it?"

"Yes," he sputters out when I squeeze his cock tighter.

"Mmmm, that's right." I resume fucking him with the toy at the same rhythm I'm stroking his cock. Slowly, he starts rocking his hips, the sweetest noises falling from his lips. "You're doing so good for me."

My body responds to every sound he makes. I'm slick, dripping down my thighs, all from giving my man pleasure. Pleasure he deserves, that he's earned. Every day for the rest of my life, I want these moments with him. When we're tired, I want it slow and sweet. When we're angry, I want him to fuck the sass out of me. When we're in the moment, I want it right then and there, no matter where we are. Desperate for each other. The way he turns me on is unlike any other. One swipe of my clit and I could combust right now.

I pick up my pace with the dildo and stop stroking his cock to smack his ass again. He groans, but takes it. "That's for telling me what to do in the kitchen." I smack him again, loving the way it makes him clench around the toy. "And that's for putting your bare ass on our counter."

"I need to come," he whines. "Please, baby."

He's been so good for me, so I resume stroking his cock and make sure the dildo drags against his prostate with every thrust. In a matter of minutes, he's a shaking, whimpering mess, coming all over the comforter in spurts.

It's a hot and heady feeling, dominating him in this way. Knowing he's given me every ounce of trust and vulnerability. He's given me all of him.

These last few weeks, he's struggled with the feelings of being a burden and the fear of not being able to provide for me the way he wants. He's so wrong, though. All I've ever wanted from him is… him. His love, his care, his devotion. He gives me that every day, and then some. Ethan is attentive, protective, and nurturing. Despite my protests and doctor's orders, he's been cleaning, working in the yard, and even made a business expansion plan for Hidden Meadow if I choose to go that route.

He rolls onto his side, careful not to fall into his cum. His body is trembling, and he's wearing the most satisfied smug grin. I run my hands up and down his back, then over his powerful thighs. They work to knead out the muscles until the trembling stops and he's relaxed. After scooting to the top of the bed, I twirl some strands of his hair before letting my nails rake over his scalp.

"You did so good for me. Thank you." I keep my statement simple, letting those words truly sink in.

When his breathing is back to normal and his grin turns into something soft, I grab a small towel from the nightstand and wipe him and the comforter as best as I can, despite his protests. "What are you smiling at?"

"You didn't even get mad about the mess."

I stare at the wet stain he left on the blanket that I'll be removing the moment he gets up. He's right. The thought of baby oil, cum, and lube covering it didn't even cross my mind, and I'm not remotely upset. "You're changing me."

"In a good way?"

"Always a good way."

He slips off the bed and takes the towel from me. "Go get in the shower. I'll clean this up and join you in a minute."

There's no protest from me. I'm getting used to being taken care of. Some might even say I'm downright spoiled now. Ethan would say I'm finally being taken care of the way I deserve. No complaints here either way.

The shower door opens while my head is under the water, and his arms wrap around my waist. He nuzzles closer to me. "I love the way you smell."

I finish rinsing out my hair. "It's my body wash and lotion."

"Mmm," he groans, kissing my neck. "You know what's even better than your scent?" He drops to his knees and, with no preamble, swipes his tongue over my pussy. "Your taste."

In an instant, I'm pushed against the shower wall, and he's putting one of my legs over his shoulder. Ethan wastes no time diving into my pussy. His tongue circles my clit before he latches his mouth onto it, sucking while still flicking it with the tip of his tongue. He builds me up hard and fast, getting me right to the edge.

My hands are gripped in his hair, holding him against me. I've been wet and ready since I walked through the door and found him naked and hard waiting for me. The foreplay of getting to fuck his ass and make him come only edged me. With his mouth on me now, it's taking no time to get me there.

Ethan must sense that I'm close because he slows his ministrations and looks up at me. "Not yet, pretty girl. Let me savor you."

He spreads my pussy open with his lips and licks his tongue in a circular motion with his mouth wide. Over and over, his tongue circles, gliding over my clit each time. It's mind-numbing, the different sensations. I'm wholly consumed by him and the things he makes me feel. His tongue moves faster and faster until my breathing is ragged and I can barely hold on. All of his attention then focuses on my clit, and I explode, coming in an array of moans and shivers.

Ethan groans against my pussy, lapping up every drop of my release. My legs are shaking, but he holds me up with ease. The month of light physical activity after his accident sucked, but it's worth the wait if this is the reward.

He carefully lowers me to my feet, then washes my body again before cleaning his own. When we're done and back in the room, I see a fresh blanket on the bed and everything put away. I can't wait to marry this man.

We climb into bed together, utterly spent and exhausted. Exactly the way I hope it always is.

michele

With a coffee tray in hand, I step into Amber's boutique. She spots me instantly, says something to the customer she's serving, and skips over to me. Without asking, she removes one cup at a time until she finds the one she likes and slips it from its place.

"Mmmm, I needed this. Thanks, bestie." She hums around the first sip.

"Who says that one was even yours?" I ask, eyebrows raised.

"It's the rules. I licked it so it's mine."

She cackles, taking the tray and walking back to the counter. We both know that was hers, since she loves as much sweetness as she can get. Amber lifts the vanilla latte out and hands it to me, leaving the third.

"That one's for whoever is working today."

"Natasha will thank you when she gets in." Her gaze travels down my body, and back, "Michele! We'll talk about your glow in a second, but are you wearing my entire store?"

I look down at the white top I've paired with a cream skirt and black-heeled booties. "Unintentional, but yes. I think half my closet's from here now."

Amber beams at me. "This is why I keep you around. Next inventory, you're coming to help me style looks again. You have the eye for it in a way I never will." Her hand waves down her body, clad in a blue lace crop top, black leggings, and blue Chucks. It's adorable and her typical style, but not necessarily what she sells.

A customer comes up to check out, so I walk around the boutique to have a look at the new items. Socks, her and Jake's cat, is sprawled on a chair by the changing rooms. I scoop him up, take his seat, and snuggle him into my chest. His purrs have me melting, ready to adopt the next animal I see. I've wanted a cat for a while. A little buddy to hang out in the garden with me, lazily following me from home to the office every morning. Maybe it's time to talk to Ethan about that.

Amber saunters over, gives Socks a quick head scratch, then starts folding a pile of shirts next to me. "Spill. What's with the glow and the impromptu visit?"

"I'm in love."

She chokes, pausing with a shirt half-folded. "Uhhhh, yes. That's typically what happens with the person you're going to marry."

I roll my eyes and snuggle Socks tighter. There's a war of words raging in my head, trying to best articulate my feelings. All it takes is one thought of Ethan, and my mind quiets, and everything aligns.

"I've known love in this life. It's the way I feel when I look at the river flowing through the valley, steady and wild in perfect harmony. In the way my flowers give me the most beautiful blooms year after year. I see it in the time my brother takes to call and check on me, even if he's in the middle of a war zone or healing a piece of his soul. I've felt it in the way we girls show up for each other every time it's needed; no matter the pain we know it may bring."

Amber puts the shirt down, not bothering to finish folding it, her soft gaze locked on mine.

"But it all started in the way Ethan's eyes lit up when he made me laugh. His desire to be near me, even if it was in silence. *Especially* in the silence. It was felt through the way he laced our fingers together, rubbing his thumb comfortingly over my knuckles. The joy he would radiate when I shared something I found exciting. It was seen in the way his gaze never left mine, no matter how silly or trivial the conversation was. I felt it in the way my body and soul were at peace when we were together. I knew what love was."

"And you didn't realize you still had that until now?" she asks, trying to follow my train of thought.

This is the scary part. But I need to talk it out with someone, and she's my go-to. "No, I knew. My body called to him, responding to his unspoken cues from the day he showed up here. My soul felt that same sense of tranquility. The underpass in a rainstorm, bringing a comforting silence to the chaos around me. But my heart... my heart *hurt*. He took his Pulaski and picked away at the walls around it until there was nothing but pebbles left in his way. The problem was, I still didn't allow him in. No barriers, but no open arms either. I was waiting for the other shoe to drop. For the moment I could surrender every part of me and trust he would see that for exactly what it is and be the fortress for me. The way I am for him."

My hands shake as they continue to pet the sleeping cat on my chest. Amber's uncharacteristically quiet, and when I turn to her, she's biting her lip with watery eyes.

"You finally feel safe enough to surrender?" she asks in a whisper.

I knew she would understand the weight of this moment for me. Love is a life force. You can have it and experience it in many different ways with many different people. Love with complete vulnerability, offering everything you possess and everything you are, is a feeling that changes you forever. She experiences it with Jake. Now, it's my turn.

Ethan gave me his heart. The burnt edges, the scared and twisted fears, the truest and purest version of himself. He's given it all to me. I don't feel compelled to give myself in return. I want to. I *need* to. Like I need my next breath, there's no stopping this desire to submit all I am to him.

"I do."

michele

The drive home to Ethan feels different. I'm confident. Ready. I've promised him my life, but now it's time to give him… me. The only thing I've wanted from him, I'm finally ready to give. His truck is out front, parked furthest from the door as always, offering his protection even in the smallest of acts.

He's on the couch watching baseball when I walk in, his face lighting up as soon as he turns to me. The sight normally makes my heart race, but today, it only makes me feel steady and sure. He senses the difference immediately. Always reading me better than I can myself.

With a confident ease, he leans forward, grabs the remote to turn the TV off, and throws it next to him before sitting back again. All while never breaking eye contact. The air is charged, electric, and my nerves are starting to thrum. Still, my heart beats in its measured rhythm.

I slip my keys on the hook, waiting for him to make a move. He doesn't have to take control; I want to give it. His eyes track down, caressing every inch of my exposed skin. There's a sly smile on his face as he leans forward again, placing his elbows on his knees and tracing his bottom lip with his thumb.

You could hear a pin drop in the silence. My hands turn clammy with the need to do something; smooth down my skirt or fix my hair, but I resist. I don't need words. He knows he's in control of this situation; he knows that I won't make a move until he tells me to.

"Michele. Crawl to me."

When he says my name, the world narrows to that single sound. No threat, no force—just gravity, pulling me to my knees before I even realize I've moved. My body obeys, desire pumping through my veins thicker than blood. The wood floor is cold and unforgiving, but my eyes never leave his. Green eyes calling like a beacon in the storm, guiding me to my ruin, only to build me up better than before.

I wait at his feet, spine straight, eyes trained on his. He takes a strand of my hair, twirling it between his fingers before stroking that same thumb over my bottom lip, pulling it open. He presses on my tongue, eyes alive with delight, before sitting back again.

"On your knees, legs spread, palms on your thighs."

There's a brief hesitation before I sit straight. Not from fear, but in the weight that suddenly feels lifted, knowing what it means to submit. The awareness that this is love in its purest form. It doesn't ask permission. It's the trust you can breathe, belonging that hums beneath your skin. The calm and the current, the grounding and the pull.

Ethan circles me, not touching, but I feel the caress of his stare all the same. He stops in front of me, reaching to pull his shirt over his head. It gets discarded to the side effortlessly, while he continues to keep his focus on me. I try to hold my position the way he always holds space for me. Unwavering. His muscles flex and shift with every movement. There may be red skin splattered across his chest, but it only adds to his raw power. His resilience painted on him like a canvas woven with strength and perseverance. With a gentle touch, he runs the back of his knuckles down my cheek with reverence.

His hands move to his pants, unbuttoning them and slipping them off. There's no break in his stare, all his attention fixed on me. He grips his briefs and pushes them down, leaving him hard and exposed in front of me. My mouth waters at the sight, desperate to lick the bead of precum glistening on his tip. The smirk he wears tells me he knows exactly where my thoughts lie. He squats, placing a tender kiss on the spot below my ear that I love.

"Arms up," he commands. I obey, shivering as he lifts my shirt over my head. My bra quickly follows when he reaches around to undo it and tosses it to the side. I let my palms rest on my thighs, waiting for his next instruction.

He sits back, sucking his bottom lip as he takes his time looking over every inch of me. His fingertips graze over my collarbone, tiptoeing down my chest until he gets to my breast. There's no hesitation as he grips the barbells and tugs, drawing out a whimper. I love the bite of pleasure and pain, mixing in a dance of sparks, shooting straight to my core.

While still playing with my piercing, his other hand dips below my skirt and swipes over my panties, undoubtedly feeling the wet spot there. A wickedly satisfied grin crosses his face. "Is this all for me, sweetheart?"

He moves my panties to the side and uses his middle finger to circle my clit before sliding it down. When he pulls his hand out, his finger glistens with my arousal, and he sucks it into his mouth.

"Chest on the floor, ass in the air, arms out next to you."

The movement is simple as I lean forward, placing my overheated chest on the cool, hard floor. My knees stay in place, ass and pussy on full display behind me. There's no thought involved.

His control leading me to that quiet place in my mind where I get reprieve from being in charge.

There's a raw honesty in being seen as the one always in charge, keeping things together, and knowing Ethan is taking this pressure for me. He's giving me the space to be free of the confines I've been living in. My freedom comes from not needing barriers, but trusting in his absolute control.

His bare feet pad across the hardwood until I can't see him, but I still hear his sharp inhale. "My perfect, messy girl," he utters, caressing over my ass and down my wet panties again. I'm surprised when his hand continues down my thighs, then across my calves until he gets to my boots. He slides them off my feet, gently removing my socks as well. Every movement is precise and laden with care.

My heart pounds against the floor, and my fingers flex, focusing on the smooth surface beneath them. Ethan unzips the skirt, tugging it and my panties down my thighs.

"Lift," he commands when he gets to my knees. I do, and he nudges them further apart when I set them back down.

Every word he gives feels like a key turning a lock I haven't touched in years. I'm not breaking, I'm opening, like the petals of a delicate flower, blooming only in the presence of the sun. It doesn't take thought; it happens on instinct. An intrinsic desire to be led.

"I have to taste what's mine." I feel his breath moments before his mouth as he wastes no time fucking my pussy with his tongue. He moans as he swirls his tongue inside me, licking up the mess he made. It doesn't take long before he has me on the edge, but he pulls back, not getting me there.

I'm naked, laid bare before him, and still my mind is at peace. I don't have to carry the weight of being perfect all the time. Of walking through this life alone, always in control, hiding the cracks in my porcelain frame.

He spreads my pussy, this time taking his time to lavish my clit and lick every inch of me. Every time, getting me to the edge, but never lets me fall all the way. I want to beg him for more. To let me come, but he's in control here. That freedom hits again as I repeat those words in my head. *I'm not in control.*

"Kneel and face me." His husky voice breaks through my thoughts. Goosebumps scatter over my skin as I push off the floor and kneel before him. He grips my chin with his thumb and forefinger, pulling my mouth open. "Tongue out. I want to feel the back of your throat."

Drool instantly pools as I obey, and Ethan gives a satisfied hum. He palms his cock, giving it a few lazy strokes, before sliding the tip into my mouth. I fight the instinct to close around him, letting him lead. *I'm not in control.*

His taste coats my tongue, and I breathe in his masculine scent. I've never been a blowjob queen. My gag reflex always kept him from going too deep, scared to hurt me. Today, though, Ethan doesn't share those compunctions. Each thrust he pushes deeper into my mouth until I'm struggling to handle his size.

He pauses with his cock touching the back of my throat, almost completely cutting off my air supply. His gaze is soft and filled with pride as he runs his thumb down my cheek, swiping the drool from my chin. I shudder when he slides that thumb into his mouth, cleaning it off.

"My good girl, taking me so well."

When he finally pulls back, more drool leaks from the edges of my mouth. It's obscene, messy, and I'm getting wetter by the minute. He continues to fuck my mouth, every drive getting deeper. I try to close my knees, needing some friction for the ache between my legs.

"You're getting desperate. Do you need to come?"

Relief washes over me as I try to nod. His use of my body in this way, his complete authority over this situation, is opening my eyes to a whole new world of play for us.

"Use your fingers and rub that pretty clit the way I would."

Before I can touch myself, Ethan grips my hair and angles my head up more, his cock still on my tongue. "Don't come until I say."

A shiver runs through me at his command. He doesn't raise his voice or growl it out. His tone is calm, measured, and reassuring. The sight of him, with his cock leaking and piercing green eyes focused on me, embodying the provider, protector, and leader I've yearned for, is astonishing.

I match my fingers to the rhythm of his thrusts. The once-quiet house is filled with my gagging as he encourages me. His gentle hand stroking over my hair is at complete odds with the way he's working my body. Every slide of his hips cuts off my air, letting me struggle, before slipping all the way back out. Saliva hangs from his dick, connecting to my tongue, before he does it all again.

It's lewd, precise, and so fucking hot that my arousal coats my thighs. He picks up his pace, fucking my mouth with fervor, slowly losing control. My fingers fly over my clit, getting myself closer to that edge.

His powerful thighs rutting into me, every muscle in his stomach bunching, and that delicious V of his hips is enough to make the drool drip down my chin and onto my tits.

"Fuck, baby, I'm so close. Take me deeper," he says through gritted teeth. Barely hanging on to the last tether of his control. I want to come, I'm right there, but I know I have to wait for permission. *I'm not in control.*

He's giving me the freedom to just… feel. Relief hits me like a tidal wave, threatening to consume me whole. So I let it. Tears gather on my lashes, and instead of wanting to wipe them away, I let them fall, unashamed. I don't have to be strong. Guarded.

Ethan sees the cracks I've spent years hiding. They're uneven abrasions on the perfect persona I lived in, but instead of recoiling, his hands are steady.

That doll that has been shattered one too many times isn't perfect, but when he looks at me with nothing but reverence, I feel whole.

His pace falters, and his thumb wipes under my eyes. "Come with me, Wildflower."

I do, my orgasm setting off as the first spurt of his salty release hits the back of my throat. Ethan groans through his release, as I try my best to swallow it all down. Tears are leaking in earnest now, as every nerve in my body frays.

My forehead lands against his thigh, catching my breath, as the flow of air comes back into the room, my body floating back into itself. I'm trembling, wrecked, and *safe*. The room exhaled with us, all heat and heartbeat, until only the sound of breathing remained.

The true feeling of release comes from the utter and complete clarity I feel. I am Ethan's. He's always been mine, but I've finally given him all of me, and he took it with surety. Unwavering confidence that he's had me all this time, fractured parts and all.

He sinks to his knees in front of me and kisses the tears rolling down my cheek. With his discarded shirt, he gently wipes my face and chest, then scoops me in his arms. He settles us on the couch before pulling the blanket draped on the edge and covering us with it.

My body is spent, my mouth sore, and my soul finally feels like it's home. His arms wrap around me, tucking me tight against his chest as he whispers my name like a prayer.

"You did so good, baby. So good for me."

His heart plays a melody against my own, beating in time to a perfect harmony. He didn't speak much; he didn't need to. Every slow touch said, "You're here, you're safe, you're mine."

He holds me close, his arm a quiet shelter around me. The doll was never perfect again, but I stopped wishing to be. The seams are visible now, rough and uneven, honest as the life that made them. They show I'm resilient, repaired, and accepted exactly for who I am. Resting against him, I finally understand; strength was never about staying whole. It was learning to live beautifully, with the evidence of being put back together.

Until my last dying breath, I'll know this type of love.

ethan

I woke early to ensure I had time to set up outside. River was already here when I snuck out at 5 a.m. with two coffees in hand. "What time did you get here?" I ask, passing over the coffee with cream.

There's no need to whisper, but the world feels too quiet right now. Low-hanging fog kisses the tree trunks in the forest, and dew clings to the petals like a lover's embrace. Even the birds seem to be singing in hushed tones, the fat bumble bees stumbling between the blooms. The fresh-brewed coffee pairs nicely with the smell of pine and roses. This little oasis Michele has built will always take my breath away.

"Less than an hour ago." He shrugs, but there's a massive grin on his face. "I couldn't sleep, I was too excited."

"Isn't that my role?"

"I can't help it if you aren't doing your job."

I scoff at him. "I told you 5:30. I need coffee, I had a long night," I whisper-yell at him.

He covers his ear with his free hand. "Lalalala. That's like my sister. Gross."

We lean against the porch railing, looking out at the back

yard. River's already started on the plans, and damn, if he hasn't done an amazing job. There are rose petals lining the edges of the path from the stairs on the porch to the front of the greenhouse. I had to scrap my original plan of proposing in our meadow. I considered doing it at Hidden Meadow Nursery, but decided that right here in our backyard would mean the most.

He takes a sip of his coffee and turns his head to me. "When Thoren called me last month…" He takes a moment to clear his throat and swallow down his emotions. "I'm really happy this day is here, and that I get to be part of it."

We haven't talked about it at all. He showed up in the hospital, ruining my pathetic proposal, and that was the extent of him acknowledging that I almost died. I never asked who made the phone calls and told who, or who had visited me and supported my girl while I was incapacitated.

When I woke up, I was scared out of my mind. All that mattered was Michele and knowing I still had her. I didn't need the specifics to know she was supported by everyone. Getting to continue my career is the cherry on top. It may look a little different. A little more hands-off, a little more from the sidelines. But I still get to do my part. River's come back twice to spend time with me when his schedule allowed, and I'm beyond grateful for him.

"Should we get started?" I nod to the greenhouse where he's stacked the boxes.

"I already started, jackass." He jumps down the steps before I can slug him.

We work in tandem to remove the table from the greenhouse first, and then we start on the decorating. I spent a few hours with Anna yesterday, clipping flowers that were going to be discarded. I tried to get one from each frame that I filled over the years, and mostly succeeded. We ended up with over six buckets full, so while River sets up LED candles on the shelves, I make little arrangements with the vases River carted over.

Over an hour later, we have the whole greenhouse decorated, flowers and candles in every corner, and rose petals littering the ground. It still doesn't seem like enough.

"You'd better get inside and distract her so I can sneak back to my car. Is everything else in place?"

"I hope so."

From the day I left the hospital, I've been planning this. I couldn't leave Michele with that terrible proposal. I wanted to be fully healed when I did it for good. Last week, I knew I would get the all clear at my appointment yesterday, so I started putting plans into motion then. Really this proposal is about ten years too late, but better late than never.

I head back into the house and sneak up the stairs to make sure Michele is still asleep. When I find her snoozing, I send a quick text to River to let him know he is good to go. Next, I pull the box from the guest room closet and set it on our bathroom counter. This part of the plan is a new addition. Ever since she found the old photo of us in my helmet, she's carried a copy of it everywhere with her. So, I found a pink dress similar to the one she wore on her sixteenth birthday, and bought it for today.

With that in place, I meander back downstairs to make her coffee. There are quite a few things on today's agenda, and I can't let my girl sleep any longer. I place her coffee on the nightstand, then plant a soft kiss on her forehead.

"Good morning."

Her hazel eyes are sleepy as she slowly blinks them open and smiles at me. "Good morning," she says, covering her mouth. "I've made a lot of concessions for you. Morning breath isn't one of them."

"Okay, baby. I made you coffee and left something for you on the counter. You have one hour before we need to leave."

She stares at me, registering what I said before jumping out of bed. She rushes into the bathroom and stops dead in her tracks when she lifts the lid on the box. With delicate fingers, she picks up the dress and inspects it before carefully holding it up to her. Watery eyes turn and look at me. "Ethan."

"I know, beautiful. Fifty-five minutes now."

She rolls her eyes and kicks the bathroom door shut, only to open it a second later to grab her coffee. There's my feisty girl. I've watched her be careful, attentive, and reserved this last month. I know she's scared of hurting me. She held my hand as the doctor listed off all the long-term effects on my lungs and the things I will need to be monitored for.

I'm not dying today, though. Hopefully not until I'm old and gray with her by my side. Seeing her starting to accept that and become herself again is a treasure. I've seen her growth in the way she skips her makeup some days and allows others to clean up messes. She boasts about her businesses with pride—both of them now. I'm so proud of her, and I'm not the only one.

By the time I've showered and dressed, I still have another twenty minutes before Michele will be ready, so I send off some messages to make sure everything is set up. Right on time, I hear heels on the stairs and turn only to have the breath stolen from my lungs.

Michele looks like a vision. The pink dress is shorter than the last one she had, the pink silk hitting mid-thigh. She paired it with knee-high boots that have my mouth watering. Her hair is falling around her in waves, and the lightest shade of pink is gracing her lips.

"Stunning," I manage to sputter out.

"Thank you. I can't believe it fits so well." She runs her hand down her front, then heads to the kitchen with her empty mug in hand. I snatch it up quickly, not willing to risk her looking out back.

"I'll put this away, you go grab your purse and a coat."

I meet her in the entryway and take her hand to lead her out to my truck. She climbs inside when I open the door and is patient until I reverse out of the long driveway. "Soooo, where are we going?"

"To brunch."

"Why?"

Reaching over, I lace our fingers together and bring them to my lips. "Because I love you."

She stares at me suspiciously but doesn't ask anymore. Instead, she relaxes into the seat while we drive into town. There's a café called The Crepe Escape that has the best breakfast around, but thanks to a little birdie, I know it's been years since she's eaten here. Michele's smile is bittersweet when I park out front.

"Everything okay?" I ask as we unbuckle and step from the truck.

"It's great," she lies, taking my hand on the sidewalk. "I just haven't eaten here without Austin. It's kind of our thing."

"Nice to know some things never change," comes a deep voice from behind her.

Michele stumbles, she spins so fast, and squeals when she spots her brother. "Hey Chele-Bell."

"Tin-Tin!" She jumps on him, holding him tight. Austin smiles over her head at me. I still have a few steps to go before earning his full trust and support, but ensuring he was here for this went a long way to mending everything. "Oh my God, what are you doing here?"

"Your boyfriend here told me it's been too long since I've visited my sister. I happened to agree."

"He's my fiancé."

"Oh yeah? Because I don't see a ring."

He knows damn well I have the ring. I video-called him and

his parents with it when I asked for their permission over three weeks ago. Suppose I do deserve the heckling, though.

Michele slaps him on the chest. "He's working on it. Can we go eat now? I've missed this place."

Austin lets go of his sister to give me a quick hug, and we all head into the restaurant. Surprise one is complete.

michele

This is the best morning ever. It's been so long since my brother visited, and getting to spend the morning eating, catching up, and laughing with him was the greatest surprise. Seeing him accept Ethan and the two of them get along might have been an even bigger surprise. He told me he would accept my choice no matter what, but I thought it would come with more than a few quick barbs.

"How long are you staying?"

Austin wipes his mouth after eating his second entrée. Yes, we've been here that long. "A week. I'm going to drive over and see Mom and Dad. And I want to catch up with Ian while I'm here, too. I might crash at his place."

"You know you always have a room in our home." I pout.

He raises an eyebrow at me, glancing between Ethan and me. "I'd rather not."

Ethan smirks, and I cross my arms. "Fine. What else did you want to do while here?"

"Can we stop by Jake's shop? I had him make me something small I need to pick up. Plus, I heard he decked Ethan for making you cry, so he deserves at least a handshake."

I gape at him, then turn to Ethan, who just looks sheepish. "Should we go?"

You know what, I'm going to drop this. Nothing is ruining this perfect day. "All right, let's go."

We decide to walk since it's such a beautiful day and downtown is so small. It's been a while since I've truly meandered down Main Street and appreciated Cedar Ridge for the unique town it is. I feel like I'm always on the go with a destination in mind, so the stroll is nice. Instead of joining the guys to see Jake, I pop my head into Amber's store next door. Socks lolls his head over his hammock perch on the window and meows, demanding pets.

"He's so needy," she quips, coming from behind the counter. "What are you up t—" Amber's words halt when she takes in my outfit. "Daaaaamn, Chele. You look hot."

"Ethan bought me this dress," I whisper, like it needs to be a secret. "And flew my brother out."

"What?" She lets out a low whistle. "What's the occasion?"

"I have no idea. We're already engaged. Unless he wants to take it to the courthouse for a wedding, but we haven't applied for a marriage license. I'm truly at a loss."

"Maybe, and I could be crazy here… but maybe he just really loves you and wants to do nice things for you."

I can't hide my stupid grin. "I really love that man."

"I think it's clear he feels the same. Well, come on, introduce me to your brother. I love a man in uniform." She links her arm through mine, leading me to the back door, and winks to Natasha, her employee. "We'll be right back."

"Jake's going to be pissed if he hears you talking like that."

She snorts out a laugh. "Oh, I do hope so. It's been a while since he punished me."

"Amber," I screech, but honestly, who am I to talk? The boys are standing in the alleyway when we walk out, talking and shooting the shit.

Jake has met my brother a time or two, but they were never close. The age gap between them was too great. You wouldn't know that from seeing the three of them now. I make the necessary introductions, and Jake steps behind Amber, giving the back of her neck a squeeze when she bats her lashes at Austin. I try to cover my chuckle with a cough, but it doesn't go over well.

We stand and talk for over an hour before Amber admits she has to get back to work, and Jake follows her cue. After saying our goodbyes, Ethan, Austin, and I head back to our cars.

"What'd you get from Jake anyway?" I ask, eyeing the small bag in his hand curiously.

"Nothing important." He shrugs. I look to Ethan, hoping he'll spill the beans, but he puts his hands up in protest.

"I asked the same thing and was given the same response."

"Fine," I grumble. "Back to our house?"

"Actually, I was hoping we could go to Hidden Meadow. I want to see what you've done with it."

"Right now?" I look down at my pretty dress.

"Real quick," Austin promises.

"I have to run by the office anyway, so I'll meet you guys back at home." Ethan grips my hip and drops a kiss to my forehead before heading to his truck.

"Oh, come on," Austin teases. "I helped you start the place. I can't help but feel invested."

We climb into his rental, and I navigate him to my nursery. He's quiet most of the drive, and it's accentuated when he parks by the greenhouse and turns off the engine. The silence is tense until he turns to me with a look of awe. "All of this is yours?"

I nod. I've sent him some picture updates over the years, but last time he was here, there were only one-tenth of the gardens there are now.

"Can we walk through?"

He looks like a kid at Christmas, and I can't deny him. "Sure. Let me change into my work boots."

We spend over an hour walking through the rows. He asks about the flowers, the business, and where I plan to take it next. We pick a small bouquet for the house, and he even ventures out to look at the bees. The weather is perfect with a light breeze and slightly overcast.

On our walk back to the car, Austin pauses. "I need to tell you something."

I stop, waiting for him to continue.

"For a long time, I was furious at Ethan for leaving you. I thought he was selfish and blamed your every change on him. It's taken me a long time to see that he wasn't the only one to leave you. He wasn't even the first. I was." He clears his throat, looking up at the sky.

"I'm not sorry for pursuing my career, but I'm sorry I left you to do it. I hardly ever came back to visit. Never flew you out to see me. I think me leaving you that way made it so much harder when Ethan did the same." He scratches the back of his neck. "Look. All this to say, I'm sorry, and I'm glad things are working out for you. You've deserved this happily-ever-after longer than anyone I know, and I'm so happy you're finally getting it."

I hug him to me, swallowing down the lump in my throat. "Thank you, Tin-Tin."

"And I'm so damn proud of you. You've really built something with your life, you know that?"

I beam proudly at him. "I know."

It's late afternoon by the time we're heading home. "Can we order something for dinner? I don't want to cook."

"It's your house, you make the rules."

I smile over at him as he turns down my driveway. "You're going to make a great husband one day."

"And you'll make a great wife." After parking up, he tips my face toward my front porch. My front porch that's covered in rose petals and lined with flickering candles.

"What's this?" I ask, tears already forming on my bottom lashes.

He climbs out of the car, opens my door, and takes my hand. "Why don't you go find out?"

I follow the roses up the stairs, and to the left. The trail continues all the way out the back and down those steps. There, the petals line the small path to the greenhouse.

It's then my eyes collide with vibrant green ones. Ethan is standing there, in the middle of my greenhouse, wearing slacks and a white button-up, undone at the top. My God, he looks so fucking handsome, smiling at me.

"Go on." My brother nudges me from behind, and I realize I've stopped and am just staring. When I take a step into the greenhouse, I'm overwhelmed by the sweet floral scent. There are flowers covering every free spot in here. Vases line the floor, the shelves, and are intermingled with candles.

The sun is barely sinking below the trees, creating the most magical colors through the windows. Reflections of the lights, candles, and flowers make me feel like I'm in an ethereal world. My hands are trembling when Ethan takes them.

"I know I already did this, but I need to do it right. I've spent so much time coming back to you the right way, I couldn't screw it all up now. Michele, you are the most beautiful, intelligent, giving, and caring woman I know. You've been my best friend, my lover, my partner, and fiancée, and I can't wait until the day I make you my wife. I will give you all that I have, all that I am, and still find ways to give you more. I love you, my Wildflower."

Tears stream down my cheeks as he gets down on one knee and reaches over to a shelf, producing a bracelet with little blue wildflowers made of blue topaz gems. He clips it onto my wrist, smiling up at me. "I needed to give you that first. Finally, a version that won't wilt."

He winks, and I cry harder through the tears. Then he pulls a small box from his back pocket and produces the most beautiful emerald-green oval ring. "Will you marry me?"

"Yes!" I shout through the tears, almost tackling him as he tries to stand in time to catch me. He spins us in a circle, whispering how much he loves me when the noise around us registers. There are catcalls and whistles, and as soon as he sets me down, I see all of our friends standing in our yard. There's not a single dry eye, even if Jake denies it, and it only makes me cry harder.

Thoren puts a squirming Griffin on the ground, who comes running at me, yelling, "Mel." Jake has Amber pulled into his chest, wiping his cheeks on her shoulder as she leans against him. My brother's wiping his eyes as he mouths "I love you" to me.

The girls demand to see the rings the minute we step out of the greenhouse. It's everything I could have dreamed of and more.

It's my happily ever after. Until our last dying breaths.

bonus - ethan

This evening has been nothing short of magical. While Michele and I changed out of our fancy clothes, our friends ordered food and got a fire going in the pit. I may have bent her over the bathroom counter and worshipped her with my axe, but that's neither here nor there.

We got to relax, celebrate, and simply enjoy having everyone in one place again. Hopefully, this is only going to start happening more often with River moving back in a few months.

Speaking of, he walked off to take a phone call a while ago, and I haven't seen him since. I excuse myself from the swing, the one I ate my girl's pussy on a few months ago, to go find him. He's pacing behind the greenhouse when I reach him. He looks pained, maybe excited, definitely nervous.

"Riv, what's going on?"

He runs a hand through his hair before leveling me with a stare. "Vanessa's pregnant."

acknowledgments

My dear, sweet, alpha readers. Phew, we made it through this book. Thank you for all that you do. Your friendship, encouragement, and laughter through the hard times means the world to me.

Ciara, my beta reader, thank you!! Your feedback, honest reviews, and wildland firefighter knowledge helped shape this story into something better and more beautiful. I'm so grateful for you.

To the wildland firefighters who answered my questions and gave me feedback, thank you. The work you do is incredible, and you are true heroes I will always admire.

Arianne, thank you for always reading and loving these stories as much as me, and making the most fun stickers to go along with them.

Katie, my incredible editor. You're the woman! Your eye and attention to detail are so appreciated, as is all your hard work on this book to make it the best that it can be. Oh, and your reactions and voice notes make me squeal like a little girl. Couldn't have done it without you.

To the one who helped me when I was stuck, talked through the emotions, the love, and the heartbreak with me. Who sent me song inspirations when I needed the right headspace, and feedback when I was just not quite hitting the mark. Who encouraged me through the editing. Forever grateful. Thank you.

To my beautiful daughter who asks all the time what chapter I'm on and how many words I wrote today. Who loves me and celebrates every small win with me. I love you B. Thank you.

To my husband who gives me the time to work on writing and editing and listens to me gripe when things aren't falling into place. Love you, and thank you.

To all of you who take the time to read my books, share my books, talk about my books and review my books… THANK YOU! You are the reason I can keep doing the thing that I love.

Coming next in the Wanderland Series:
River and Ivy's story

about the author

Etta Lane is a married mother who loves to read spicy romance as much as she loves to write it. She loves the outdoors, adventures, and game nights with friends. When she isn't reading or writing, you can find her spending time with her family, gardening, or Facetiming her sister.

connect with etta

Instagram: @ettalane.author
Facebook: Etta Lane
TikTok: @etta.lane.author
Facebook Reader Group: Etta Lane's Reader Group
Email: ettalanewrites@gmail.com